THE PAINTIN' PISTOLEER

Justin Other Smith, known as the "Paintin' Pistoleer" for his skill with water-colors and Colt alike, lives happily in the little town of Apache. With his friends — including Sheriff Rimfire Cudd (who couldn't shoot a hole in a barn wall even if he was inside the barn); Curly Bill Grane, barkeep at the Bloated Goat (who maintains — in the face of all evidence — that he runs a highly refined establishment); and Lew Pirtle, Overland Telegraph operator (who enjoys nothing so much as shouting the contents of private communications all over town) — he must contend with such surprising arrivals in Apache as a baby delivered on the Arizona Flyer, a mail-order bride, a charlatan rain-maker, and a sharpshooting monkey ... all whilst dodging the beady eyes of the Ladies' Knitting & Peach Preserves Society, self-appointed moral guardians of the town.

THE PAINTIN' PISTOLEER

WALKER A. TOMPKINS

First published in the United States by Dell Publishing

First Isis Edition
published 2018
by arrangement with
Golden West Literary Agency

A catalogue record for this book is available
from the British Library.

ISBN 978–1–78541–549–4 (pb)

Published by
F. A. Thorpe (Publishing)
Anstey, Leicestershire

Set by Words & Graphics Ltd.
Anstey, Leicestershire
Printed and bound in Great Britain by
T. J. International Ltd., Padstow, Cornwall

Contents

Tattoo or Not Tattoo

No, sir, nobody paid much attention to this Justin O. Smith when he first showed up in Apache, with his folding easel and box of paints slung behind the saddle of his crowbait pony.

It wasn't long, though, before he become famous hereabouts as the "Paintin' Pistoleer," and after he single-handed saved the whole county from going bankrupt, well, Smith could write his own ticket anywhere. Folks is still augering as to which caused the biggest commotion, his pistol or his paintbrush . . .

The reason Smith didn't drift on through was because Curly Bill Grane felt sorry for him and offered him a week's board and room to paint the big picture of Chief Sittin' Bull which hangs over the back bar in the Bloated Goat Saloon. Curly Bill got the best of the bargain, because Smith seemed to be a consumptive who'd come out West to regain his health or else die, with the odds on the latter.

Leastwise, Smith was a sallow, sunken-cheeked bag of bones when he first rode into Apache. His eyes were feverish bright, he was stooped over like he had his galluses buttoned on backward, and he had a racking

1

cough. There were some who claimed he packed a 'dobe brick in his hip pocket to keep from being blowed away by a dust-devil.

Yes sir, Justin Other Smith was a character.

He was a plumb likable cuss, though. The day when Lemuel Quincy, the bank president, was hoorawing him because he ordered a glass of buttermilk at Grane's bar, the pilgrim explained how he come by his name.

Seems when he was born, the youngest of a family of 13, back on a share-cropper's plantation in Alabama, the doctor had grumbled about being routed out of bed to deliver "just another Smith." His Ma was running out of names by that time, so she christened her latest offspring "Justin Other Smith." Or so the pilgrim claimed.

There was two things Justin O. Smith was expert at, though. Give him a piece of paper or a flat board, and he could sketch the spittin' image of a man in less time than it took to tell it — a likeness you'd swear was as true as a photygraph.

And he could shoot.

Tipping the scales at less than 100, that summer he first rode into Apache, Smith couldn't have licked a postage stamp. But he packed a Colt .32 on a .45 frame, and he wasn't long in demonstrating that the hardware wasn't just for ornament.

Like when Sol Fishman swapped him stable space for his pony in return for painting that big lynching-bee picture for Sol's O. K. Mercantile, and everyone agreed the outlaw with the rope around his neck was a dead ringer for Lemuel Quincy, the banker. Quincy, he took one look at the painting and vowed he would perforate Smith's hide the minute he cut Smith's sign.

Curly Bill warned Smith to light out of town, because Quincy was pizen mean when he got tanked up on Blue Bagpipe whisky, the private stock he paid Curly to import from Scotland for him.

Smith didn't light out, though, not even when the boys from the Bloated Goat warned him that Quincy had downed a pint of Blue Bagpipe, neat, and had left the saloon hunting for Smith.

Quincy located his prey out behind the livery barn. Justin O. was busy writing his name on a barrel head with that .32 six-shooter of his, at a range of 20 yards.

The banker waited until Smith dotted the i in his last name, and then he slunk off to kill the rest of that bottle of Blue Bagpipe. Nobody heard Quincy bragging about perforating anybody's hide after that. But he hated the pilgrim and roweled him in ornery little ways, ever' chance he got.

Smith picked up a few dollars painting desert scenes and flaming sunsets behind mountain peaks for the cowboys, which dinero he invested in grub and a camping outfit at Sol Fishman's.

Then he lit off across the desert toward the Devil's Playground over in the Sacatone Mountains, and Apache figgered they had seen the last of Justin Other Smith. He'd cough hisself to death out in them badlands, if he didn't get lost and starve first.

But that Paintin' Pistoleer, as he become known as, he surprised everybody by sashayin' back to Apache about a year and a half later, on a spankin' palomino.

Nobody knew him at first. He'd put tallow on his ribs, his cough was gone, and there was a good healthy tan on his face. Filled out, he made a right handsome young sport.

Seems the high dry air of the Sacatones had cured his lungs, give him a ramrod back and put tone in his muscles. He'd been over to Phoenix, painting what he called mural panoramas in the State House, and he brought back a roll of money that would have choked a horse. Which same he deposited in Quincy's bank.

The Paintin' Pistoleer rented hisself a room upstairs over the Longhorn Saddle Shop, on account of it had what he called north light, and commenced painting Arizona scenery. He'd mail a canvas off, ever' so often, to a publishing house back east. None of the paintings come back, either, except on fancy calendars and on the covers of mail-order catalogues. A nice little balance began piling up to Justin O. Smith's account over in the Stockman's Bank.

Smith was in the bank depositing a check one Saturday about closing time, when the alley door batted open and two masked hombres come into the lobby, brandishing sawed-off shotguns.

Lemuel Quincy happened to be out of town at the time, on a trip to Tucson, so his cashier, Jim Groot, was the only man in the bank besides the Paintin' Pistoleer.

The bandits must have figgered to hit the bank just before Groot closed the vault, so they could clean out the payroll money that the big Diamond X Cattle Syndicate had brung in that morning. But they figgered it wrong. Seems Groot had already closed the big vault,

4

and couldn't open it because nobody but Lemuel Quincy knowed the combination. Quincy wouldn't be back till Monday, which was too long for them to wait around.

The masked fellers didn't calculate to let that stop them, though. They gagged and hog-tied Groot and Justin O. Smith and hid them behind the teller's cage. Then one of the bandits fished in a gunny sack he was carrying and brought out some nitroglycerin, and went to work.

The vault was an old-fashioned job, and when the nitro went off, it like to lifted the door clean off the hinges. The masked hombres busted in through the smoke and raked up what currency they could find into their gunny sack.

Of course the boom of the explosion roused the town, but Sheriff Rimfire Cudd was the only one who figgered out it come from the Stockman's Bank building. The bandits heard Cudd a-pounding on the front door, and in their hurry to make a getaway, the nitro expert catches his shirt on a stovepipe damper and like to ripped it clean off his back. He didn't let the mishap slow him down none, but as he was high-tailing it for the back door of the bank, both Jim Groot and Justin O. Smith got a good look at his chest.

Tattooed acrost this bandit's wishbone was a red cowboy on a blue buckin' bronco, the like of which Jim Groot, at least, had never seed before, and which they both knowed they'd recognize if they ever laid eyes on it again.

Well, the bandits had horses waiting out back, and they had vamoosed hell-for-leather into the mesquites before Sheriff Rimfire Cudd managed to bash in the front door. He come around back and discovered Smith and the cashier lyin' there hog-tied.

Soon as the Paintin' Pistoleer got the gag out of his mouth, he says to the sheriff, "Sheriff," he says, "there's no sense trying to trail those buscaderos, and riskin' being drygulched. You slap a hull on your horse and ride with me. I'll show you where them robbers is holed up."

Well, Rimfire knew the job it would be tracking anybody acrost the lava beds with night a-comin' on, so he listened to what Justin O. had to tell him.

"It's like this," the Paintin' Pistoleer explained. "Last year I headed into the Devil's Playground huntin' scenery nobody had ever painted before. I run across a prospector's shack at the end of a canyon back there, where a feller name of Buckaroo Benson was livin'. Buckaroo claimed he was a prospector. Anyhow, he had a red cowboy straddlin' a blue hoss tattooed on his chest. Buckaroo Benson was one of these here bank robbers."

Rimfire had quite a stake in recovering the bank loot, him being one of the board of directors, so he took Smith at his word and saddled a fast bay. Before Apache knowed their bank had been cleaned out, Smith and the sheriff was gone.

But they didn't head northeast in the direction the robbers had took. They cut due west, toward the Sacatones. By sundown they were in the foothills, and

Justin O. Smith was leading the sheriff into the roughest part of the badlands, over trails that nobody had used since the Injun days.

He had some more information for the sheriff. Seems when he was over in Phoenix on his painting job, he happened to see Buckaroo Benson's face on a reward poster in the State House. Only it give Benson's name as Slickfinger Pete, wanted for safe-cracking back in Nebraska. Slickfinger was on the dodge, Smith figgered, and was holed up back in the Devil's Playground, pertending he was a prospector. Smith hadn't had any idea Benson would still be there, so he hadn't said anything.

Well, they rode half of the night before Smith located the canyon and the prospector's shack. It was a natural spot for a wanted owlhooter to hole up, all right, with plenty of grass and a spring of water and all.

They stashed their horses in a side draw and hid in the cabin to wait. Sure enough, a little after daylight, a rider come up the canyon, his horse ganted and footsore. Slickfinger Pete, alias Buckaroo Benson, was astraddle the horse, and his shirt was ripped dang near off his back. But he was alone. His partner wasn't to be seen nowheres.

The sheriff, he come blustering out of the shack with his hogleg at full cock. Buckaroo Benson went for his gun, and the sheriff drilled him betwixt the eyes. Nacherly, Rimfire was surprised at his own unaccustomed marksmanship, but he never batted an eye.

"You hadn't ought to have done that," Justin O. Smith complained. "Now we'll never know who Benson's partner was."

They had a look-see in the gunny sack Benson had tied to his pommel. It had about $5,000 of the Stockman's Bank haul in it, but that was barely enough to cover the payroll the Diamond X Cattle Syndicate had deposited before the robbery.

"Easy enough to figger out what happened," the sheriff lamented. "Somewhere back in the desert the two robbers split the booty and separated. Only Benson's partner got the lion's share, because I know for a fact the bank's liquid assets totaled around forty thousand, me being on the board of directors."

Well, they buried Benson, after taking a good look at the bronc rider tattooed on his chest. The Paintin' Pistoleer, he poked around the cabin, putting a few pieces of paper in his pocket that interested him, and paying particular attention to a pile of empty liquor bottles he found in the woodbox. When him and the sheriff hit the trail back to Apache along about noon, Justin O. Smith asked Rimfire to do him a favor.

"Don't tell nobody in town about Benson havin' that bronc rider tattooed on his hide," he urged the sheriff.

So Rimfire Cudd, he kept his lip close-hobbled about the tattoo when they got back to Apache. He claimed him and Justin O. Smith had trailed the bank robbers back into the Devil's Playground and tallied one of them. Rimfire hogged most of the credit for himself, which suited Smith fine.

That was a Sunday. The next morning, Lemuel Quincy clumb out of the Tucson stagecoach. When he heard his bank had been robbed during his absence, he was fitten to be tied. He called an emergency meeting of the board of directors, and they took a tally and reported that the bank had been cleaned out except for the measly $5,000 the sheriff had recovered from Benson back in the Sacatones. That left 30-odd thousand dollars unaccounted for, and the news hit Apache folks like a bolt of lightning. The life savings of half the town were in that bank, including Justin O. Smith's pile.

When Lemuel Quincy tacked up a notice saying the depositors would be paid off pro rata on what was left, and the bank would lock its doors permanent, great were the lamentations to be heard throughout Stirrup County.

Lemuel Quincy, of course, made a beeline for the Bloated Goat that night and bought a bottle of his imported Blue Bagpipe whisky. He got so drunk that Justin O. Smith found him passed out cold as a fish in a privy behind the saloon. The Paintin' Pistoleer managed to haul Quincy over to Ma Jiminez's boarding-house where he lived, and put Quincy to bed, clothes and all. Which was right decent of him, considering how ornery Quincy had always treated him. He poured some black coffee down Quincy's throat, and then he took a *pasear* over to the Bloated Goat to roundside with Sheriff Cudd and the boys.

Jim Groot was there, bragging as how he'd know the missing robber any day of the week, if he ever got a gander at the hombre's tattoo. But that was loco talk, as Sol Fishman pointed out, because no bank robber is going to peel off his shirt to let the world check up on his brand and dewlaps.

The sheriff got in his cups a little, which was rare for him, and admitted that Justin O. Smith had been responsible for their tallying one of the robbers, on account of Smith had recognized Buckaroo Benson as a prospector he'd run across during his wanderings through the Sacatone badlands the year before, and had taken Rimfire on a short cut to Benson's hide-out. The way Smith had put on meat, Benson hadn't recognized him during the holdup.

Of course, that made the Paintin' Pistoleer a hero, but he wouldn't accept any drinks. He still stuck to buttermilk. He was swigging down a glass of the moo juice when Lemuel Quincy come staggering in through the batwings, cold sober, but red-eyed and disheveled-looking and sore as a brimmer bull.

"This town hates my guts because the bank got wiped out," Lemuel Quincy says sullen-like, looking the crowd over hostile. "Soon as I wind up my affairs, I'm headin' back to Omaha where I come from and curry the sticky-burrs out of my mane. I don't know why I come to Arizona Territory in the first place."

Nobody pays much attention to Quincy, except Jim Groot, the cashier, who offers to buy him a drink. Curly Bill Grane got out his last bottle of Blue Bagpipe Scotch and passed it across the mahogany to Quincy.

"I'd know that bank robber anywhere," Groot kept parroting, feeling his oats because the holdup had put him in the limelight and he didn't aim to be shoved out of it. "He had a red cowboy astraddle a blue bronco tattooed acrost his briskit. I run across that hombre's sign anywhere the rest of my life, I'll know the jasper."

Just then Justin O. Smith speaks up, in a lull in the talking. "That bank robber is right here in this saloon this minute," he says, in that soft Alabama drawl of his.

It was like another bottle of nitroglycerin had shook up the town, the way the barroom crowd reacted to the Paintin' Pistoleer's statement. They knew the pilgrim wasn't given to much joshin'.

"You repeat that last remark?" invited Curly Bill Grane, scowling as he mops the mahogany with his bar rag. "You accusin' the Bloated Goat of caterin' to bank robbers?"

Justin O. Smith nods emphatic, sipping his buttermilk and staring down Curly Bill over the brim of his glass. "That bank robber is right here in this barroom now," the painter says over again, slow and distinct. "Only he wouldn't take off his shirt for no money, on account of Groot an' me would spot his tattoo pronto."

Well, the sheriff being in his cups, the first thing you know, he peels off his shirt to expose a chest as bare and scrawny as a picked chicken's. Curly Bill was half mad, and he unties his bar apron and rips open *his* shirt, to reveal a briskit as hairy as a boar ape's. Both men being innocent of any tattooing, it goes without saying.

"I never saw such crazy goings-on," sneers Lemuel Quincy, pouring himself another slug of Blue Bagpipe.

11

"Smith brays like a jenny-ass full of loco weed after he's had a few buttermilks."

The sheriff screws an eye toward Quincy and levels a long finger at the banker. "Supposin' you peel off yore shirt, Lem!" he challenges the banker, with a hiccup. "I aim to see (hic) the chist of every galoot in this saloon before I (hic!) leave here tonight!"

Quincy was just drunk enough to be ugly and mean. Exposing his naked chest to a barroom crowd was beneath his dignity, but the boys didn't cotton to the banker's snobbish ways nohow, and they begun to close in, seeing a chance to spook Quincy.

Jim Groot, who had taken plenty of rawhiding from his boss during the years he had slaved behind a teller's cage for 12 bucks a week, he seen the temper of the crowd and it egged up his courage. He lays a-holt of Quincy's collar and makes like he's fixing to rip the banker's shirt off.

"All right — anything to please you damned yokels!" Quincy says, slapping Groot's hands off him. "You fellers lost the shirts off'n your backs when my bank got cleaned out. Take a look at *my* chest, if it pleases you any!" So he unbuttons his shirt and underwear and spreads 'em wide. Then he takes a look at his reflection in the back-bar mirror, and his face turned the color of a jackrabbit's tail.

Plain as day across Lemuel Quincy's hairless chest was a red cowboy forking a blue bucking horse!

Quincy was shocked cold sober. Every man in the barroom was paralyzed, staring bug-eyed at that tattoo.

12

Everybody, that is, except Justin O. Smith. He was watching Quincy's gun hand like a hawk.

"Lem stuck up his own bank!" bellers Jim Groot, breaking the silence. "He pertended to be over in Tucson for the week-end, and he come back and robbed his own bank!"

Lemuel Quincy dug for his gun then. He started backing toward the door, his eyes as wild as a hog-tied steer's. He cocked his .45, too, but he didn't get a chance to shoot anybody.

Farther down the bar the Paintin' Pistoleer had set down his buttermilk. His little .32 cracked like a whip. The slug tore the big peacemaker out of Quincy's hand.

The banker wilted when Sheriff Rimfire Cudd come to his senses and jabbed a gun in his belly. "Okay — you win the pot," Quincy groans, like a man who sees the jig is up. His brain was still addled by too much Blue Bagpipe, or he'd have knowed he had been framed. Instead, he kept talking.

"I been juggling the books for a year," he confessed. "You'll find the rest of that money in my bank up in Omaha. I knew the examiners would be here next week to audit my books, so I hired a friend I knew in Nebraska who savvied how to crack safes, and we pulled off that holdup to hide the shortage."

Then Quincy rubs a finger acrost his chest. You could have bowled him over with a toothpick when the red lines on that tattoo smeared off on his finger!

The rest of the boys began to catch on, then, that the Paintin' Pistoleer had "tattooed" Quincy with red and blue paint when he was putting the banker to bed earlier that evening. In his drunken stupor, Quincy never even felt the paintbrush tickling his ribs.

Quincy hollered "double cross" and "frame-up" even after Rimfire Cudd locked him up in the county jail, but he had palavered too much to back out by then.

The sheriff got the shakes, though, when he buttonholed Justin O. Smith back at the Bloated Goat a little while later. "What if Lem hadn't confessed?" the sheriff wanted to know. "We'd a been left holding the dirty end of the stick. Quincy would have closed up the bank and pulled stakes for Nebraska without nobody being the wiser."

Justin Other Smith shook his head. He reached in his pocket and took out the papers he'd brung from Buckaroo Benson's cabin over in the Sacatones. "I put two and two together before we left Benson's hide-out yesterday morning," he explains. "In his shack I found these here receipts for grub an' supplies bought at the O. K. Mercantile store, and debited against Quincy's account."

Sol Fishman let out a squeal like a stuck shoat when he seen them papers. "Quincy told me he was grubstakin' a prospector!" Sol yells. "That's why I gave the stranger credit."

"And," Justin O. Smith went on, "I found a couple of Blue Bagpipe whisky bottles in the woodbox up at Benson's place. That was proof that Quincy had done some drinking with Benson lately. He always bragged he's the only man in the Territory who imports that particular brand."

14

Curly Bill Grane come up with his jug of buttermilk then, but the Paintin' Pistoleer waved it away.

"I aim to celebrate," he says loftily, thumping the bar with his palm like he'd seen the heavy drinkers do, "on account of getting my savings back from the Stockman's Bank. Pour me three fingers of Scotch and hold the chaser, will you?"

Curly Bill made it Blue Bagpipe, on the house.

Monkey See, Monkey Do

Pegleg Pillpoot was shrewd, all right, when he brought his sharpshooting monkey to Apache on the very day when town was crowded with jackleg miners from the Bonanza Syndicate diggings, come to collect their month's pay and spend it. They rose to the bait fast when Pillpoot offered a $1,000 prize to any man who could beat this monkey, Jub-Jub, in a shooting match, with no strings attached.

Now the miners knew something Pillpoot didn't know — that the champeen pistol shot of all Arizona lived right here in 'Pache; the young artist feller named Justin Other Smith, better known hereabouts as that Paintin' Pistoleer.

With the miners placing wagers on Smith, who couldn't lose if he tried, and Pillpoot coppering all those bets because he said Jub-Jub was unbeatable — well, there you have your immovable object meeting your irresistible force. Something's got to give. As it turned out, it cost Apache some bloodshed and near bankruptcy before the thing was over, and a murder mystery to boot.

The Syndicate's paymaster, Jake Grubb, always paid off the muckers in Apache, because he claimed it was too risky to ride back into the Sacatone foothills with such a fat payroll. So the custom was for Grubb to ride over from Tucson on the Wells-Fargo stage, and pay off the boys on the front porch of Sol Fishman's O. K. Mercantile store.

No doubt Pegleg Pillpoot and his shooting monkey had an eye on the profit angle by timing their arrival to jibe with payday, when $100 bills was thicker than corkscrews at a camp meetin'. On this particular afternoon, the miners showed up from the diggings around two o'clock, aiming to use their credit at the O. K. Mercantile and the Bloated Goat Saloon and the other places in town, which meant the bartenders and barbers and gamblers would glom onto the Bonanza payroll even before it got to Apache.

Sheriff Rimfire Cudd was making the rounds of the main street in the interests of law and order, because these mischief-making miners had a habit of tipping over backhouses and shooting out window lights and putting burrs under the saddles of cowponies hitched at the racks, and all that kind of devilment.

That was why, in all the payday excitement, Rimfire didn't notice the long red tent that was being pitched in the alley between Lew Pirtle's telegraph office and the Longhorn Saddle Shop. The tent was up and a freckle-faced button about 13 was rigging up a big canvas sign over the front before the sheriff finally sashayed over to the alley for a look-see.

This sign was a gaudy affair, all faded and crinkly from being rolled and unrolled so often. It looked like a circus sideshow poster, and showed a picture of a red-haired chimpanzee holding a pair of six-shooters with flame spittin' out of the bores. This monkey was wearing a John B. hat and had a ca'tridge belt strapped around his belly.

Big gold letters over the sign said *Shooting Gallery — Pegleg Pillpoot & Son, Managers*. And underneath this picture of the gun-slinging monkey was bright red printing that said: *$1,000 Reward to Any Sharpshooter Who Can Beat the Score of Jub-Jub, the World's Only Monkey Marksman!*

Well now, that was too much for Sheriff Rimfire Cudd to swaller without chawing; so he takes a *pasear* over to where this kid is tying a guyrope to a tent peg and braces him.

"You mean to stand there with your bare face hangin' out and tell me you got a monkey who can shoot guns like a human?"

"That's the gospel truth, Sheriff," the kid says, ogling Cudd's platter-sized star. "My dad's inside feedin' Jub-Jub now. Go on in. Dad's blind as a bat, but he'll be glad to see you, Sheriff," the kid says.

So Rimfire Cudd goes inside the red tent, his eyes popping like a tromped-on frog's, the way they allus do when he figgers somebody's hoorawing him. He sees a counter loaded with .22 rifles, at the far end of the tent, with planks set up as a backstop to catch bullets, and targets hanging from nails in the planks — clay pipes and pigeons and bright little tinsel balls like what come on Christmas trees.

Parked just inside the front of the tent is Pillpoot's canvas-hooded Conestoga wagon, painted a bright red that is dimmed considerable by traveling acrost the desert, with the words *Pillpoot & Son Shooting Gallery* painted in gold letters acrost the box, like a circus wagon.

The sheriff hears a chattering noise, and he hunkers down to look under the wagon. There between the wheels is a wooden-legged man wearing a long-tailed frock coat. He's busy feeding bananas to a monkey, said monkey being hitched to a bolster-rod with a piece of brass chain.

"Are you," speaks up the sheriff, "Pegleg Pillpoot?"

The man hands the monkey a banana, which it skins and chomps down before you can bat an eyelash, and turns around. Rimfire sees the man is wearing a pair of black spectacles.

"In person," he says, standing up and bracing his left elbow against the wagon box while he sticks his right hand out toward the sheriff. The hand is off at an angle, though, which indicates to Cudd that Pegleg Pillpoot is stone-blind.

"I'm the sheriff here in Apache," Cudd says importantly, glowering at the monkey while he shakes Pillpoot's hand. "If you wasn't blind and a cripple, I'd clap you in jail for fixing to swindle money under false pretenses in our mee-tropolis."

Pillpoot just smiles. Even Jub-Jub, the monk, lets out a sneering laugh, and then he gives a hop up to the wagon wheel, takes a good holt with his long toes, and reaches out and whips off the sheriff's Stetson.

Cudd bellers like a brimmer bull when Jub-Jub runs his hairy fingers over Cudd's head, hunting for fleas.

19

The chimp gives up in disgust, though, chattering monkey cusswords when he discovers that Rimfire Cudd ain't got no more hair on his noggin than a spittoon has.

"A swindle? False pretenses?" repeats Pegleg, as the monkey flies through the air and lands astraddle of his shoulder. "And what would our esteemed minion of the law be insinuating by such harsh language as that, Jub-Jub?"

The monkey answered that one by peeling off Pillpoot's stovepipe hat, exposing a dome as bald and shiny as the sheriff's, and planting a big slobbery kiss on Pillpoot's left ear.

"Listen, Baldy!" the sheriff rips out, feeling superior because naturally Pillpoot can't see Cudd is a baldy too. "That billboard your kid is riggin' up outside says this gorilla of yours can shoot firearms. Any galoot knows that's a damn lie — besides bein' against the statutes. Or something."

"Jub-Jub can do anything a man can do," Pillpoot boasts. "We been touring through Arizona an' New Mexico an' Texas for going on ten year now. Nobody's shot as good a score as Jub-Jub, so far. Would you want him to demonstrate?"

Rimfire Cudd almost swallers his chaw while he's thinking that over. He sees Jub-Jub hop off Pillpoot's back and skin under the canvas wagon-hood. The monkey pops his head out of the oval opening in the back a minute later, and he's carrying a little nickel-plated .22 pistol in one hairy paw.

"Hey — don't point that pop-gun at me, you damn fool!" yowls the sheriff, backing off. Then he looks sheepish. "You mean that monkey can really handle a hawgleg?" he asks.

Just then the kid comes in, tossing his wooden mallet and some extry tent pegs into the Conestoga. "Of course he can shoot, sheriff!" pipes up the button indignantly. "We've got one thousand dollars cash that says he can out-shoot any gunnie you got in this flea-bit burg!"

Now Rimfire Cudd has got plenty of civic pride. He's not worth a plugged *peseta* when it comes to shooting hisself, but he realizes that Apache would be the laughingstock of Arizona Territory if any long-tailed critter like this Jub-Jub was to come out ahead in a shooting match with a local citizen.

"I hope you got that thousand bucks with you this trip, Mister Pillpoot!" the sheriff says to the blind man, "because you're going to lose it. We got a man here in 'Pache who can out-shoot that monkey blindfolded!"

Pillpoot and his younker just laugh out loud and say nothing.

"Did you ever hear of Justin Other Smith?" Cudd asks.

Pillpoot looks vague, the way a blind man can. "Can't say as I have, Mister Sheriff. Lute and I have known lots of Smiths, so I guess we could have missed just another one."

Rimfire Cudd chortles kind of sly-like, and plays his ace. "Justin O. Smith," he says proudly, "happens to be the champeen shot west of the Pecos, in addition to being the best artist in the whole You-nighted States. The Paintin' Pistoleer, we call him. He'll give your monkey odds and rake in the pot!"

Pegleg Pillpoot reaches under the lapel of his black coat and fishes out a wallet. He thumbs out two $1,000 bills and waves them under the sheriff's nose — which ain't so much of a feat even for a blind man, as Rimfire's proboscis protrudes like the muzzle of a double-barreled shotgun anyhow.

"Put some money where your teeth are," challenges the shooting gallery man, "and we will double our offer. Jub-Jub has never been bested in a target match. Bring on your Paintin' Pistoleer, Mister Sheriff!"

Well, that made the sheriff see red. Two minutes later he was leading Pegleg Pillpoot out of the tent, and Pegleg was leading Jub-Jub on a leash. The kid, Lute, had fixed a little ten-gallon sombrero — only it was more of a ten-pint model — onto the monk's head with a rubber band, and had buckled a pair of ca'tridge belts around the monkey's little pot belly, with two holsters that carried a pair of sawed-off .22 target pistols. Jub-Jub looked cuter than a suckin' shoat in that git-up.

"Don't worry about Jub-Jub shooting anybody on the street," Lute assures the sheriff. "His guns ain't loaded except when he puts on his act here in the tent."

A crowd of miners had gathered in the alley to read the sign in front of the shooting gallery, and they rubbered and guffawed when they seed the sheriff escorting a blind man and a strutting monkey out of the tent.

Rimfire Cudd leads Pillpoot and Jub-Jub into the Longhorn Saddle Shop next door, and upstairs to where Justin O. Smith has his artist's studio.

But when the sheriff got up there, he found the Paintin' Pistoleer had gone out some place. The studio was all littered up with canvases on easels, and the walls was hung with paintings of desert scenery and snow-clad mountains and Injuns in war bonnets and cowboys on bucking broncos and gorgeous sunsets.

"It's a pity you can't see," the sheriff remarks. "This Justin O. Smith can sling paint almost as good as he can shoot. And at shooting he is a champeen of which there ain't no whicher."

"Next to Jub-Jub," Pillpoot mutters smugly. "Jub-Jub can —"

"We'll cross over to the Bloated Goat Saloon," cuts in the sheriff. "I forgot it's three o'clock. That's when the Paintin' Pistoleer goes out for his glass of buttermilk."

Quite a mob of kids foller them acrost the street, the monk screaming and spitting at them, and scaring hell out of a drunk cowpuncher who's got himself surrounded by a porch pillar. He figgers he's got the delirium trimmin's for shore.

Sure enough, the Paintin' Pistoleer is at the brass rail, roundsiding with the miners and drinking his usual glass of buttermilk. You'd never know to look at Justin O. that he had been about dead with consumption when he first hit Apache two years before. The desert air had fixed him up so he was as husky as whangleather and about two shades browner.

The news of the shooting monkey had already got to Curly Bill's barroom, so a big crowd was on hand when the sheriff introduced Pillpoot and Jub-Jub to the Paintin' Pistoleer, basking in the reflected glory of these here celebrities.

Justin O., he takes a gander at the two $1,000 bills which Pillpoot shows him. Then he looks at the monkey, which has scrambled up on the mahogany and is slapping a bar rag at his reflection in the backbar mirror, his tail anchored around Curly Bill's skinny neck.

Smith listens to Pegleg's challenge, and shakes his head.

"You ain't yeller, are you?" says Lew Pirtle, the Overland Telegraph agent, in a sort of dismayed tone. "You ain't a-scairt of bein' beat by a bat-eared baboon, are you?"

Smith flushes at that. "No-o," he says in that soft Alabama drawl of his, "but it wouldn't be right to take money from a —"

"From a blind man?" grins Pillpoot. "My friend, you are competing with Jub-Jub, not with me. This two thousand dollars represents only a small portion of my anthropoid's winnings. I assure you Jub-Jub can afford to gamble, since he never loses."

Well, the miners and cowpokes start hoorawing the Paintin' Pistoleer, and the upshot of it was that he scribbles off a check to cover Jub-Jub's bet and hands it to Jim Groot, the banker, who will hold the stakes. The next thing you know, every galoot who can crowd into the shooting-gallery tent has done so.

They all watch the blind man scramble up into the Conestoga and fetch a box of .22 shells, which he loads into the monkey's pistols. That makes a few of the boys nervous and they skin out, not wanting to be pinked by a bullet from no hairy ape, although Lute guarantees that Jub-Jub is never reckless with firearms.

"Oh, he's shot a few jackrabbits out on the open range, just to keep in practice," Lute admits, "but otherwise, Jub-Jub has been trained to shoot at just one thing — a bright red ball."

Well, the audience crowds back along the sides of the tent, while Lute sets up the targets. He puts a gunnysack loaded with sand on the shooting-gallery counter, and on the outside of this backstop he pins a couple dozen tinsel balls, the flimsy kind that come on Christmas trees.

These balls are in all colors — yeller, silver, blue, red, green, purple — with the red balls scattered around with the others.

"Okay," says Lute, when everything is ready. "Mister Smith, you will be allowed six shots — Jub-Jub the same. You will fire alternately, tossing for first turn. The bargain is that you are to shoot at any bulb *except* the red ones. Red is the only color Jub-Jub will shoot at. Is that understood?"

Well, that's fair enough. Justin O. Smith flips a coin with Jub-Jub, looking perty foolish. That is, the monkey flips the coin and the Paintin' Pistoleer calls it. He wins, and elects to shoot first, so as to show Jub-Jub the competition he's up aginst.

Justin O. is using his own gun, a .32 Colt on a .45 frame. It's quiet enough in the tent to hear a bumblebee belch when Justin O. takes his stance straddling the tongue of the Conestoga wagon. The tent is about 30 feet long, and the Christmas-tree balls are only an inch in diameter, which is a tolable small target even at that short range.

"I'll take the purple ball with the gold spots," Justin O. announces casual-like. Everybody's head cranks around to look at the sand bag and spot the target that the Pistoleer says he figgers to draw a bead on.

Without even lining his sights, Justin O. squeezes off a shot from the hip. The purple ball with the gold spots disappears with a little tinkling sound, and the crowd applauds. Even Jub-Jub claps his hands. Of course, nobody in Apache was surprised by that shooting; the Paintin' Pistoleer wasn't even warmed up yet. But what would Jub-Jub do?

Well, Lute, busy covering side bets with the customers, he gives the monkey a whistle signal. Pegleg Pillpoot is back inside the Conestoga hood, out of sight. The monkey clumb up onto the driver's seat and hauls a pistol from leather.

Jub-Jub juggles the .22 pistol in a kind of twirl around his long black finger, and it went off with a little popping sound in comparison to the roar of Justin O. Smith's Colt.

Rimfire Cudd squints up at the roof of the tent, expecting to see a bullet hole in the canvas. He had his mouth open to call a halt to the whole she-bang as being a fraud and a dangerous thing for any bystander in range of that orey-eyed orangotang.

But before the Sheriff could yell, he seen the Paintin' Pistoleer's jaw drop open. Smith was a-starin' at the target, and lo and be-gosh, one of the red tinsel balls was busted to smithereens!

"Your turn, Mister Smith!" sings out Lute Pillpoot from the sidelines. "The score is now even Stephen, one and one."

For the first time in his life, Justin O.'s gun-hand was trembling a little, and who could blame him? "The green-striped ball," he croaks out kind of hollow-like, and ears back the hammer of his Colt.

He pulls trigger. The crowd groans when it sees a silver-colored ball just above the green-striped one vanish in a puff of flying tinsel. Smith had aimed a hair too high.

"A miss!" calls Lute, inspecting the sandbag targets. "You're a crack shot, Mister Smith, but mebbe you'd better quit calling your shots — All right, Jub-Jub — take your second turn."

This time the monkey turns a summersalt in mid-air, jumping off the wagon seat onto the whiffletrees and firing his .22 while he's whirling through space.

The crowd really went mad with excitement then, when they seen another red ball smashed by Jub-Jub's bullet. Men who had been busting themselves to place side bets with Lute began pulling back into their collars when Lute announced that the score now stood two to one — in Jub-Jub's favor!

Well, it was all over in a hurry. Justin O., looking kind of green around the gills, continued to call his shots regardless and even switched to his left hand for the next four tries, hitting the called target ball every crack.

But the monkey punched out four more red balls too, from a variety of damn-fool angles — hanging from his tail from the ridge pole of the tent and the like of that.

The crowd like to yelled its lungs out when they seen banker Jim Groot pass Smith's check up to Pegleg Pillpoot, who was leaning over the driver's seat of the wagon. Blind, he couldn't see the shooting, but he knew Jub-Jub had won from all the noise.

Pillpoot took the check and shook the Paintin' Pistoleer's hand, and even offered to give him back half the money because it was the closest Jub-Jub had ever come to losing, but of course that was adding insult to injury.

The Paintin' Pistoleer lurched out of the tent and went over to the Bloated Goat Saloon, looking sort of dazed. Curly Bill Grane, who had locked up his place to attend the shooting-match, knew without asking that this was a special occasion when Justin O. needed something more fortifying than buttermilk, so he got out a bottle of Blue Bagpipe whisky and poured Smith a long one, on the house. Smith needed it, that's for shore.

The miners plumb forgot their impatience about waiting for the payroll to show up, in discussing Smith's disgrace. They went over to Pillpoot's tent, aiming to try their own skill with the shooting-gallery's arsenal of .22's, but they had lost all their money to Lute and their credit was no good until the paymaster showed up. So Pillpoot cleared out the tent and said they would open for business later in the evening.

Pillpoot's kid went over to the Stockman's Bank and cashed Justin O. Smith's check, and along about sundown Pegleg went over to Dyspepsia Dan's restaurant to eat supper. He left Lute to watch the tent and take care of Jub-Jub. That's where Justin O. Smith found the kid when he went over to the shooting-gallery.

"Jub-Jub beat me fair and square this afternoon," the Paintin' Pistoleer admits, game as they come. "Mind letting me look at his smoke-poles? I'm sort of interested in firearms."

Lute allowed that was okay, and when the Paintin' Pistoleer went back upstairs to where Rimfire Cudd and Sol Fishman were waiting in his art studio, he was shaking his head, looking plumb miserable and considerable perplexed.

"It don't stand to reason a monkey could shoot so accurate," he says, "but I could find no evidence of trickery. Jub-Jub's revolvers were regulation stock models and were loaded with standard .22 short ammunition. It beats hell out of me how a blind cripple could train a simian to shoot like that. Pillpoot could clean up a fortune in New York —"

Just then a yell went up from the street below and the sheriff and Sol Fishman hurried out, the news getting out that the Tucson stage was pulling in with the paymaster aboard.

The Paintin' Pistoleer, feeling down in the mouth and knowing his rep as a sharpshooting champ was blowed higher than a kite by this migratory monkey, strolls over to the window of his studio and watches the Concord pull up in front of the Wells-Fargo office.

It was pretty dark by then, but he saw Jake Grubb, wearing a red hunting-shirt and two six-guns, step off the coach with his briefcase full of greenbacks to pay off the miners.

The muckers were jostling each other for position in the payline over on the porch of the O. K. Mercantile, so nobody but Justin O. was paying much attention to Jake Grubb.

Justin O. watches the Syndicate man head for Sol Fishman's store. And then something happened. As Grubb was passing the alley between the Wells-Fargo office and the O. K. Mercantile, a club whizzed out of the shadows and caught Grubb on the head.

Grubb went down like a pole-axed steer on the board walk, and then a big hombre in batwing chaps and a black Mexican hat leaped out of the dark alley and yanked the payroll case out of Grubb's hand. In plain sight he angles across the street, sprinting like a turpentined terrier.

Justin O. Smith's mind worked like greased lightning then. He leaned out of the upstairs window and takes a quick shot at the robber, who was wearing a bandana mask over his face.

Jake Grubb staggered to his feet, rubbing his sore skull and yelling bloody murder. Then he dragged his two six-guns from leather and took off acrost the street after the bandit.

The holdup had happened so quick that nary a man had budged by the time the Paintin' Pistoleer got downstairs and headed into the alley where Grubb had chased the desperado. Lamplight from a saddle-shop window fell into the alley and as Justin O. Smith passed by, he seen a big black Mexican sombrero lyin' in the dust, with a bullet hole punched through the crown. He figgered that his snap-shot had knocked off the bandit's skypiece, anyhow.

By the time Smith reached the back of the saddle shop, all he could see was a trail of dust where Grubb had chased the payroll robber around the corner. The Paintin' Pistoleer cocked his .32 and headed in that direction, expecting all the time that the robber would veer off into the bull-tongue cactus patch, where he probably had a getaway horse stashed in the mesquite chaparral.

He was approaching the back end of Pillpoot's shooting-gallery tent when he heard a couple of shots inside. Smith lost a little time locating the fly in the back of the tent. When he finally clawed his way inside, he saw Jake Grubb sprawled over the counter where the Pillpoots had put the sand-loaded gunnysack for a backstop.

The Syndicate paymaster was dead as a tick dunked in sheep-dip. He still clutched his smoking .45's, but blood was leaking from a bullet hole in his red shirt, square over the heart. A little hole, the kind a .22 bullet would make, Smith saw at a glance.

The Paintin' Pistoleer looks around. The tent was brightly lighted by the ceiling lanterns, but it was deserted except for clouds of dust and gunsmoke. The payroll robber had ducked into the shooting-gallery and gone out the front way.

And then Justin O. Smith seen that the tent wasn't empty after all. Jub-Jub was chained to the wagon at the other end, and in his right paw was a smoking .22 pistol.

Lute had gone over to Dyspepsia Dan's to eat a snack of bait, so the Paintin' Pistoleer clambered up into the wagon and found a bunch of bananas. He swapped one of them for Jub-Jub's pistol. It had a fired shell in the breech.

Apache buzzed like a hornets' nest. Sheriff Rimfire Cudd showed up, late as usual, and listened to Justin O. Smith's story. Everybody come to the conclusion that the monkey had shot and killed the Syndicate paymaster.

"I can't jail a monkey," Cudd groaned, "but I can sure as blazes arrest Pillpoot for owning a dangerous animal —"

Well, Pegleg Pillpoot and his son Lute come back from Dyspepsia Dan's restaurant, and they carried on something fierce when they found out what their pet monkey had gone and done.

"Jub-Jub never done a thing like this before," Lute kept whimpering. "It was a case of monkey see, monkey do. Grubb was swapping shots with this robber, and Jub-Jub did like the robber did and took a shot at

Grubb. That red shirt — Jub-Jub is used to shooting at red targets, you know —"

The whole town curried the 'squites for a trace of the missing robber, but by midnight they hadn't turned up so much as a set of tracks. The miners were hopping mad over losing their pay, especially to a robber who was most likely a cowboy; but at the same time public opinion was dead set agin Sheriff Cudd arresting a poor blind cripple for something his pet monkey had done.

Jub-Jub would have to be destroyed, of course, but that wouldn't help solve the mystery. After all, Pegleg Pillpoot and his whelp had to eat supper; you couldn't blame them for leaving the monkey on a leash inside the tent out of harm's way.

It was a little after midnight when the Paintin' Pistoleer mosied into the shooting-gallery tent where Pillpoot and his son Lute was hugging and kissing poor Jub-Jub good-by before Rimfire Cudd had to lead it out into the chaparral and kill it.

Justin O. Smith was carrying the Mexican sombrero he had shot off the robber's head earlier in the evening. "Look inside this hat, Sheriff," the artist says in that easy-going Alabama drawl of his. "Notice anything peculiar?"

Cudd looks, but aside from the bullet hole in the peak, he allowed the Mexican hat had no identifying marks in it, no initials in the sweatband or anything.

"No hairs, either," Justin O. points out. "An ordinary hombre sheds hair inside a sweaty beaver hat like this one. The robber's head was as bald as a peeled onion, you can bank on that."

Then Justin O. did a funny thing. Quick-like, he reached out and jerked the black specs off of Pegleg Pillpoot's eyes. Pillpoot blinked twice, and then Justin O. hauled off and clipped him an uppercut on the jaw that laid Pillpoot out alongside the wagon tongue, cold as a fish.

"Hey!" bellers Lute. "You can't slug a blind man —"

The sheriff was about to holler at Justin O. likewise, but the Paintin' Pistoleer was squatting down beside Pillpoot and pulling back his frock coat. That was when the sheriff seen that Pillpoot's left leg wasn't missing at all, but was just doubled back and strapped to his thigh, with a fake wooden pegleg buckled to the knee, the whole hoax hidden by Pillpoot's long coat.

"There's your thief, Sheriff," Justin O. says calm-like. "And that ain't all I got to show you." With which the Paintin' Pistoleer clambers up into the wagon box and comes out with a B-B air rifle mounted on a tripod.

"The monkey was shooting blank shells," Justin O. explains to the goggle-eyed sheriff, "while Pillpoot, who ain't any more blind than you are, plugged those red balls with this noiseless air rifle, from inside the Conestoga where nobody could see him. A B-B shot could bust a tinsel ball as easy as a real slug. I noticed this B-B gun earlier in the evening when I was hunting up a banana for Jub-Jub. When I seen Pillpoot's pupils react to the light after I whupped off his specs, I knew my hunch was okay."

34

Afterward Smith found Jake Grubb's payroll case stuffed inside the sandbag backstop, where he was putting it when Grubb caught him. Pillpoot had handed his smoking .22 to the monkey as an alibi, along with his fake pegleg and blindness. The gunnysack revealed a lot of B-B shot, which Lute confessed was the secret of Jub-Jub's so-called shooting ability.

Anyway the miners got their pay and Rimfire Cudd clapped Pillpoot in jail, hogging all the credit for the arrest, as usual. It turns out that Lute wasn't Pillpoot's kid, but a orphant who was forced to work for this swindler, so he was let off.

The whole town trooped over to the Bloated Goat around daylight to see Jub-Jub put on another show. The Paintin' Pistoleer had found out that Jub-Jub liked whisky, and he poured Blue Bagpipe down that simian's gullet until the poor monk was plastered tighter than wallpaper.

Having got back his $2,000, Justin O. could afford to feed Jub-Jub imported Scotch, although Curly Bill Grane allowed it was degrading for such monkey-business to go on inside a high-toned establishment like the Bloated Goat.

Could be.

Here's Mud in Yore Eye!

Justin Other Smith, this young artist feller they call the Paintin' Pistoleer around Apache, was setting up the boys to a round of Blue Bagpipe Scotch whisky when this red-whiskered stranger come stomping into the Bloated Goat Saloon.

He was tall and tough and had a chip on his shoulder as big as a sawlog. There was alkali dust on his Stetson and bluish-green mud dried to his spurred cowboots, and he looked saddle-ganted the way a man does after a long ride acrost the desert.

The boys say howdy but he ignores 'em, hooking a muddy boot over the brass rail and staring down at the bottle of Blue Bagpipe what he seen Justin O. Smith was treating the boys to. Smith, he always drinks buttermilk, the same as he was doing now.

"Give me a dram o' that," the stranger says. "Raw."

Well, Curly Bill Grane, the barkeep, he explains polite as pie how this Blue Bagpipe was a rare brand which this artist feller had shipped from Scotland, and it was up to Justin O. Smith whether he wanted the stranger to have a shot of it.

"A tinhorn sport, huh?" bellers the stranger, sizing Smith up and down in the backbar glass like he would a horny toad.

Smith had come out West for his health a year or two back, and while he was as tough as whangleather now, he was only five-two and weighed about a third what this boogery stranger weighed.

"Well," the bully says, "when Red Graw orders a special brand o' likker, he don't ask permission from no milk-swiggin' runt!" With which this Red Graw hombre shoves aside Sol Fishman, who runs the O. K. Mercantile acrost the street, and Jim Groot, the banker, and that brings him face to face with Justin O. Smith.

"Ordinary, I'd say you was welcome to my Blue Bagpipe," the Paintin' Pistoleer says, looking up at Graw without batting an eyelash. "But your domineerin' attitude rubs my fur the wrong way, Graw. I got a strong dislike to bein' called a runt, especially a milk-swiggin' runt."

Graw grins like a cat with a mouse under its paw. He gives his big gun harness a hitch. Then, without warnin', he sticks a muddy boot between Smith's ankles, pushes him in the face with a palm, and the Paintin' Pistoleer trips sprawling at the feet of Rimfire Cudd, who happens to be the sheriff.

Before Cudd could help Smith to his feet, Graw grabs the bottle of Blue Bagpipe offn the bar, spins on his heel and heads for the door, guffawing to himself.

Sheriff Cudd don't make a move, although Graw had committed assault and battery and petty larceny right in front of his eyes. Not because Rimfire was yaller, but he reckoned Smith could take care of the situation better than he could.

Graw was just pushing through the batwings when Justin O. reaches for his gun, a Colt .32 on a .45 frame. Nobody seen his draw, it was so swift, but the next instant the bottle exploded into a hundred pieces in Mister Red Graw's fist, and whisky sprayed in all directions.

Graw stopped. He stared down at the jagged bottle neck in his hand. He sniffs the fumes of that precious stuff that had come all the way from Glasgow just to be spattered over the sawdust floor of the Bloated Goat Saloon. And then he looked around to where Justin O. Smith was settin' on the floor.

"I reckon I made a mistake," Graw says, chucking the busted bottle neck into a sandbox. "I made the mistake of turnin' my back on a gun-toter. Next time I cut your sign, Runt, you won't be able to get offn the floor." With which Red Graw spins on his heel again, and starts through the door a second time.

Without appearing to aim his six-gun, the Paintin' Pistoleer squeezes off another shot, and nicks the lobe of Graw's left ear as neat as you please, just enough to draw a little drop of blood.

"You forgot to pay for that likker," Justin O. reminds him, reasonable enough. "Blue Bagpipe sets Curly Bill back twelve bucks a quart, wholesale. I figger you owe him a sawbuck."

Well, Graw scratches his bleedin' ear, and then he sees the tin star on Rimfire Cudd's vest, and he decides not to copper Smith's bet. That law badge made him pull in his horns pronto.

"My dinero is out in my saddle pouch," he grumbles. "I'll ante a double sawbuck to the kitty and be driftin' yonderward."

Curly Bill Grane decides it's about time he dealt himself in, so he comes out behind the bar counter with his sawed-off buckshot gun, and escorts Graw out of the Bloated Goat. A lathered-up pony is hitched to the rack out front, and Grane stands by while Graw unbuckles an alforka bag and reaches a hairy paw inside.

He fishes out a 20-dollar bill, so new and crisp that Curly Bill holds it up to the sun, thinking it might be counterfeit. But it's the McCoy, and the smallest Graw's got. Curly Bill forces him to take 11 bucks change, and the last Apache sees of Mister Graw, he's lopin' off into the desert, still thirsty.

Justin O. Smith polished off his glass of buttermilk like nothing had happened, dusted his pants off, and goes back to what he calls his studio, upstairs over the Longhorn Saddle Shop, where he paints the pictures he sells to calendars and catalogues.

Well, a couple hours later, Sheriff Rimfire Cudd rattles his hocks up to where the Paintin' Pistoleer was busy daubing away at a canvas on his easel, painting an ocotillo in full bloom.

"Looky at this here wire that Lew Pirtle just got offn the Overland Telegraph!" Cudd hollers, shoving a piece of paper under Smith's nose. "Wouldn't that set your cork to bobbin'?"

This message was from the sheriff of the next county over east. It said that the Wells-Fargo stagecoach from Tucson had been held up last night by three masked bandits, who had vamoosed for parts unknown with a strongbox containing an even $5,000 in brand-new 20-dollar bills, said dinero being consigned to a big mining outfit up in Nuggetville.

"You savvy what I do?" Cudd pants out. "That red-whiskered skunk who tried to bully you in the Bloated Goat this afternoon was one of them stage robbers! New twenty-dollar bills, it says. And Curly Bill allows this Red Graw had a saddlebag full of 'em!"

Justin O. Smith wipes his hands on a turpentined rag and pulls his lower lip, in a habit he's got when he's thinking hard.

"Just what," he asks, "do you want me to do about it?"

That takes the wind out of Cudd's sails. Ever since young Smith figgered out who robbed the Stockman's Bank here in Apache, the sheriff sort of looked up to him as a detective or something.

"Well," Cudd says sheepishly, "I reckon I ought to light out after this Red Graw galoot. But with that wind whippin' acrost the desert, his trail is colder'n a polar bear's rump by now."

The sheriff bowlegs his way downstairs. Through his window, the Paintin' Pistoleer watches Cudd fork his saddler and ride out of town, heading west, looking plumb dejected.

After the sheriff was gone, Justin O. Smith got to scratching his head. Finally he goes over to a kind of cupboard where he keeps a lot of his old canvases and sketchbooks and what-not. He scrabbles around through the trash awhile, and comes out with a charcoal sketch he'd made over in the Sacatone badlands a year or so ago, when he was curing himself of some lung trouble.

Justin O. Smith had built up his reppitation by painting country nobody else had ever painted before, country nobody but owlhooters and Injuns had even traveled in, for that matter.

This here rough sketch he'd dug up was one of them pictures, that he'd just blocked in, as he called it, and aimed to finish from memory later on. It showed a canyon full of willowbrake and scrub cottonwoods, with Thunderbird Peak in the background, and a lot of crags and buttes and gulches in the distance. Smith had writ in with pencil the right colors to use on the cliffs and such, and the location of this scene — 20 mile north of Wagonwheel Springs.

Well, after considerable cogitating, the Paintin' Pistoleer tucks the roll of canvas under his arm and takes a *pasear* over to the Bloated Goat. A bunch of the boys was in there roundsiding about this stage robber drifting through town, when Justin O. Smith ambles in.

"Curly," he says anxious-like to the bartender, "I hope you ain't swamped out the barroom recently."

Curly Bill Grane eyes him reproachfully and scowls. "Are you criticisin' the housekeeping I do in the Bloated Goat?" he asks, his feelings hurt.

But Justin O. Smith ignores the question, and walks over to where Red Graw had tripped him off his feet.

He squats down and pokes around in the sawdust and quirly stubs there for a spell, and finally he comes up with a little chunk of bluish-green mud, the size of your little fingernail.

"This mud," he says, very much pleased, "fell offn that stage robber's spur. You got any objections to me taking it?"

Curly Bill reaches for his jug of buttermilk and pours the Paintin' Pistoleer a brimming glass. "On the house," he says. "And you are welcome to all my sweepin's any day of the week, friend," he says. Curly Bill still feels indebted for that big masterpiece of Chief Sittin' Bull that the Paintin' Pistoleer made for him in exchange for a measly week's board and room, when Smith first come to town.

Smith gulps down the buttermilk, and then he tucks the hunk of bluish-green mud carefully in his pocket, and unrolls his sketch and studies it a spell, without offering no comments.

Then, imitating Red Graw, he spins on his heel and walks out. He goes over to the livery barn and saddles up Skeeter, his prize palomino, and straps on a bedroll and his painting gear and a gunnysack of grub, and the next thing people know, the Paintin' Pistoleer is riding out of town. That ain't onusual, though, because Smith is always taking a notion to go out into the desert for days at a time, hunting for pictures you see later on calendars and magazine covers.

There was a sandstorm blowing across the desert, whipping up so much dust it blinded Smith, but he knowed the general direction of Thunderbird Peak and he steered thataway, giving the palomino his head.

He camped that night in the edge of the Sacatone foothills, and during the night the storm blowed itself out. He set off toward Wagonwheel Springs, and around noon he spies a smudge of dust a few miles south.

Using a pair of field glasses he carried slung around his saddle horn, Justin O. Smith made out that it was Sheriff Rimfire Cudd, heading back toward Apache. He didn't have no prisoner in tow, either. The way he sat his saddle, the sheriff looked like he had the burden of the world's woes on his shoulders.

The Paintin' Pistoleer decided against riding back to head off Cudd, preferring to travel solo anyhow. He camped that night at Wagonwheel Springs, and he found fresh sign where somebody had dunked a campfire with coffee grounds. That might have been the sheriff, but Justin O. had his doubts, on account of Rimfire Cudd had lit a shuck out of Apache without taking no vittles with him. He figgered Red Graw had camped here.

It was pretty rough going through the lava country, so Smith only covered about 15 miles before it got dark. He was heading north toward Thunderbird Peak.

Next morning, though, he was in familiar country. He passed a spot where he had camped a week to paint Thunderbird, a picture that was spread all over the country on the back of an almanac now — country that an ordinary man wouldn't ever see.

A couple hours later he was gigging the palomino down a hogback toward the mouth of a twisting canyon where green stuff was growing. The palomino had already sniffed the water that lay ahead and broke into a canter, when Smith seen two riders heading his direction, from the north and quite a ways off yet. Through the glasses, the Paintin' Pistoleer seen that they was hard-looking cases, a half-breed and a feller who looked like he might be a Navajo Injun. They was armed to the teeth and their horses was limping like they'd been ridden hard and far.

Justin O. Smith looked around for cover but didn't see any. So he piled out of his saddle and quick-like set up his folding easel, and stretched out the unfinished canvas he'd sketched of this same canyon mouth more'n a year ago, at about this spot.

He was busy smearing paint when the two riders spotted him, on their way into the canyon. They swung their broncs around and come beating up the ridge toward him, the sun flashing off the Winchesters they had unlimbered from their saddle boots.

Smith, he was painting for all he was worth when the two riders galloped up and reined in. They took a gander at the picture Smith was working on, and couldn't make much out of it.

"How long you been here, feller?" asks the breed, finally.

The Paintin' Pistoleer was wearing an affair he calls a smock, all splotched up like a rainbow with different colored paints, and he unbuttoned it so he could reach his .32 when he seen that the Navajo Injun was working his horse around behind him. It looked like these riders was fixing to get him between them, which wasn't a healthy sign a-tall.

"Oh, three-four hours," Smith says, meek as milk. "I'm painting a picture of that mountain peak. Perty, ain't it?"

The breed and the Injun scratch their heads, puzzled, and finally the breed speaks up:

"You're squattin' on private property, stranger," he says. "You gather up your gear and go back to wherever you come from."

Smith's hands started shaking like he had a touch of palsy, and he began throwing his gear back into the paint box in a hurry.

"I d-didin't know this land belonged to n-nobody," he stammers, apologetic as all hell. "I'll get out pronto."

He rolled up his canvas and folded up his easel and the two hard cases sat their saddles, watching while he packed his smock in a saddle bag, and then fixed to mount.

Then the Injun shook his head. He had had his eye on Smith's palomino hoss ever since he rode up.

"Me take-um cayuse," the Injun says. "We make-um trade."

The Paintin' Pistoleer yelped like he had been stung by a yallerjacket at that, because to him the palomino was people, and he had trained that pony until it was almost human.

But the redskin levered a shell into his .30–30 and pointed the bore down Smith's throat, practically, so there wasn't a thing he could do but strip his kack off the palomino and swap Skeeter for the broken-down flea-bait pony the Injun was forking.

"Now, keep riding, tenderfoot!" orders the breed, when Smith was astraddle the Injun pony. "If we ketch you grazin' on this range agin, Sleepin' Beaver here will lift yore scalp."

They tooken him for a dude, and Smith acted out the part, trying to play scared when he was really boiling mad over having a mangey Navajo buck steal the best palomino in Arizona right out from under him.

He coaxed the Injun's cayuse into motion and headed back toward Wagonwheel Springs as fast as he could make the spavined, string-halted critter go, which wasn't much more than a trot. When he had put a couple of ridges between him and the hoss-thieves he made himself a dry camp and ate some cold bait just to keep his strength up for the job he aimed to do as soon as it got dark. No flea-bitten redskin, especially one with a name like Sleeping Beaver, was going to get away with his hoss, he'd be teetotally danged if he was . . .

The Injun's cayuse was too stove up to be much good, so he decided to picket him out and pick him up later. As soon as the moon come up, Justin O. Smith started on foot back toward the canyon he had been painting, taking his field glasses with him. The badlands looked so ghostly beautiful under the moonlight that the pilgrim's fingers got to itching for his paints and brushes, but that would have to wait.

Around midnight, he had worked his way to the mouth of the canyon, with Thunderbird Peak out of sight beyond the rimrocks. He jacked open his .32 Colt and made sure all the chambers was loaded, and then headed into the willowbrakes and dwarf cottonwoods that grew in the canyon.

Around a bend, he come in sight of a campfire. It was plumb late at night for anybody to be up and stirring, but through his glasses, Smith seen three men moving around the fire, saddling up their horses. The three hombres was what he called silhouetted against the fire so he couldn't exactly tell who they was, but he knew he was on the right track when he recognized his Skeeter hoss picketed with the other two.

The three campers was getting ready to hit the breeze, but Smith remembered from his last trip that this canyon ended in a blind box, so they would have to pass him coming out. He hid himself in some quaking aspen scrub and scrooched down in the mud, the whole bottom of the canyon being a sort of swampy ground from a spring that was dribbling out of the cliff farther up.

Pretty soon the campers doused their fire and started riding three abreast out of the canyon. When they rid out of the shadow of the cliffs, Smith seen that the Injun wasn't riding his palomino. A strapping giant of a man was astraddle of Skeeter, and in the moonlight Smith recognized his red whiskers.

It was Red Graw, all right, and it showed Justin O. Smith that he had figgered plumb correct before he pulled out of Apache and headed for this canyon. The breed and Sleeping Beaver was flanking Graw's stirrups.

Down on his hands and knees in the black thicket, the painter waited until the three riders was right opposite him, talking low between theirselves. Then he put his fingers in his mouth and give a loud whistle.

Skeeter pricked up his ears, and before Red Graw had a chance to pull leather, that palomino arched his back like a busting clock spring and swapped ends, like Smith had trained him to do when he got the whistle signal. Graw went flying tail-over-tincup to crash into a patch of prickly pear cactus.

The Paintin' Pistoleer had his .32 ready before the other two riders knowed what had happened. He took aim a little more careful than usual, and triggered a bullet at the spot where Sleeping Beaver's eagle feather was stuck into his hair.

The Navajo hoss-thief slid from his pony like a coat dropping off a hook. His hair had a part in it where there hadn't been a part before. He was a Sleeping Beaver for sure when he lit flat on his belly in the mud.

Justin O. Smith come scuttling out of the quakers with his gun spitting lead so close to the halfbreed's ears that it discouraged the breed from finishing the job of hauling his Winchester out of its scabbard.

Red Graw was picking hisself groggily out of the cactus when Smith charged up and clouted him one acrost the noggin with his Colt. The breed had his arms up and was hollering for mercy, but Smith just unbuckled Graw's shell belts and chucked the artillery over into the cactus out of reach.

Then he made the breed hogtie Graw's arms behind his back with the Mexican reata he carried, and likewise for the Injun, who was still taking his mud bath without knowing same. Smith whacked off what was left of the lass'-rope and took care of snubbing down the breed his own self.

It was around four o'clock the next afternoon when Sheriff Rimfire Cudd looked up from where he was whittlin' a stick in the shade of the jailhouse in Apache, and seen four horsemen coming down the main stem like something out of the apocalypse. He blinked his eyes.

It was Justin O. Smith, riding herd on Red Graw, the halfbreed, and Sleeping Beaver.

"Here's your Wells-Fargo money, sheriff," the Paintin' Pistoleer sings out wearily, tossing Rimfire a pair of saddlebags. "It's all there, except that sawbuck Graw squandered on Blue Bagpipe booze the other day."

Well, Cudd locked up the three stage robbers pronto, and got Lew Pirtle to telegraph the sheriff in the next county that the bandits and the Nuggetville syndicate's dinero was in his jail, not mentioning that he hadn't had much to do with same. Then Cudd lit a shuck over to the Bloated Goat Saloon, to get in on what the Paintin' Pistoleer was explaining to Curly Bill and Sol Fishman and the other boys.

"Seems those robbers separated to confuse their trailers after the hold-up," Smith was saying, "all agreeing to meet at their secret camp over in the Sacatones. Graw carried the loot, and he cut acrost the desert, aiming to stop at Apache for a snort of rot-gut.

49

If he hadn't hoorawed me about being a milk-swiggin' runt, he wouldn't have been forced into shelling up one of those new twenty-dollar bills that give him away."

Rimfire Cudd realized he looked mighty foolish, after coming back empty-handed from a round trip to the Sacatones thataway. "But how in thunderation," he wants to know, "did you know exactly what spot in all that country to find Graw's camp?"

The Paintin' Pistoleer feels in his shirt pocket and draws out the little gob of blue-green mud he found on the floor of the Bloated Goat.

"I've only run across one spot in Arizona with dirt this particular shade of color," he says. "Any artist would recognize it as being plumb distinctive. It comes from a canyon over Thunderbird Peak way, where a spring has washed out this peculiar bluish-green mineral.

"When I remembered seeing that funny color on Graw's boots, it set me to thinkin'. I'd made me a sketch of that canyon a year ago, when I was over in that country, and after I dug it out of my files, I seen enough landmarks was on my sketch to guide me back there."

The boys seen, then, where Justin O. Smith's boots were caked with this same bluish-green mud, the same as Sleeping Beaver seemed to have wallowed in from head to foot.

"It shore beats the bugs a fightin'," Sheriff Rimrock Cudd says, scratching his bald head, "what Smith can accomplish with only a little bitty chunk of mud to go on."

Curly Bill reaches under the bar and hauls out a bottle of Blue Bagpipe Scotch. "This here calls for something more nourishin' than buttermilk," he grins. "Belly up, folks — the drinks are on the house!"

The Paintin' Pistoleer flips the little gob of dried mud into a spittoon, and hoists his dram of Scotch for a toast.

"Well," he says in that soft Alabama drawl of his, "here's mud in yore eye!"

Object Matri-Money

You'd think a Jasper in Sheriff Rimfire Cudd's shoes would let well enough alone, after reveling in the blessings of bachelorhood for 60-odd years like he has. Nobody in Apache enjoyed more of life's pleasures or had less to offer a bride.

Rimfire had a rent-free shanty behind the jailhouse to live in, the county furnished him a fair-to-middlin' saddle horse and all the ca'tridges he needed, and his credit was good for a beer at the Bloated Goat Saloon any time.

But in spite of all this bounty from Lady Luck, old Rimfire had to up and swaller the bait he seen in the *Cattleman's Journal* about this here "Lonesome Hearts Club," which outfit rustles up wives for unsuspecting single men, and dabs a wide loop on husbands for old maids and grass widders.

Rimfire must have felt a mite sheepish about the deal, at that, because the old fool never let on to nobody about it except this young artist feller name of Justin Other Smith.

Anyhow, Justin O. was busy daubing away at a canvas in his studio upstairs over the Longhorn Saddle Shop one day, working on a pitcher of Custer's Last Stand for a cowboy bootery up in Denver that aimed to use the pitcher on its next year's catalogue, when who should come clambering up the stairs, blowin' like a fish, but Sheriff Rimfire Cudd. He brung with him a tore-up copy of the *Cattleman's Journal* he had found out behind the Feedbag Café.

"Smith," Rimfire wheezes after he's ketched his breath, "I want you to sketch a pitcher of me to send to my future bride."

The Paintin' Pistoleer lays down his brushes and comes over close to take a sniff of the sheriff's breath, nacherly figgering Cudd had hoisted one too many over at Curly Bill Grane's Bar.

"Bride?" Justin O. guffaws, thinking Rimfire is joshin' him. "What she-male would take a moth-eaten old galoot like you?"

Which same made Rimfire bristle up. He shows the Paintin' Pistoleer this here Lonesome Hearts Club advertisement in the magazine, which listed a batch of would-be brides all the same as a stock breeder announcing an auction sale.

"I picked this one and writ her a letter," the sheriff brags, pointing to a paragraph he had ringed with a soft-nose .45 bullet. "She sounds like a fittin' companion to share my sunset years."

Right then Justin O. Smith realizes Cudd ain't joshing, and what was worse, the old rapscallion had gone in too far to back out. Smith reads the description of Rimfire's choice:

Wealthy Socialite, 35, blonde, statuesque beauty, cultured Boston background, college degree, excellent cook, seamstress. Desires correspondence with Western gentleman of similar station. Object: matrimony. Address (Miss) Bedelia O'Tooligan, Box F, care of Cattleman's Journal.

"Great day in the mornin'!" Smith manages to blurt out. "No Beacon Street beauty would think of moving sight unseen out to an uncurried neck of nowhere like Apache, Arizona, to marry you, Sheriff — not even if your nose was full of nickels!"

Cudd preens his tobacco-stained handlebar mustaches and dances a little buck-and-wing jig, which shows what love can do to an old codger who is usually so stove up with rheumatiz that he has trouble h'isting a laig to reach the stirrup.

"Is tha-a-t so!" Rimfire snorts, giving his galluses a snap. "Well, I writ her, offerin' my hand in holy matrimony. She ain't exactly ascepted my bait, but she's nibblin' powerful hard. I got her letter here somewheres to prove same."

Sure enough, Rimfire produces a perty purple-colored envelope which has a Boston postmark, and it smells sweet as a bull-tongue cactus after a spring rain. The address is writ in a neat feminine hand, with lots of fancy curlycues:

> *Sheriff Rimfire Cudd, Esquire,*
> *Suite 3, Calle La Boose Arms,*
> *Apache, Arizona T.*

"Callaboose Arms!" Smith howls. "Suite 3! That's a newfangled way of describin' a leaky-roofed lean-to behind the county jail, danged if it ain't."

Cudd rolls his eyes like a sick calf and teeters up and down on his cowboots, grinning like his throat's cut from ear to ear. "All's fair in love an' war," the sheriff smirks. "I told her I owned a gold mine, too. Go ahead an' read what Bedelia has got to say."

The Paintin' Pistoleer gives Rimfire a sidewise look like he figgers the sheriff's been eating loco weed, and unfolds the letter. A tintype falls out, and when Smith sees the girl's face he lets out a whistle you could have heard plumb acrost the Border.

This Bedelia O'Tooligan is a lulu, all right, with a fancy head of blond curls that reminds Smith of the cancan girls at the Birdcage Theater in Tombstone. She's got big blue eyes, shiny as the seat of a drummer's pants, and sassy little rosebud lips, and a button nose that any artist would say belonged on a statoo of a Greek goddess,

"You sure picked a gorgeous filly," Smith has to admit. "Let's see what she's got to say:

"*Dearly beloved Rimmy-Cuddles,*" Smith reads out loud, and has to wait a minute till he gets over a choking spell. "*Your epissle of the 10th inst. convinces me that at last I have found my bold Lochinvar from out of the West. I am sure you are a Lochinvar when you tell me you own a dashing white steed that you will carry me away on to the love-nest you have built for us out where your gold mine is.*"

That's too much for Justin O. to swaller without chawing.

"'Dashing white steed!'" he groans. "You ain't by any chance referrin' to that spring-halted bone bag you been ridin' lately, are you? And this love-nest wouldn't be spelled boar's nest, would it? The last time I was inside your shack —"

Rimfire Cudd can stand a hoorawin' as good as the next man, but he shows signs of getting boogered. "You know how women are with the mushy talk," he blushes. "Go on. Read the next page. She's just gettin' warmed up."

Smith fans the perfume out of his nose and finishes reading Bedelia's tender message: "*I enclose a picture of myself. It doesn't do me justice, but I am sure you are not wooing me for my beauty, Rimmy darling, any more than you are attracted by my personal fortune. It goes without saying that you being the owner of an Arizona gold mine is a mere bagatelle to me —*"

"It may be a mere bag o' shells to Bedelia," the sheriff cuts in, "but it was a whoppin' big lie to me — yak! Yak!"

"Shut up," growls Smith, and goes on reading: "*As an evidence of your good faith, Rimmy-Cuddles, would you please send me by return mail a recent photograph of your dear face, and a certified check in the amount of $200? This is the train fair from Boston to Arizona, and I ask you for it only because it would not be seemly for a maiden of my refinement to pay her own way. — Eagerly and devotedly your own loving Bedelia (O'Tooligan).*"

Justin Other Smith hands the sheriff back his letter, and scratches his head, trying to figure out a gentle way to bust the idea that has occurred to him.

"I'll be glad to sketch a portrait of you, Sheriff," he says, "because that won't cost you anything. But don't be a danged fool and mail her one penny of dinero. If Bedelia's wealthy, she won't need it. If she ain't got the price of train fare West, then she is a fraud and a swindle, and you don't want to tangle with her."

Well, they augered back and forth for quite a spell, and finally the Paintin' Pistoleer give in. He had this rush job to do on the catalogue cover, and it was obvious that Rimfire Cudd had made up his mind, such as it was.

So Justin O. has the sheriff hunker down on a box by the window, and picks up a pencil and a pad of paper, and in less time than it takes to tell it, he had drawed a spittin' image of Rimfire and handed it over.

The sheriff looks at it, and his Adam's apple bounces up and down like a rubber ball. It's as natural-looking as his reflection in the backbar mirror over at the Bloated Goat, no denying that. Smith hadn't flattered him none, and he hadn't detracted from Rimfire's masculine qualities, neither.

But like Smith said later, Michelangelo hisself couldn't have done much to glamorize Rimfire's big nose, which looks like the muzzle of a sawed-off shotgun at best, or his noggin, which is as bald as a bedpost and twict as shiny. He was practically a gummer, that is to say he only had two teeth that met, and his eyes bugged out like a tromped-on toad-frawg's. Rimfire's ears looked like leather flaps on a suitcase and his neck resembled a bar rag that had been twisted around a mopstick.

Well, Rimfire folds up the picture, and mumbles his thank-yous, but Justin O. ignores all that, having turned back to his easel to make up for lost time. After all, if Rimfire wanted to throw 200 bucks down a rathole, at his age, that was his business.

The sheriff knowed what would happen to his budding romance if Bedelia O'Tooligan saw this monstrosity Smith had drawed. Cudd looks around the studio, and his eyes light on a little postcard-sized portrait that the Paintin' Pistoleer had turned out in color for Lew Pirtle, who runs the Overland Telegraph.

This here pitcher made Lew look like one of them handsome sports you see in the flannel-drawers pages of the mail-order catalogues, his hair all spruced up slick like, his mustache trimmed just so, and his neck fixed up fancy with a celluloid buckwing collar and a string cravat. Lew Pirtle aimed to give this pitcher to his missus on the tenth wedding anniversary they had coming up, as a surprise, and hadn't gotten around to calling for it yet.

Well, Rimfire Cudd slips Lew's painting under his vest on his way out, without the Paintin' Pistoleer being none the wiser. He sneaks over to the jail and wraps it up, along with $200 in greenbacks he had scraped up from friends around town, a little here and a little there. The upshot of it was that the next outgoing mail stage carries a package addressed to Miss Bedelia O'Tooligan in Boston, Mass., and Rimfire settles back to await developments.

Lew Pirtle was fit to be tied when his wedding anniversary rolled around two weeks later, and Justin O. Smith had to confess that he had mislaid the portrait he had fixed up for the missus. Missus Pirtle must have tooken it perty bad, not getting a present from her old man, because Lew showed up at the Bloated Goat that evening with a mouse on one eye, and swigged rotgut until around midnight, when Missus Pirtle and the nine little Pirtles come by and dragged Lew out by the ear.

Justin O. Smith happened to be in the Bloated Goat one afternoon about a week after that, having his usual glass of buttermilk while he played chess with Sol Fishman, who runs the O. K. Mercantile, when the batwings slam open and Lew Pirtle comes bustin' in, all het up the way he gets when a telegram comes in addressed to Apache station, which ain't often.

"Where's Rimfire Cudd?" Lew bellers, looking around the barroom. "I got a telly-grum here from the future Missus Cudd!"

Well, it so happens that Rimfire ain't in the saloon, being busy in his lean-to behind the jailhouse, papering his bedroom with colored pages he's tore out of mail-order catalogues. Nobody knew why the sheriff was busting out with this rash of fol-de-rol in this boar's nest he batches in, excepting Justin O. Smith, who by this time has figgered that the sheriff has heard the last of Bedelia O'Tooligan and his $200.

But it seems that the Paintin' Pistoleer had been a mite harsh in his judgment of the young lady from

Boston. Lew Pirtle could hardly wait to spring the news, although he got real huffy when Curly Bill Crane, the bartender, wanted to open the telegram.

"That ain't ethical!" Pirtle says, shocked. "This message is for the sheriff an' nobody else. Besides, it come collect."

Curly Bill had his swamper light a shuck out to fetch back the sheriff, and in the meantime Lew wet his whistle a couple of times with the Bloated Goat's forty-rod special. This likker has a habit of loosening a man's tongue, so Justin O. Smith and the others knew what was in Rimfire's telegram before the sheriff had a chance to get back.

"*Rimmy-Cuddles,*" Lew Pirtle quotes the message he had tooken off the wire, "*your pitcher has won my heart completely. Your princess will arrive in Apache on July tenth, in a gilded chariot drawn by six white chargers. Forever your adoring Bedelia.*"

About that time the sheriff shows up, pop-eyed with curiosity. The Paintin' Pistoleer loans him a sawbuck to pay for the message, and Rimfire goes over to a corner and makes a big mystery out of reading what it says. He comes back to the bar pertending that the telegram come from the Texas Rangers, warning him to be on the watch for a desperado who's heading west, armed to the teeth.

"Aw, come off, Sheriff!" says Lew Pirtle, who by now is so drunk his back teeth is floating. "We're all your friends. If you're expecting your sweetheart to show up on the tenth — hell's fire, man, that's tomorrow! And there ain't even a minister o' the gospel in town to tie the knot!"

Well, that let the polecat out of the bag, but Rimfire was game. He set up the house to free beers, and shows off Bedelia's tintype. He brags about how good she can cook, and how he already had a new stove coming C.O.D. from the mail-order house as a wedding gift for his bride, and he goes so far as to offer Bedelia's services in sewing on buttons or darning socks for any of the poor single men around town.

The Paintin' Pistoleer was the only hombre in the saloon who was cool-headed enough to figger out that Bedelia's golden chariot drawed by six white chargers was nothing more or less than tomorrow's regular weekly Wells-Fargo stagecoach from Tombstone.

Missus Jim Groot, the banker's wife, gets wind of the news and sends an urgent telegram calling the circuit rider over from Bisbee, and she gets the Apache Ladies' Knitting & Peach Preserves Society busy dolling up the lodge hall with sage blossoms and ocotillo wands and mesquite brush, making a wedding bower.

Justin Other Smith, still unable to figger out how a queen like Bedelia could bring herself to marry a repulsive old nincompoop like Rimfire, joins in the spirit of the thing and volunteers to paint a wedding portrait of the happy couple.

Sol Fishman decked out the sheriff in new overhalls and star boots and a new Stetson, and the livery stable chipped in a buggy and a team to take the newlyweds over to Tombstone for their honeymoon.

The July tenth stage was due at Wells-Fargo Express at noon. By 11:30 everybody in Apache had turned out to greet the bride from Boston. Cowboys from outlying spreads, and jackleg muckers from the Sacatone diggings, and a batch of Cheery-cow Injun bucks and their squaws, all dolled up in their Sunday feather bonnets and brightest blankets, was jammed around the stage-coach depot.

Well, the stage showed up on time for once, and it was kilted over at an angle like it had a big load of passengers aboard. The sheriff was waiting, his mustache washed and waxed and his stubble shaved off for the first time in five years, and his tin star shined up like the Arizona sun. He was as proud an' happy as if he had laid an egg single-handed.

Lew Pirtle, who was sort of acting as Rimfire's best man for the coming nuptials, was on hand in his Prince Albert to open the door of the Concord before it rattled to a halt.

Well, it turned out there was only one passenger, and it was a lady on the far side of 40 who must have weighed in the neighborhood of 300 pounds. The Concord tilted over on its thoroughbraces as this lady steps out, almost spilling the driver off the boot when it rocked back to a level keel.

Rimfire Cudd's face fell down to his belt buckle when he seen that Bedelia O'Tooligan must have missed connections back along the line. This passenger couldn't be the girl of the tintype. Her head was a bloated sausage set on a stack of double chins, and her hair straggled out from under her hat like stuffing from a busted sofa, and what appeared at first glance to be an oversized bustle — well, turned out it wasn't a bustle after all.

Well, this elephant in the pink dress hides her face coy-like behind a fan, and looks around at the crowd. The stage team let out a snort of relief, like they'd pulled a load of ore down from the mines and was glad the haul was finished.

Lew Pirtle was poking his head through the window of the coach, looking for another passenger who would fit Bedelia's description, when this walking lard barrel caught sight of him.

"Rimmy-Cuddles, precious!" she squeals like a shoat caught in a rail fence. "Come to your little Bedelia, my beloved! You look exactly like your picture — I'd have known you anywheres!"

Lew Pirtle jumped like a hornet had stung him under his tail coat, but he was too late. Bedelia reached out a pair of hands that looked like inflated rubber gloves and caught Lew in a bear-hug, kissing him with a big flabby mouth that Lew said later felt like a leppie-calf slobbering in a milk bucket.

Everybody was so busy watching Pirtle struggling with that silk-skirted octopusk that they didn't see Rimfire Cudd sneaking out for parts unknown. The sheriff's face looked as green as it did the time he found the dead mouse in his beer.

By the time Bedelia let Lew go, the best man looked like he'd come off second best in an augerment with a buzz saw. Before he could say anything, though, Missus

Lew Pirtle storms up like a stampeding brimmer bull with blood in its eye.

Missus Pirtle hauled off and bopped Bedelia in the face with the boquet she had aimed to give the bride-to-be on behalf of the Ladies' Knitting & Peach Preserves Society. Bedelia lost her balance and sat down with a thump in the open door of the stage coach, and like to capsized it offn the running gear.

"Floozy! Husband-stealer! Home-wrecker!" squalls Missus Pirtle, and then she turned toward Lew and give him a backhanded slap that knocked his store teeth gally-west and sent poor Lew tail-over-tincup.

Missus Pirtle followed up, hauled her husband offn the adobe by both ears, and the next thing Lew had ducked behind the stage and was lighting out for his Overland Telegraph office, with his Missus and her nine kids strung out behind him like the tail of a kite.

Well, Bedelia O'Tooligan picked herself up, clawed rose petals and baby-breath ferns out of her chins, and glares around for somebody to light in on. The Injun bucks give out with a war whoop and busted into full retreat when they seen the Boston lady sizing them up.

Nobody in Apache would have tackled Bedelia with a 20-foot horse whip just then, but Justin Other Smith, who smelled a rat the size of Adam's off ox by this time, remembering the pitcher of Lew Pirtle that had disappeared from his studio, comes out of the crowd and doffed his hat.

"Madam, you made a slight mistake, is all," the Paintin' Pistoleer says in that courteous Alabama drawl of his. "I can explain everything. The gentleman you thought was your intended groom was, in reality, the best man."

Bedelia was puffing like a cow bogged down in a mud-hole, but Justin Other Smith was a handsome young sport who had a way with women, and his big grin cooled her off pronto.

"Sheriff Rimfire Cudd is the man you're looking for, and he's twice as handsome as Lew Pirtle," Justin O. prevaricates, figgering that the sheriff had buttered his bed and be danged if he oughtn't to lie in it. "Right now your intended groom is out in the desert tracking down a bandit by the name of Two-Gun Timothy, the Terror of the Territory. Rimfire will be back, draggin' his prisoner behind him — you can depend on that."

Well, Bedelia just cooed like a mud hen in a hog-waller when she heard the reason why her beloved wasn't on hand to greet her. "If you will be so kind as to pay the stage driver ten dollars and thirty cents," she gurgled, "I will go to a hotel and tidy up after my journey. I wish to look as charming as possible when my Lochinvar returns."

Justin O. wasn't one to turn down a lady in distress, so he takes out his poke and pays off the Wells-Fargo jehu. By this time the good ladies of the Knitting Society have taken the bride in tow, and hustled her off to Jim Groot's home.

The Paintin' Pistoleer was as busy as a cat on a tin roof after that. He sashayed over to the jailhouse and found evidence to prove that Rimfire Cudd had high-tailed in a big hurry, leaving only a note for somebody to cancel his order for the cookstove. His horse was missing from the county stables, but Justin O. had a perty good idea where the bridegroom had vamoosed to.

Smith rounded up Sol Fishman and the other boys at the Bloated Goat, and swore 'em to secrecy, and they had a powwow. Then he tossed a kack on Skeeter, his palomino, and lit out of town in the direction of the Sacatones and the Mexican Border.

Sure enough, he located Rimfire Cudd hiding out at his brother's soddy in a sheep camp over in the foothills. Rimfire allowed he would bed down there for the night, and then he was heading for the Mexican Border and didn't intend to come back to Apache, ever.

"That overstuffed witch tricked me," Rimfire groaned. "That photygraph must have been tooken around 1492 B.C. I woulda jailed her on a fragrancy charge, only I knew corrallin' her would be worth more than my life."

The Paintin' Pistoleer whips out his .32 Colt on a .45 frame, the gun he had made famous throughout Arizona Territory for his trick target-shootin'. "Runnin' out ain't the honorable thing to do, Sheriff," the Pistoleer says, sounding disappointed. "You're takin' a *pasear* back to Apache and do right by your Bedelia. She come all the way out from Boston to marry her Lochinvar, and she ain't going to be jilted — not so long as there is a spark of chivalry in the wild and woolly West. Where's your sense of honor, Rimfire?"

The sheriff looks at the cocked smokepole in Smith's hand, and unbuttons his shirt to bare his skinny chest. "Go ahead and shoot, cuss you!" he begs. "I wouldn't hitch up with that overgrown hippopotamus ifn she was worth her weight in gold dust. Which would amount to a right considerable sum."

Justin O. clicks his gunhammer to show he means business. "Rattle your hocks, Sheriff," he says. "The weddin' is scheduled for eight o'clock an' you're goin' to be there."

Well, it was getting along toward dusk when Sheriff Rimfire Cudd rode back into Apache. He was towing a masked man who was handcuffed and had a lass'-rope around his neck.

Bedelia O'Tooligan was trying on her bridal gown in Mrs. Jim Groot's parlor when the sheriff rode past, and the ladies heard somebody holler that the sheriff had dabbed his twine on Two-Gun Timothy, the Terror of the Territory.

That did it. Bedelia lets out a whoop and goes lumbering at a gallop over to the jail, her veil blowin' in the breeze like a loose shirt tail, in time to see her hero get offn his dirty-white steed and march his prisoner into the calaboose.

"Two-Gun Timothy, yore days as the Terror of the Territory are over!" Rimfire hollers, after he claps his prisoner into a cell. "I'll delay yore hangin' just long enough to get myself married to the pertiest gal who ever drawed a breath."

Rimfire comes out of the jail and meets Bedelia face to face. She looks sort of stunned for a second, remembering what Justin O. Smith had said about his good looks, but she was dead game. The next thing

Rimfire knowed she was hugging him fit to bend every rib in his body and wetting him down good with kisses.

"My adorable he-man!" she cooed. "Will it make any difference to you if I confess something naughty?" she says, fluttering her eyelashes.

Rimfire was too tuckered to say a word just then.

"I'm bankrupt, Rimmy-Cuddles!" she whimpers tearfully. "My fortune was in mining stock, and just before I left Boston I found out my mines had petered out and left me a pauper. Does that make any difference in our love, my Rimmykins?"

It must not have, because the word got out that the sky pilot from Tombstone would perform the nuptial rites over in the lodge hall prompt at eight o'clock, and the horse and buggy was all slicked up outside, waiting to take Mr. and Mrs. Cudd on their honeymoon trip.

The lodge hall was packed by seven o'clock, with Injun bucks off the Cheery-cow reservation dangling from the rafters and peerin' in the winders. Rimfire Cudd, dolled up in the new overhalls Sol Fishman had donated, was waiting with the preacher. He looked more like a cheap job of embalming than he did a happy groom-to-be, though.

Jim Groot, the banker, and Lew Pirtle, the latter pretty well skinned up, were posted in the background with their six-guns ready, just to make sure Rimfire didn't try stampeding at the last minute.

Prompt at eight o'clock Missus Pirtle thumped out the wedding march from Low & Grin on a piano they had brought over from the Busted Flush Dance Hall for the occasion, and everybody stood up when Bedelia

O'Tooligan waddled into the hall on the arm of Sol Fishman.

Sol had to drop behind, though, the aisle not being wide enough for both him and a bride of Bedelia's dimensions, but in due time the sky pilot was reading the marriage ceremony, using one arm to help hold up the sheriff, who was already depending on his Bedelia for support.

"Do you, Bedelia Penelope O'Tooligan, take this man to be your lawful wedded spouse?" the sky pilot wants to know, shutting his eyes and shuddering.

"If I don't I'll have had a long trip for nothin'," Bedelia titters, beaming down at the sheriff. "You bet I do, Reverend."

The preacher gulped and turned to Rimfire. "And do you, Rimfire Cadwallader Cudd, take this woman —"

Just then the glass window behind the rose bower smashes open and a masked man in batwing chaps and a ten-gallon sombrero straddles over the sill, brandishing two six-guns.

"Two-Gun Timothy!" bellers Rimfire Cudd, coming to life. "The Terror of the Territory has busted jail — and I ain't heeled!"

The preacher keeled over in a dead faint at Bedelia's feet.

"You're spendin' your honeymoon in Hades, Sheriff!" yells Two-Gun Timothy. "I'll give you five ticks to say yore prayers!"

And then the masked bandick cuts loose with a dazzlin' display of fancy shootin' that told everybody in the lodge hall except Bedelia O'Tooligan that it was the

Paintin' Pistoleer masqueradin' behind that git-up. Nobody in the world except Justin Other Smith could have shot up the place as expertly as this "Two-Gun Timothy" did then.

His left-hand gun shot a vase of flowers offn the piano. His right-hand gun knocked feathers off an Injun buck's bonnet up in the rafters. He kept shooting, fast as fire-crackers popping off — windowlights, wall pictures, a couple of lamps. And then he turns his smoking guns on Rimfire Cudd, who was braced for the shock like the hero he was.

"I got one slug left in each gun," Two-Gun Timothy snarled, "and they got yore name writ on 'em, Sheriff!"

Bedelia let out a scream as she seen the masked man shoot point-blank at her prospective groom, and Rimfire Cudd toppled over to the floor like a coat spilling off a hook.

That was enough for Bedelia O'Tooligan. She lit out for the side door. It was latched, but that didn't mean a thing for her 300-odd pounds. She crashed outdoors in a shower of kindlin' wood.

The Paintin' Pistoleer sprinted outdoors after her, sheddin' his mask and his guns on the way. He caught up with Bedelia out at the fence. She was squalling like a baby, and for a minute Justin O. feels guilty for the trick he'd pulled off, until he found out what she was crying about.

"If that blankety-blank outlaw had waited one more minute," she cusses like a muleskinner, "I would have been Rimfire's legal widow and could have settled up his estate for my poor, dead lover!"

Justin O. Smith hands her a one-way stage ticket to Tombstone, her not stopping to wonder how come he had it so pat-handy. "It so happens that the stage you came in on hasn't left town yet, on account of the driver staying around to see Rimfire get married off," the Paintin' Pistoleer says sympathetic-like. "You just got time to make it, unless — unless you want to stick around for poor old Rimfire's funeral. The least you can do for the poor dead boy is take care of his burial expenses."

But Bedelia O'Tooligan left on the Concord, wedding gown and all. It seems she hated funerals, preferring to remember the late lamented sheriff as he had looked in life — a dashing Lochinvar on a handsome white steed.

So Apache's loss was Boston's gain, and the boys adjourned to the Bloated Goat. Rimfire Cudd got his chance to strut and be the toast of the town after all, thanks to the two blank ca'tridges which the Paintin' Pistoleer had "shot" him with in the lodge hall.

It was such a gala occasion, this celebration of the sheriff's narrow escape from a fate worse than death, that the Paintin' Pistoleer consented to down a shot of Blue Bagpipe whisky when Curly Bill Grane got around to setting up the house in Rimfire's honor.

Funny thing, but Curly Bill was the only man in the house who wasn't grinning fit to split. Bartenders ain't supposed to go on crying jags during business hours, but Curly Bill was mighty close onto it.

"I can't get that Bedelia out of my mind," he blubbers. "She looked so sweet an' innocent an' perty standin' there in front of the altar. Say, Rimfire — you still got her Boston address, ain't you?"

Blood's Thicker Than Watermelon

Now for a cow town that ain't no more'n a fly speck on the map of Arizona Territory, Apache has got its share of beetle-brained citizens. But for plumb foolishness, it would be hard to beat this here "Watermelon Derby" deal which Slickfinger Balch, the gambler, enviggled old Hector Coddlewort into.

Heck held the permanent rank of General in Apache's army of the unemployed, you might say. He wasn't exactly lazy, but his idea of work was betting his shirt on any loco idea that come along — like how many flies Curly Bill Grane would find when he cleaned out his beer keg at the Bloated Goat Saloon, or the outcome of next week's dawgfight.

Seeing as how Missus Coddlewort supported Heck and their six kids by taking in washing for the cowboys and miners hereabouts, nobody blamed her for being riled when she found out that this tinhorn, Slickfinger Balch, had hornswoggled Heck into staking their family house and home on the outcome of a melon-growing contest.

It might seem queer to outsiders, but when Samanthie — that's Missus Coddlewort — went looking for somebody to help her, she didn't go to Rimfire Cudd, the sheriff, or even to Gospel-Truth McGulp, the Baptist sky pilot. No sir, she went to this young artist feller named Justin Other Smith.

Anybody else in her fix would have done it, because Justin O. has got Apache folks out of more predicaments than a bartender at a temperance meeting would get into. Even though Smith was practically a yearling, only having voted once, folks took their troubles to him.

One morning in April, Samanthie Coddlewort sets her basket of washing down on the porch of the Longhorn Saddle Shop and waddles her way upstairs to where Justin Other Smith is busy in his studio painting a picture for next year's calendar. When he seen that Samanthie was about to blubber over, she was that mad and scairt, he sets his brushes aside and drags up his stoutest chair for her, and listens to her tale of woe.

This Slickfinger Balch was a shifty-eyed no-good who run a poker game down at the Busted Flush Casino, fleecing the wages offn cowboys and Sacatone miners with his educated pack of cards. Where he thought up his Watermelon Derby idea was hard to say, but Heck Coddlewort had shore swallered the bait.

Heck and Balch had gone over to Sol Fishman's O. K. Mercantile the day before and bought a packet of watermelon seed, and they had planted five seeds apiece at the same time — Heck planting his in a corner of Samanthie's garden patch, and Balch planting his out in the mesquites where he lived with an old Mexican wood chopper name of Pablo.

The bet was to see who had the heaviest watermelon come noon on the first day of August. If Balch's melon was the biggest he would take over the Coddlewort house and lot down past the stage depot. If Heck's melon tallied out the biggest, he was to win Slickfinger's white Arabian saddle horse and a diamond cravat pin, shaped like a horseshoe, which same Coddlewort had coveted ever since the tinhorn came to Apache.

"You see the way things stack up, Justin," Samanthie sniffles. "Heck's too lazy to water his melon seeds, let alone hoe the patch or spray the bugs off when an' if any vines sprout. The old fool has already handed over the deed to our home to Lew Pirtle, over at the telegrapht office, who's holding stakes. Slickfinger Balch is already bragging how, come August, he's going to evict me and my younguns and move into my house with a little half-breed dancin' girl from Tombstone that he aims to marry up with."

Well, the Paintin' Pistoleer says he'll do his best to auger Balch into calling off the bet, and Samanthie goes back to her washboard perked up considerable. But Justin O. ain't long in finding out that the Watermelon Derby is on in dead earnest, and that there's no more chance of stopping it now than there would be of batting a slug back into a gun barrel.

Slickfinger Balch shows his fangs like a rattler in dog days when Smith tells him he ought to be ashamed of hisself, fixing to take the roof offn the heads of pore Missus Coddlewort and her six younkers.

"It's a gentlemen's bet, and Lew Pirtle is holding the stakes," Balch says nasty-like. "Hell's fire, Smith, my diamond stickpin alone is worth as much as that Coddlewort shanty. Besides which, I don't cotton to your rammin' a horn into my private affairs."

Well, the Paintin' Pistoleer moseys over to the Bloated Goat for his afternoon dram of buttermilk, and runs across old Heck handing over his silver-buckled belt to Jim Groot, the banker, who'd won it in a checker game. From here on out, Heck would have to hold up his pants with piggin' strings, because he moved checkers around a board with about as much judgment as a stink bug uses pushing a ball of mud over the ground.

"You old coot, you should be hosswhipped for not consulting your wife before you staked her home in this damn-fool melon marathon," Justin O. scolds Coddlewort.

Heck gets huffy at that, saying he has growed watermelons out in Californy that took a hoss and wagon to haul off of the field, and that no dude cardsharp like Balch was going to best him in such a contest. That white Arabian and the diamond pin was as good as won, Coddlewort says.

Justin O. sips his buttermilk and looks downright glum. "It ain't a case of farmin' ability," he says. "Slickfinger Balch is first and last a tinhorn, and tinhorns don't gamble on anything but a sure thing. Heck," the Paintin' Pistoleer warns the old swamper,

"Balch will cold-deck you sure as I'm setting here if your melons show signs of outstripping his."

Well, it don't take long before the whole county knows about the Watermelon Derby, and the boys beat a path from the Bloated Goat over to Missus Coddlewort's garden patch, and then acrost the 'squite flats to Pablo's place, waiting and watching for developments.

Coddlewort collects a few side bets when his vines sprout first, and Balch's pushes through the 'dobe a day later. For the next couple of weeks the vines grow neck and neck.

Curly Bill Grane, who is making a few side bets on Heck's melon to romp down the chutes with a winner, almost spoils things when he gives Coddlewort the bright idea that irrigating his vines with prime whisky would "stimulate their growth." Without discussing the matter with nobody, Curly Bill donates a pint of Blue Bagpipe Scotch to Heck, who puts same in a bottle his wife uses to sprinkle clothes with before she does her ironing and he sneaks out to his melon patch that night and douses 'em good.

The only thing that saved Coddlewort from being out of the running complete, there in early June, was that most of the fertilizing solution went down his gullet instead of onto the garden. As it was, four of his five vines withered right up with acute alcoholism the next day.

This makes Apache set up and take notice. By this time everybody in town was in the pot one side or t'other, with Slickfinger Balch covering all bets that come his way. Lew Pirtle, the stakeholder, he told Justin Other Smith confidential that Balch had over 1,000 bucks covered at two-to-one odds, which put this Watermelon Derby plumb into the big-business cattygory.

With Slickfinger having five vines to Heck's one, and with good healthy blossoms on same, Justin O. figgered Samanthie was as good as headed for the poorhouse, come August first.

Well, trouble come on the Fourth of July, when a bunch of jackleg muckers from the Sacatone diggings come to town. They didn't cotton to Slickfinger Balch, on account of his card-marking talents in their stud games lately, and they taken a liking to Hector Coddlewort, who by now was strutting around liken he owned the town, bragging about how his one melon vine was thriving. Nobody had seen Heck struttier or braggier since Samanthie presented him with triplets a couple years back.

These here miners were tough hombres and their consciences didn't bother them much, so the night of the Fourth they mixed up a batch of brine over at the livery barn, by soaking a block of stock salt in hot water, and they sashayed over to Balch's melon patch after dark with their buckets, all set to cook the tinhorn's goose permanent by salting down his ground.

Sheriff Rimfire Cudd was roundsiding with the boys in at the Bloated Goat when he heard the explosions he knowed was too loud for giant firecrackers. He hauls out his old .44 and gallops outdoors, just in time to get hisself run down and trompled on by these Sacatone miners stampeding hell-for-leather out of the brush.

It seems that Slickfinger Balch knew a few tricks with salt too. He had loaded a scatter-gun to the muzzle with rock salt, and when the miners clumb over the fence he'd built around Pablo's garden track to keep the stray critters from grazing there, Balch let go with both barrels from the door of Pablo's woodshed.

The miners were a sorry sight, with their backsides peppered with salt. But of course Sheriff Rimfire Cudd didn't have a legal laig to stand on. After all, Balch had been protecting his property agin trespassers.

After that Balch took to hiring old Pablo to guard his melon patch day and night, and nobody got within six-gun range of his melons from then on. He did allow a committee composed of the Paintin' Pistoleer, Sol Fishman, the sheriff, and Lew Pirtle to visit his patch every other day, though, to report how Balch's melons was coming along.

His vines had an even dozen watermelons growing fat and sassy on the five vines, each one of 'em the size of a leppy's head and growing fast. The committee went over to Heck Coddlewort's place next, and what they saw didn't stack up too good for Samanthie keeping a roof over her head come August first.

Heck's lone vine had three melons on it, two fair-to-middlin' size and one cull. Any way you figgered it, Balch had better than a four-to-one edge over Coddlewort. It was a dern shame and a pity, but there wasn't much anybody could do, seeing as how old Heck had the house title made out in his name.

Rimfire Cudd, he knowed Balch had notches on the backstraps of his six-guns, which proved he had been a gun hawk before he drifted into 'Pache, but he couldn't find no owlhooter in his batch of reward posters whose earmarks and dewlaps matched Balch's.

One night when the Derby had only 15 days to go, a nanny goat got over the six-foot board fence Heck had built around his garden patch. The goat cleaned out Samanthie's onions and reddishes and young squash, and only a full appetite saved Heck's precious melon vine from winding up in that goat's elementary canal. How that goat got over such a high fence, nobody could figger out, but everybody had their private ideas regarding same. Rimfire Cudd took to watching Balch like a hawk, when he'd saddle up his Arabian *blanco* and ride over to Tombstone to call on his girl, who worked as a percentage dancer in a honkytonk there.

A couple days after the goat business, this girl showed up on the Tombstone stage. She was a dark-eyed little hussy name of Rosita Mendoza. It seems Rosita honed to size up Samanthie's house, so she could fix curtains for the windows and such-like before she married Slickfinger and moved to Apache to live.

Well, she'd no more than got out of the Concord and kissed Balch hello, when this stray nanny goat come traipsing out of the chaparral where Heck and his oldest boy Percival had chased it, and began bleating and cavorting around Rosita like a pet puppy.

Heck Coddlewort happened to be snoozing on the porch of the Bloated Goat Saloon acrost the street and when he seen how this nanny goat knowed Rosita, he was fitten to be tied. He seen Balch turn pale around the gills, trying to shoo the goat away from Rosita, but it stuck to her feet like a cocklebur.

Coddlewort ducked into the saloon and come out with the sawed-off shotgun that Curly Bill Grane kept under his bar to maintain peace and quiet with. He aims the buckshot gun at this nanny goat, and then Rosita done a foolish thing.

She lets go Balch's arm, and drops down on her knees beside the nanny goat, and hugs it, and whimpers in Spanish, "Don't you dare shoot my precious little Chiva!"

Well, Coddlewort had gone plumb besmirk, and he bellers out that he'll give Rosita five ticks to get out of the way before he yanks triggers. She don't budge a particle.

Slickfinger Balch draws his guns then, and there wouldn't have been a judge and jury in the whole Territory who would have hung him for salivating old Heck, the way things was shaping up.

Just then a gunshot blasts out from somewhere acrost the street, and *ker-wham!* the shotgun flies out of Heck Coddlewort's hands. Rosita jumps to her feet and the nanny goat lights a shuck for the brush.

"Hold it, Slickfinger!" a voice sings out.

Balch turns around and stares up at the window over the Longhorn Saddle Shop. Leaning acrost the sill was the Paintin' Pistoleer, wearing his artist's smock, and in his hand was his famous .32 Colt on a .45 frame, with smoke curling from the bore. Talking it over afterward,

Apache agreed that there wasn't another man in Arizona who could have shot the buckshot gun out of Heck's hands at that bad angle and long range.

"Holster them guns and move along, Balch!" Justin O. Smith warns in that soft Alabama drawl of his. "Heck, you come closer than a gnat's knuckles of making Samanthie a widow, you know that?"

Well, Balch cusses some but he backs down and him and Rosita Mendoza head off down the street to the Coddlewort house.

There, Rosita has the gall to ask Samanthie for a tape measure so she can see how big to make her curtains and rugs. Samanthie was up to her ears in a washtub at the time, but she skims the soapsuds off her arms and grabs the handiest thing she could lay hands on, a big skillet, and whams Rosita over the noggin with it.

"No dance-hall jessie-bell can set foot in my house as long as I'm running it," Samanthie says. "Ske-daddle, you she-skonk!"

Rosita shows fight, calling Missus Coddlewort an old she-blister and some other names in Spanish lingo, but Samanthie picks up a lump of homemade lye soap and pops it in Rosita's mouth, which same makes Rosita rattle her hocks back to the front gate where Slickfinger Balch is waiting for her. Rosita's mouth is foaming like a hydrophoby skunk, and she ketches the stage back to Tombstone pronto.

Sheriff Rimfire Cudd was the last one in town to hear about the ruckus, as usual, and he wanted to run Slickfinger Balch into the calaboose for such a low-down trick as fetching in Rosita's nanny goat to clean out Heck's garden patch, but you think old Coddlewort would allow it?

"Not by a dang sight!" he bellers. "I got two melons that are going to beat that dozen of Balch's, you wait and see. I aim for my son Perc'val to get that white Arabian for his birthday, and I aim to be sporting that di'mond cravat pin, soon as I can rustle me a cravat. No sirree, Sheriff, you leave this Watermelon Derby lay the way she was dealt. I ain't going to lose."

Well, Heck was the only one so optimistic about his chances. The warm days and cool nights was doing wonders to Balch's dozen melons, the committee was forced to report. The August first deadline was only ten days off, and Samanthie Coddlewort began looking peaked like she wasn't sleeping much of nights, and Slickfinger Balch took to looking over the wedding rings in Sol Fishman's showcase, fixing to buy one for his Rosita.

As a matter of fact, a jerk-line muleskinner comes into town with a couple wagonloads of stuff Rosita and Balch had had shipped in from Phoenix — tables and chairs and chiffyniers and rugs and such-like, all ready to move into the Coddlewort house when the melon derby paid off. Balch stored the stuff in the empty shed back of Dyspepsia Dan's restaurant.

Well, there was only one measly week to go in the Watermelon Derby when the committee discovers that two of Coddlewort's three melons had died on the vine, leaving only the runt of the litter, a nubbin that was about the size of a whisky bottle, quart size.

"I got a fat chance of beating Balch now," old Heck sobs. "One thing shore, I'll never gamble agin as long as I live. I wouldn't blame Samanthie and Perc and the triplets ifn they up and left a wurthless old dunce like me."

The boys nicknamed Coddlewort's melon "Fat Chance." Slickfinger Balch got permission of the committee to take a look-see over the board fence at Heck's melon, and he seed for himself that the Derby was as good as won. That same day he bought Rosita's wedding ring at Sol Fishman's.

That night the Paintin' Pistoleer took a *pasear* over to Samanthie's house, and he brung the two dead watermelons back to his studio. With nobody there to see what he was doing, he cut into the two melons like an undertaker making an autopsy.

He found something that made his dander rise, too. Down close to the stems, he seen where a tiny hole had been punched through the melon rinds, and then stoppered over with beeswax so nobody could see they had been tampered with. Inside the pink meat along with the seeds was a cupful of turpentine.

"Balch clumb over the fence and doctored the two best melons," he says to himself. "But proving that ain't going to be so easy."

Well, Smith piddles around his studio awhile, frowning the way he does when he's rassling with a problem, and finally he sticks the watermelons in a gunnysack and goes over to Sol Fishman's house. After a while, him and Sol make a trip into the O. K. Mercantile together.

84

It was the very next day that the miracle began to happen. Coddlewort's "Fat Chance" melon doubled in size overnight. The committee hung their chins over the board fence and seen the proof for themselves. This watermelon was big and dark-green and shiny, and where it had been a measly foot long the day before, it must have been two foot long today, easy.

Curly Bill Grane takes a cake of soap and writes a score board down on his back-bar mirror every day that week. It looked something like this:

Balch's Biggest		Heck's Fat Chance
15″	MONDAY	12¼″
15½″	TUESDAY	23″
16″	WENSDAY	27″

Heck Coddlewort, he took to guarding his melon patch 24 hours a day, not letting nobody inside his fence with the younguns fetching him his grub and coffee, and him spreading his soogans alongside old Fat Chance of nights.

Samanthie begin grinning like she was cut from ear to ear, and her children started playing with the other kids agin, and didn't look red-eyed and squally all the time.

Slickfinger Balch, escorted by the committee, took a trip over to the Coddlewort garden every morning to see how Fat Chance was doing. Heck kept the vine covered from view with a little tent he'd made out of a horse blanket, but he'd lift up one corner and let Balch

85

watch for hisself while Justin Other Smith, as official referee, would go into the garden with a yardstick and take the melon's measurements.

On July 31, the day before the Derby was to wind up, the score on the backbar mirror at the Bloated Goat stood like this:

Balch's	Heck's
Biggest	*Fat Chance*
17½″	31″

Well, the Paintin' Pistoleer was in at the Bloated Goat roundsiding with the big crowd that night, when the old Mexican wood chopper, Pablo, busted through the batwings, plumb excited.

"*Señor* Balch has *vamoosed!*" he bellers. "He saddles up hees *blanco* and hit off eento the desert, *si!*"

The boys all stampeded over to the Mexican's shack, and sure enough, they seen that Balch had taken his bedroll and his war sack full of fancy duds, and had skipped town.

Justin O. Smith, he gets an idea then, and he grabs the sheriff and they gallop over to the Overland Telegraph office. Sure enough, they find Lew Pirtle, the stakeholder, lying on the floor hog-tied and with a gag stuffed in his mouth. His company safe was yawning wide open and his telegraph instruments had been smashed up considerable and the outside wires cut.

"Slickfinger come in here and pulled a gun on me," Pirtle explains to Rimfire Cudd. "He makes me open the safe, and got out his diamond stickpin and the money he'd bet with the boys. That Arabian stud of his was waiting out back at the time."

Rimfire Cudd blows his big nose like a bugle and gives his galluses a hitch. "That welsher seen he'd lost the Watermelon Derby so he lit out for the Border," the sheriff says. "I'll dab my loop on the son before he gits very far."

And, dumb coot that he is, Sheriff Cudd rounds up a posse and takes off into the desert after the absconder. Which was a loco idea, seeing as how there wasn't a moon out, and Balch had an hour's head start. But Rimfire and everybody who had a nag to fork, they took off hell-for-leather toward the Border.

Everybody, that is, except the Paintin' Pistoleer. He stayed up most of the night helping Lew Pirtle patch up his telegraph outfit. Then he has Lew send a message to the marshal over at Tombstone, describing Balch and his white Arabian stud, and asking this marshal to keep a stirrup eye peeled on a certain Señorita Rosita Mendoza, who was a fandango dancer at the Oriental Palace in Tombstone.

Well, the sheriff and his boys drifted back to Apache along toward daylight, empty-handed. They were a woebegone-looking passel of rannies, too, because every man in the posse had a stake in the dinero Slickfinger had vamoosed with.

They all went to bed, and it was around high noon, the hour set for the Watermelon Derby to finish, when Lew Pirtle shags over to the jailhouse and wakes up Rimfire Cudd, handing him a telegram he'd just tooken off the wire.

This message was from the marshal of Tombstone, and it said that he was holding Slickfinger Balch in his calaboose, along with his loot, for Rimfire Cudd to pick up at his convenience. Thanks to Justin O. Smith's astootness, Balch had been arrested when he rode up to the Oriental Palace on his white horse, to get Rosita Mendoza to head south of the Border with him.

Well, that called for a celebration in Apache. It was a toss-up whether it would be Blue Bagpipe whisky from the Bloated Goat, or a big watermelon feed. Since women and kids would be in on the deal, the watermelons won the vote.

Sol Fishman takes a wheelbarrow and goes over to Balch's melon patch, and since Pablo wasn't guarding it any more, Sol come gallivanting back with 12 luscious watermelons, which same he dumps in a horse trough to cool.

The whole town fell into the spirit of the thing, and the menfolks hitched up a couple of wagons and went over to the shed back of Dyspepsia Dan's restaurant, and loaded up the furniture and rugs and stuff that Slickfinger had bought for his bride-to-be, and duly installed same over in Samanthie's parlor.

Samanthie was fit to bust for joy, it being the first new stuff she'd had in her house since she'd married old Heck 30-odd years before.

"Not only that, but when Heck gets Balch's diamond stickpin back from Tombstone, he's fixing to make me a lavyleer out of it," Samanthie says, giving Heck a nice slobbery kiss on top of his bald head. "Heck always was a mighty good provider."

That last was stretching things a point, but in two ways old Coddlewort was a changed man. You could offer him ten-to-one odds that the sun wouldn't rise tomorrow and you couldn't tempt him to gamble, he had got that bad a scare. And it wasn't long before he got a job over in the mines, and Samanthie quit her taking in washing. But that's getting ahead of the story.

Well, picnic tables was set for the watermelon feast out in the Coddlewort's back yard, and after Gospel-Truth McGulp, the Baptist preacher, finished asking the blessing, he says that the main piece of resistance should be the biggest watermelon that Arizona Territory had ever produced, namely the derby winner itself, old Fat Chance.

The Paintin' Pistoleer grins to himself when Samanthie hands him a butcher knife and a washtub, and everybody follows him out to the board fence while Heck, chuckling over some little joke of his own, unlocks the gate.

Sheriff Cudd, who wanted to get a belly full of watermelon before he started for Tombstone to fetch back his prisoner, he remarks to Justin O., "That there melon must weigh fifty-sixty-odd pounds. I better help you tote that tub over to the table."

The Paintin' Pistoleer walks across the garden and lifts the horse blanket tent off of the vine, giving most of the spectators their first glimpse of the miracle melon. There she set, old Fat Chance, in all her glory. As long as a man's arm and green as grass, with yellow stripes running from stem to tip.

89

"I think I can manage okay," Justin Other Smith says, shooting a wink at Sol Fishman. "I'll plug her to see if she's ripe."

With which Justin O. slips his butcher knife into old Fat Chance, and *ker-blam!* That champeen watermelon blowed right up in his face with a hollow popping noise and vanished right before everybody's eyes!

Then the Paintin' Pistoleer reaches down and picks up a limp, flabby-looking thing that looked like an old rag lying on the ground.

"It's a rubber balloon Sol Fishman give me over at the O. K. Mercantile the other night," Smith says, and goes on to explain how he found where Balch had doctored Heck's melons with turpentine, having bought said turpentine the same day from Sol hisself.

"In view of the vital issues at stake," Smith goes on to point out, "I figured a few tricks might help our side. So I took this toy balloon up to the studio and painted it to look like a watermelon, and every night I'd blow a little more air into her."

Everybody busted out laughing and cheering fit to split a gut then, all except Curly Bill Grane, the bartender. Folks thought at first that Curly Bill was unhappy because he knowed his presence at the picnic was about as popular as a weasel in a hen house so far as Samanthie was concerned. Entertaining a saloon keeper would embarrass Samanthie next time she met with the Apache Ladies' Knitting and Peach Preserves Society.

But that wasn't what was bothering Curly Bill. He wipes the drool offn his mouth and looked downright doleful.

90

"That melon shore would have tasted delicious," he moans. "Them culls from Balch's vines won't hold a candle to old Fat Chance. I don't think I'll even have a slice."

But Curly Bill gorged hisself into a nice spell of colic, it turned out. Samanthie seen to that.

Souse of the Border

You wouldn't have thought a sawed-off little runt like Whisky Pete Krumb could have wrecked the Bloated Goat Saloon like he done, but when he got through smashing up everything in sight it wasn't worth setting a match to.

Pete was a sheepherder from over in the Sacatones, so short and bandy-laiged it seems like he's standing in a hole, and he looks like a little elf out of a kid's fairy-tale book with his long yeller whiskers, full of sticky-burrs and tobacco juice and dangling to his bootstraps.

He had fixed hisself up a still back in an old prospect hole where he brews up this concoction he calls "Panther Perspiration." About once a year Pete gets more of a load than he can handle and comes down to Apache on a toot.

Them trumpets which caved in the walls of Jericho couldn't have played second fiddle to one of Whisky Pete Krumb's toots. Just like a lightning bolt, nobody knows for sure just where he is going to strike when he shows up in town aboard his jenny mules, with a jug of his homebrew under one arm, and a shooting-iron in each fist.

92

This particular toot, Whisky Pete had got the idea that Curly Bill Grane's saloon was an eyesore which ought to be tore down and that he was the hombre to take on the contract. First thing he done was to shoot the backbar mirror full of holes, to clear out the customers so he could have elbow room. When Curly Bill took offense at Pete tipping over his piano, Pete rammed a brass cuspidor over Curly Bill's bald head which taken a blacksmith to pry loose.

Whisky Pete grabbed a pool cue then and clubbed hell out of a stuffed moose head on the wall, laboring under the impression that he was lambasting Sheriff Rimfire Cudd. After a little more horseplay the like of that there, he straddles his mule and heads back to his sheep camp, singing a gospel hymn at the top of his lungs.

Well, the decent citizens of Apache crawled out of hiding and rousted Sheriff Rimfire Cudd out from under his bed over at the jailhouse, where he claimed he was fixing to bait a mousetrap, and threatened to lynch the sheriff if he didn't track down Whisky Pete and arrest the old souse.

Sheriff Cudd started trailing Krumb around midnight, but Sunday morning comes and he ain't back yet with his prisoner, and the town begins to wonder ifn they shouldn't have sent a good-sized posse out to dehorn Whisky Pete.

Anyhow, Curly Bill is in his saloon this Sunday morning, sizing up the shambles Whisky Pete had made of the place, little knowing that his run of bad luck hadn't even started yet. He was hunkered on the edge of a busted poker table, looking at his reflection in the beer which covered the floor from a barrel that Whisky Pete had shot full of holes, when the batwing door which was still hanging by one hinge give a squeak.

Curly Bill looks around to see who's there, hoping it's the sheriff with Whisky Pete safely hog-tied for branding. But it was Lew Pirtle, who runs the Overland Telegraph. Lew has a telegram in his hand, but he makes off like he's a-scairt to come in.

"If you're fetchin' bad news there, fork it over!" Grane moans pitiful-like. "After survivin' Whisky Pete's toot, it's plumb erysipilas to me ifn you got a wire from the Gov'nor saying I'm to be hung next week."

Pirtle sidles in, wading through the beer-soaked sawdust, and hands Curly Bill this telegram liken it was a bull rattler he had aholt of and was afraid to let go of.

"You better take a shot of red-eye before you read that, Curly," Lew warns him. "I am the bearer of evil tidings."

Curly Bill grunts and reads this here telegram Lew had just tooken off the wires from El Paso:

One of my circus performers took sick and can't care for year-old baby. Am sending infant to you on Arizona Flyer arriving Apache Tuesday morning. Will pick up baby when my circus goes through one month from now by which time its mother should be recovered.

Uncle Coot

94

Curly Bill didn't even bat an eyelash. He pats Lew on the shoulder and says, "Don't let this worry you none. It's a josh. My Uncle Coot, he runs a little two-bit circus show and he's famous for his practical jokes. Hell, he'd know better than ship an unweaned critter to an old bachelor like me, Lew."

But Pirtle digs in his pocket and fishes out another telegram. "This'll frost yore eyeballs," he says. "It's a telegraphic money order, writ out in your name to the amount of one hundred chips. It's to cover yore expenses in playin' nursemaid to this slick-ear younker until Coot's circus shows up in 'Pache."

Well, this news really set Curly Bill's cork to bobbing. The draft can be tooken over to Jim Groot at the Stockman's Bank and swapped for hard cash. Next to his practical joking, this Uncle Coot is famous for being a tightwad of the first water. This draft proves the old pinch-penny has actually shipped the baby.

"But I don't know nothin' about kids!" Curly Bill gets panicky. "I wouldn't even know how to take aholt of one."

Well, just then in walks Justin Other Smith, the young artist feller who has his studio upstairs over the Longhorn Saddle Shop. He's come over in hopes that Whisky Pete's binge hadn't smashed up the buttermilk jug, so he can get his morning swig.

Smith listens to Curly Bill's story and he reads Uncle Coot's telegram, and he gives a long, low whistle.

"This is horrible," he admits. "Me, all I know about infants is that they got an appetite at one end and no responsibility at the other, me being the last of Ma's litter. Howsomever," Justin O. gets a bright idea, "we can sashay over to Dyspepsia Dan's restaurant and talk to his Chinee cook, Aw Gwan. I understand Aw Gwan is the father of quite a brood back in California."

So Curly Bill and Pirtle and the Paintin' Pistoleer, they hike over to Dyspepsia Dan's Feedbag Café and find Aw Gwan out back churning up a batch of butter. Aw Gwan is a moon-faced little cuss with a greasy pigtail and a friendly grin, and tacked up on the wall of his kitchen is a tintype of six little slant-eyed tykes that Aw Gwan claims he is the father of.

"What," asks Justin Other Smith, "did you feed your young-uns to put all that tallow on their ribs, Aw Gwan?"

The Chinee leans on the dasher of his churn a minute and answers through his nose in his funny Asiatic sing-song, "Lice!"

Curly Bill gags like he'd swallered a live cockroach. "Lice? You mean common garden-variety crawlers like Whisky Pete Krumb soaks his whiskers in sheep dip to get rid of?"

"Lice pudding," Aw Gwan corrects him, "with cleam an' sugar."

"This is no time for joshin', you misbegotten heathen!" snaps Curly Bill. "No child of mine will get such a diet."

Lew Pirtle pipes up and says he don't think a year-old brat is ready to eat rice pudding yet. They head back toward the Bloated Goat, feeling pretty glum about the whole business, when who should come riding out of the brush but Sheriff Rimfire Cudd, towing Whisky Pete at the end of a lass'-rope.

Whisky Pete is cold sober now, and he is a pathetic sight astraddle of his jenny mule, with Rimfire's handcuffs on his wrists, and his long yeller beard rolled up like a bib and tucked inside his butternut shirt.

"Curly Bill, old friend," Whisky Pete whimpers, "I'll make good that damage the sheriff claims I done last night, ifn it takes the last peso I get from my wool crop this spring. I applegize."

Well, Rimfire Cudd almost has to pull a gun to keep Curly Bill from hauling that little dwarf offn the mule and stompin' him six feet into the 'dobe.

"The law'll shut Pete's water off for him," the sheriff says. "He'll get a ten-year stretch at Yuma pen, at least. By the time he gets through busting rocks, he won't be thirsty for no more Panther Perspiration. Mebbe he'll fergit how to make the stuff."

Well, the sheriff gets the story then from Curly Bill about how his Uncle Coot has shipped a circus woman's baby to Apache for Curly Bill to ride herd on for a month. And by a miracle, old Rimfire comes up with the first intelligent proposition so far.

"We got to think of the pore lil critter's welfare before yourn, Curly Bill. This stacks up to me like a squaw's job. There's plenty of womenfolks here in Apache who'd do the job for half of that dinero your uncle sent you. Samanthie Coddlewort, or Jim Groot's woman Hernia, or mebbe your wife, Pirtle."

But Curly Bill flies into a huff at such a suggestion. "You know danged well every she-male in this burg belongs to the ladies' Knittin' & Peach Presarves Society, Sheriff," Grane points out. "Which same Society is dead set on closing up the Bloated Goat, claiming booze is an abolution unto the Lord and the town should go on a bone-dry basis. No sirree — I don't want ary woman in town to know I'm expecting a baby come Tuesday."

The sheriff, who likes his nip as well as the next one, he realizes how them temperance-minded Apache ladies are out for Curly Bill's scalp, all right. He goes on to remark that the hull kit and kaboodle of the Knittin' & Peach Presarves Society are a bunch of she-blisters who ought to have a bung-starter rammed up their prying noses.

Lew Pirtle, whose missus happens to be president of said Society, he knows he ought to get his back up at such insulting talk, but when he sees how the others agree, he gives a sickly grin and nods emphatic, thcm being his private sediments likewise. Just then they overhear Whisky Pete babblin' to himself.

"It's too bad I'm goin' to be shipped off to the penintentiary," Pete blubbers, "on account of I've riz more younguns than you could shake a stick at. Yessir," Whisky Pete says loudly, "you wouldn't think it to look at me, mebbe, but I know more about the care an' feedin' of childern than ary wet-nurse in the county!"

Well, that's a hoss of a different color. Curly Bill stares at Whisky Pete, and then looks at the sheriff, and a grin starts spreading under his handlebar mustache.

"Mebbe this pesky sheepherder desarves one more chanct to go on the water wagon," Curly Bill braces the sheriff. "Mebbe if Whisky Pete was to groom an' grain this circus woman's kid until Uncle Coot shows up, I'd cancel my bill for damages."

Seeing as how critical the situation is, with Apache's likker supply at stake, Sheriff Rimfire Cudd is reasonable. Everybody is swore to secrecy, to make sure none of the biddies from the Knittin' & Peach Preserves Society get wind of what's happening, so as to give them another black mark to chalk up agin the Bloated Goat Saloon. Whisky Pete gets his dewclaws unlocked pronto.

The old galoot ain't bluffin', neither. After he swamps out the barroom so it don't look quite so much like an earthquake had hit it, he decides that Curly Bill's private poker room out back is *muy bueno* for a baby's nursery, especially since no woman would be caught dead with a foot inside the Bloated Goat.

Sunday afternoon, over in his jail cell, Pete gets busy and makes a crib out of a beer barrel, by sawing a big square hole in the staves and nailing rockers to the bottom from a barroom chair he'd broke into kindlin' wood the night before. The Paintin' Pistoleer fetches his box of paints over from his studio, and works all day Monday fixing the nursery room up fancy, with pictures of Mother Goose and such like on the walls.

Whisky Pete says the kid will need lots of three-cornered britches, as most likely he ain't been house-broke at his age, so Sol Fishman, who runs the O. K. Mercantile, is let in on the secret and he donates a bale of gunnysacks which Whisky Pete allows will work fine and dandy.

The question of feeding the younker comes up. Nacherly, Curly Bill says that whisky is the best nourishment for man or beast, regardless of age.

"You must be plumb loco," jeers Jim Groot, the banker, all riled up at such an outrageous suggestion. "No one-year-old kid could hold a whisky bottle. Any dumb ranny with the sense God give a crowbar knows we'll have to give him his whisky with a spoon."

But Whisky Pete, irregardless of his agreeing with Curly Bill about the merits of alcohol in any manner shape or form, he vetoes the idea after some serious thought.

"Milk is what we need," he explains. "Not the cow variety. Goat's milk. Now, I got me a nanny over in my camp who come fresh last week. If the sheriff here will let me take a *pasear* over to the Sacatones tonight, I'll smuggle my she-goat back to 'Pache without the old hens from the Knittin' Society bein' none the wiser. How about it, Rimfire?"

Well, the sheriff gets his back up. He's plumb dubious about the wisdom of turning Whisky Pete loose, knowing the old warthog has that still in the back of his prospect hole. He sneers at Whisky Pete's solemn oath that he'll never bend an elbow again, which same is an old story with Pete after he's been on a toot.

"I'll escort you over to camp personal," Rimfire compromises, "and we'll fetch back this nanny goat tonight."

So far as the womenfolks in town knows, Whisky Pete is being kept under lock and key at the calaboose, awaiting trial. But after dark Monday night, Rimfire Cudd saddles up Pete's mule and his own crowbait.

Sam Guff, the local medico, who happens to be sobering up from a drunk in the cell next to Pete's, he gives the old souse a bit of free medical advice when the sheriff comes for Pete.

"Whisky Pete, you're a border-line case so far as going to a padded cell in a bughouse is concerned," the saw bones give it to him blunt. "Ever hear of delirium tremens? Mebbe the very next drink you pour down your gullet, you'll get the D.T.'s. You'll see snakes and pink elephants and all sorts of horrible hallucinations. When you do, Pete, it means your brain has gone soft. You'll be locked up for the rest of your misspent life in a straitjacket."

So when Whisky Pete rides out of town with the sheriff that night, he's in a mighty repenting mood.

They're due back in Apache by midnight at the latest, but by sunrise Tuesday they ain't showed up, and everybody is worried plenty that something went wrong at Pete's sheep camp.

Just after daylight, the Arizona Flyer stops at the Apache station to unload a passenger. It is the first time in five years the train done that, which was why nobody was waiting at the depot except Curly Bill and Justin O. Smith, nobody else being up yet.

Well, those two worked so fast and so secret that not even Sol Fishman or Lew Pirtle or the other boys in on the baby deal know what's happened until it's over. All they can find out is that Uncle Coot's circus woman's baby showed up on the Flyer, all right, and was whisked off down to the nursery room at the Bloated Goat. Not a woman in town is wise to what happened, which is good.

The boys gather at the barroom and try to pry some information out of Curly Bill Grane, but he ain't talking, and he looks perty mad and desperate, probably because the baby is on his hands now and his nursemaid, Whisky Pete, is long overdue getting back to 'Pache with the milk goat.

"Well, is the younker a girl or a boy?" Sol Fishman insists on knowing, because he hones to present the kid with either a rag doll or a B-B rifle.

"It's a bouncin' baby boy," Curly Bill admits. But he refuses to take the padlock offn the nursery door long enough to give anybody a glimpse of the weaner he's tucked into the crib Whisky Pete had made. He's taking no chances on rumors leaking out to reach the ears of the ladies.

And the Paintin' Pistoleer ain't around to give out any news, him being up in his studio working on a picture of a beef roundup he's painting for a cowboy-boot catalogue over in Coffeyville, Kansas.

Smith is busy daubing away when he happens to look outn the window, and sees a cloud of dust coming acrost the desert from the direction of the Border. Perty soon Justin O. makes out that it's Sheriff Rimfire Cudd, riding hell-for-leather toward town. And he's alone, traveling 'way too fast for Whisky Pete's mule and the nanny goat to keep up.

Smelling trouble, the Paintin' Pistoleer sashays downstairs just in time to see the sheriff pull up in front of the Bloated Goat. Old Rimfire looks like undertaker bait.

"There's hell to pay, men!" the sheriff pants, orey-eyed. "When we got over to Whisky Pete's camp last night, we found out that rustlers had drove his band of sheep acrost the Border. We couldn't locate hide nor hair o' them woolies, including the goat."

Well, that was a balled-up howdy-do, for sure. By now that baby boy hid in the back room is probably howling for his groceries, let alone a change of britches. But Rimfire Cudd ain't give Apache half the bad news yet.

"Whisky Pete snuck over to that prospect hole where he keeps his still, and swigged down a gallon of his joy juice," the sheriff confesses, miserable. "He got hisself pickled up in a way to make all his past toots look like a Sunday School picnic. Men, that little heller is on his way here now, soused to the back teeth, with a smokepole in each hand. He aims to shoot this cow town plumb offn the map, and I can't see no way to prevent it. My advice is to take to the hills while there's time."

The boys look plenty boogery at that, and commence looking around for suitable spots to fort up and weather the storm. Ifn they'd had their druthers, every man in town would druther have outrun a stampede of long-horns in a box canyon than tangle with Whisky Pete when he was fixing to get strung out on one of his toots.

"Why in tarnation," the Paintin' Pistoleer hollered, "didn't you keep your loop dallied on that old toss-pot?"

Rimfire Cudd looks sheepish. "Matter of fact, the little galoot whopped me on the noggin with the flat of an ax blade and when I come to, my holsters was empty," the sheriff confesses. "Come to think of it, boys, the guns Pete is packin' are my forty-fours."

Well, everybody eyes the south skyline, thankful that Pete is slowed down by his string-halted jenny mule. Rimfire Cudd says he's got to leave town for the day, to collect some taxes from the cow spreads up in the north end of the county, and he rattles his hocks yonderward without tarryin' for breakfast.

The town takes its cue from the sheriff and scatters. All except the Paintin' Pistoleer, who runs over to the O. K. Mercantile and finds Sol Fishman hid in the feed shed behind some baled alfalfy.

"I got work to do before Pete shows up," Smith yells. "You got to help me, Sol. It's a matter of life or death for Apache."

Well, it's less than an hour before a big rumble like a cyclone blowing up reaches Apache. It's Whisky Pete, and anybody can see this toot is going to be a ring-tailed rip-snorter.

"I'm a curly black wolf on the high ol' prod," his yell drifts acrost the mesquite flats. "My fangs cain't be drawed an' I'm looking for a man for breakfast! This is my day to howl an' when I'm finished this town will look like a heap o' mine tailin's! Yippee! Let 'er buck! Ride 'em cowboy! Whoooopee-de-whoop!"

Whisky Pete busts into sight from the alley betwixt the Wells-Fargo station and the Busted Flush dance hall. He spurs his jenny mule out into the main stem and lets go with both of Cudd's six-shooters, knocking a tin rooster offn the weathervane of the blacksmith shop roof, just to limber up his shootin' eye.

The mule, she bucks and sunfishes and piles Whisky Pete tail-over-tincup into a waterin'-trough. But the sheepherder crawls out, wrings his whiskers dry, and proceeds to shoot the seat out of a pair of red flannel drawers which Samanthie Coddlewort has hanging on her clothesline.

The streets are plumb deserted, natural. Rimfire Cudd ain't expected back before tomorrow. It looks like Apache is going to get its lid pried off sure as hell has hot hinges.

Just then the door of the Bloated Goat fans open. Justin Other Smith comes strolling out, chewing a toothpick. Folks watching from the windows of the Stockman's Bank breathe easier when they seen that Smith is packin' his famous Colt, a .32 on a .45 frame. If anybody in Arizona can pin down Whisky Pete's hairy ears today, that man is the Paintin' Pistoleer.

Whisky Pete thinks he sees two of Smith and he starts bellerin' at both of 'em as he comes down the street on a zigzag, taking potshots at every stray chicken and dog in sight.

The town knows he's still got ca'tridges in his .44's, though, when he staggers up to where the Paintin' Pistoleer is waiting for him in the middle of the main drag. Justin O. hasn't even made a move toward his own gun when Whisky Pete circles him a couple of times like a banty rooster flirtin' with a pullet. Finally Pete draws a shaky bead on Smith's shirt with them cannons he stole offn the sheriff, and gives a beller you could hear plumb to the Border.

"I'm goin' to blow a hole in yore belly an' wade through in my bare feet, draggin' my canoe behind me!" Pete says. "I'm honin' to see ifn you'll bleed buttermilk, young feller."

Well, the Paintin' Pistoleer don't turn a hair. He's got more guts than a butcher's meat wagon.

"Before you make this experiment," he says in that soft Alabama drawl of hisn, "suppose we step inside the Bloated Goat and hoist a drink first. Not buttermilk, either. The best in the house. Blue Bagpipe Scotch — on me."

Well, that proposition appeals to Whisky Pete, seeing as how he had busted his jug of Panther Perspiration when the mule bucked him off back yonder. His tongue is dry as a bootsole and hanging out like a latigo strap.

"Okay," he agrees. "Then I'll blow that hole through your mangey hide, Smith, an' see if you bleed buttermilk, what say?"

The whole town holds its breath when they seen the Paintin' Pistoleer and Whisky Pete go into the saloon. They dassn't come out, though, knowing showdown is going to bust any second now.

Curly Bill Grane is standing behind the bar, looking like he wished a hole would cave in the floor and take him with it. There ain't a solitary soul in the barroom, besides him.

"Wh-wh-what'll it be, g-gents?" he stammers. "Name yore p-pizen, gents."

106

"Blue Bagpipe, neat!" Whisky Pete hiccups, making several stabs at hooking a boot on the brass rail and finally giving up.

Curly Bill is tremblin' like a cat spittin' peach seeds but he manages to reach under the bar and bring out a quart bottle. He sets it on the bar in front of Whisky Pete and pulls the cork.

Whisky Pete reaches for the bottle like he's dying of thirst, but then he lets go of it like it's a hot branding-iron. His eyeballs bug out like a tromped-on toad-frog's. Because out of the neck of this here bottle squirms a little green snake, its forky tongue flickering in and out like mad.

Whisky Pete lays his guns careful on the floor and rubs the drool offn his mouth. He drums his fingers on the edge of the bar for a while, and finally he turns around and looks up at the Paintin' Pistoleer, beckoning for Smith to bend down so he can whisper something in his ear.

"Smith, old pal, you an' me been friends for a long time," Whisky Pete whispers confidential. "Tell me — do you see anything peculiar about that there bottle?"

Well, the Paintin' Pistoleer leans down for a close look, his nose almost touching the snake's. Then he straightens up.

"Curly Bill didn't dust it off very good," he says. "Otherwise it looks like prime imported Scotch to me, Whisky Pete. Bill wouldn't try to ring in any watered trade likker on us."

By this time the snake has crawled outen the bottle and is wiggling acrost the bar toward Whisky Pete, who backs off a couple of yards and scrubs his eyes back into their sockets.

"It's like Doc Guff warned me," mumbles Pete. "My brain is turnin' soft. I'm seein' Lucy Nations, shore as hell."

Curly Bill gives a start like he's set on a hornet. "Lucy Nations?" he echoes. "Is she ary relation to this here Carrie Nation who's goin' around busting up saloons with a hatchet?"

Whisky Pete don't answer. Sweat is a-popping out of his pores like juice from a squoze lemon. "It's the delirious trimmings," he sobs. "The D.T.'s! I got 'em!"

Whisky Pete turns around, looking for some place to run, when he freezes dead in his tracks. He sees something, or imagines he sees something, which makes him jump clean up on the bar, snake or no snake. Smith and Curly Bill stare at each other, like they're puzzled.

Around the far end of the bar waddles a cute little elephant about three feet tall, pink as a rose petal, with big bile-green dots speckled all over it. This pink elephant shuffles down the bar, flapping its pink ears like fans, and samples the contents of a cuspidor with its little garden hose of a trunk.

Whisky Pete don't wait for his eyes to focus any. He gives a yelp and makes a flying leap to the floor, bounces like a rubber ball, and scales off in a swan dive that carries him through a glass window. His bandy legs are thrashin' like windmills by the time they hit the ground outdoors.

108

Before the Paintin' Pistoleer can reach the front door for a look, Whisky Pete has vanished in the brush, heading for the Border like a turpentined terrier.

"Now what in hell," Smith says, "could have got into him?"

Curly Bill thought his troubles was over, after that. Three weeks roll by without a trace of Whisky Pete. One night his Uncle Coot's circus train pulls in at the Apache siding and the baby is offn Curly Bill's hands, in strict secrecy so far as the town's womenfolks is concerned.

But it turns out that Grane's troubles are far from over. Fact is, they're just beginning.

The good ladies of the Knitting & Peach Preserves Society know all about Whisky Pete's latest toot, of course, and they start their temperance drive in dead earnest, aiming to force a special election come fall and vote likker out of 'Pache forever.

They ding-donged and heckled away at their campaign all summer, and finally, the week before election, they announced they was bringing in Professor Peedle, a famous temperance man and anti-saloon reformer, to lecture 'Pache's menfolks on the evils of Demon Rum.

The whole county turned out to hear the Professor when he give his spiel at the lodge hall. Peedle claimed to have been a confirmed drunkard who had seen the error of his ways and was devoting the rest of his life to converting tipplers into teetotalers.

He was an ugly little tush-hawg, with a tomato nose and no chin to speak of, but he was a right powerful talker and he managed to coax a passel of jackleg miners from the Sacatone diggings and a few cowboys from outlying ranches up on the stage, and got 'em to publically sign a pledge never to touch alcohol agin in any form, whatsoever.

This brought a cheer from the Knitting Society hens in the audience, for they were depending on winning Curly Bill's cash customers to their side. When Professor Peedle took up his collection and adjourned the meeting, it looked as if the Bloated Goat Saloon would have to close up and be turned over to the Knitting Society women to hold their rummage sales in.

Professor Peedle was herded over to Missus Hernia Groot's house to be guest of honor at a pink tea, but all of his converts to teetotalism drifted over to the Bloated Goat to hoist a few last drinks in honor of their victory over temptation.

The Professor managed to give Missus Groot's party the slip around midnight and he shows up at the Bloated Goat, sneaking in through the back door. The Paintin' Pistoleer was the first to see him, and he orders a glass of buttermilk for the Professor.

"Whisky Pete Krumb, you sure have changed!" Justin O. Smith chuckles. "Nobody in town recognized you tonight without your long yellow beard. I ain't so sure your crusade was as successful as your disguise, howsomever."

110

Well, Sheriff Rimfire Cudd almost keeled over in a faint when he realized who this Professor Peedle really was. But not Curly Bill Grane. The bartender hauls his sawed-off shotgun out from under the bar and pokes it in the Professor's ribs.

"Whisky Pete, if you've come back to 'Pache to smash up my saloon ag'in," Curly Bill hollers, "I'll blast your brisket with buckshot an' bust a bottle o' Blue Bagpipe over your boothill buryin' plot every Memorial Day, so help me Hannah!"

The Professor grins meek-like, takes a wallet out of his swallowtail coat, and throws a fat bankroll under Curly Bill's nose.

"I hope this dinero will cover the damages you got coming as a result of my past indiscretions," he says. "I make purty fair wages lambasting John Barleycorn on these here lecture tours, so I can afford to settle up my accounts. You see, Bill, your Bloated Goat is a sort of personal shrine for me. It was under this same roof that I seen the Lucy Nations which put me on the straight an' narrer path before I wound up in a booby hatch."

Well, Sol Fishman comes over and hands Whisky Pete a little bill which the Professor owes the O. K. Mercantile. It reads:

To Junior Coddlewort for loan of pet garter snake . . . two bits
To three gallons of pink paint for elephant . . . $1
To Justin O. Smith for labor . . . no charge.

111

The Professor looked kind of puzzled, but he shells up what he owed Sol like a real sport. He casts a disappointed eye at his converts, who by now are pretty far gone in their cups, and remarks that he's got a speaking engagement over in Bisbee tomorrow and he'd better light a shuck, before he looks like he's picked up a hangover from an all-night bender.

As he is turning to leave, he remembers something. "Curly Bill," he wants to know, "how did you ever make out with that baby your uncle sent you? I've had that on my conscience, running out on the poor little tike like I done."

Curly Bill starts to choke and he signals the Paintin' Pistoleer, who hustles Whisky Pete outdoors.

"You almost give away a secret that Curly Bill doesn't want to leak out, on account of it would make him the laughing-stock of the town," Justin Other Smith explains. "But it seems this baby boy was one of Uncle Coot's famous practical jokes. When the Arizona Flyer showed up in Apache that morning, the infant turned out to be a five-hundred pound baby elephant!"

Hell-Bent for Election!

Rimfire Cudd had been sheriff in Apache for so long that the old coot had thought serious of having his star tattooed on his briskit. For years, people had tooken for granite that Cudd had staked out a permanent claim on the office and the penny-ante salary which went with it.

Which was why Rimfire like to of had hisself an appleplectic stroke that morning when Jim Groot's wife, Hernia, tacks a big red poster smack in the middle of the jailhouse door.

This here poster carries a true-as-life portrait of the muleskinner named "Fearless" Peerless, owner of the Border Freight Line which has its stable and headquarters in Apache.

What is printed under Peerless's picture makes Rimfire Cudd gag and swaller his chaw of tobacco:

ELECT PEERLESS SHERIFF!
Stirrup County has suffered the disgrace of inadequate law enforcement for over 20 years. The incumbent, Rimfire Cudd, is a cowardly, drunken ignoramus who has wasted our taxpayers' money long enough. Bring law & order back to

*Apache! Vote the FEARLESS PEERLESS FOR
SHERIFF ticket at the forthcoming election! Our
candidate is honest, upright and temperant.*
Campaign sponsored by
LADIES' KNITTING & PEACH PRESERVES
SOCIETY
ANTI-ALCOHOL COMMITTEE and WIDE-
AWAKE CITIZENS LEAGUE

Rimfire Cudd hadn't had any competition for his job
for 15 or 20 years, on account of the salary wouldn't
keep a tush-hog in wallerin'-mud. One time ten years
back, Curly Bill Grane got drunk and said he aimed to
run for sheriff, and he got a smattering of writ-in votes
from the Sacatone miners and a few cowhands who was
joshing Cudd by voting agin him. But otherwise, Cudd
had the sheriff's job by the tail on a downhill pull.

Well, after Rimfire recovers from his first
flabbergastment, he squints closer at this portrait of
Fearless Peerless, and discovers that it ain't a
photographt, but a painting signed by Justin Other
Smith.

This hurts Rimfire's feelings plenty, for Smith was
his favorite amigo. He tears Hernia Groot's sign offn
the calaboose door and lights a shuck over to the
Longhorn Saddle Shop and stomps upstairs to Justin
O.'s studio, where Smith paints covers for mail-order
catalogues and almanacs and calendars and such-like.

The sheriff is gruntin' like a brood sow feeding its
litter by the time he reaches the studio. He finds the

Paintin' Pistoleer daubing away at a canvas showing a Pony Express rider in action.

"You dad-blasted traitor!" Cudd bellers, waving Peerless's poster under Justin's nose. "You snake in the weed pile! You've teamed up with the old hens in this burg to see that jerkline bullwhacker roust me out of a job. Danged ifn I oughtn't to whittle you down to my size, you paint-slingin' polecat!"

Smith looks at the poster and allows he's plenty surprised. "I drawed this," he admits. "Fearless Peerless swapped me a month's stable room for my hoss over in his barn in return for this portrait. I swear I didn't know the womenfolks would make a cut out of it and print up a batch of election posters, though. I don't even see why he'd want to be a candidate nohow. His wagons keep him too busy for sheriffin'."

Cudd blows his nose a honk and looks plumb scared. From the front window of Smith's studio, he sees that the Ladies' Knitting & Peach Preserves Society plastered signs all along the main street, thicker than buzzards at a hog-killin'. On the porch of Sol Fishman's O. K. Mercantile, and on the batwing doors of the Bloated Goat Saloon, and in the window of Dyspepsia Dah's Feedbag Café, and on a pole in front of Lew Pirtle's Overland Telegraph station.

Fact is, the womenfolks has hired young Percival Coddlewort to ride all over the county tacking up posters on fence posts and barn doors, which same Cudd doesn't hear about till later.

"I don't know what I'm worryin' about, anyhow," Rimfire Cudd scoffs, hollow-like. "It's tooken for

115

granite I'll wear the sheriff's star around these parts until they lay me in boothill. I don't reckon this two-bit bullwhacker has got an outside chance of beatin' me at the polls next month, you think so, Justin?"

The Paintin' Pistoleer tries to laugh, but his heart ain't in it a-tall. This Fearless Peerless is a handsome sport over six foot tall who weighs as much as a longhorn bull and handles a gun about as expert as he does a blacksnake whip, which is to say that the Paintin' Pistoleer is the only man in the county with a faster draw or a deader eye at drawing a bead.

On the other hand, everybody in the Territory knows that Sheriff Rimfire Cudd couldn't shoot a hole in a barn wall ifn he was inside the barn. Rimfire must be close onto 70, and the only thing he is expert at is not being handy when trouble breaks. Not that Rimfire ain't honest as the day is long, but he's too ganted up and half-blind to make a good saloon swamper, let alone a qualified keeper of the peace.

Well, before the week's over Apache sees that Fearless Peerless is going hell-bent to win this here election. He hangs a big canvas banner acrost the main street between the Stockman's Bank and the lodge hall, which says *Common Sense Will Provide a Peerless Landslide. Chew Up Cudd on Election Day!*

Rimfire threatens to arrest Peerless for putting a traffic obstruction acrost the main stem, claiming the sign is dangerous on account of it might knock a driver offn the boot of an incoming stagecoach after dark. But this just makes Rimfire a laughing-stock, because the

116

banner is a good 20 feet off the ground and Wells-Fargo ain't hiring giraffes to tool their Concords as yet.

When election day is two weeks off, Samanthie Coddlewort and her Wide-Awake Citizens' League passes out handbills which say that Fearless Peerless challenges Rimfire Cudd to a public debate, which same is to take place at nine o'clock Saturday morning in front of the old rodeo grounds grandstand north of town.

The Paintin' Pistoleer was roundsiding with the boys in at the Bloated Goat Saloon Friday afternoon when Fearless Peerless come into the barroom, passing out free cigars with his name on the gold bands.

The ladies of the Anti-Alcohol Committee don't know it, but Peerless has been setting up the boys to free beers for quite some time now, as a means of getting better acquainted with what he calls his "future constituents." What with the beer and the cigars, Peerless is getting to be mighty popular around 'Pache.

As for the womenfolks, to hear them she-blisters brag, you'd think Peerless didn't cuss, chaw, smoke, or spit, and made his own dresses. Whereas they claimed Rimfire Cudd wasn't fitten to hold public office on account of his liking a nip now and then.

Well, Rimfire Cudd was in the saloon when Peerless come in, as spruced up as a tinhorn gambler, with perfume on his clean-shaven plowshare jaw and his boots shined and a clean shirt on, which same he changed every week whether he needed to or not.

"Challenge me to a public de-bate, will you?" snarls the sheriff, taking the cigar Peerless offered him and

117

crumpling it into a spittoon. "I'll out-talk you tomorrow, you bile-complected horny toad. All the votes you'll git is the old maids' and widders' who are jealous because I'm still a bachelor."

Peerless just grins and winks at the boys. "I got my doubts," he grins, "ifn you'll even show up at the political rally tomorrow," and walks out chuckling.

Well, next morning at nine o'clock the rodeo grandstand is loaded to capacity. The old hens from the Ladies' Knitting & Peach Preserves Society marches to their block of reserved seats in a body, waving signs which says *Vote for Peerless, the Paragon, No Man With Red Blood Will Waste a Vote on Cudd, If You Have to Choose, Take a Man Who Hates Booze*, and the like of that there.

In fact the only woman who don't show up is Samanthie Coddlewort, head of the Wide-Awake Citizens' League, who overslept.

Jim Groot the banker's wife, Hernia, welcomes Fearless Peerless to the platform, and sets down to preen herself and blush over Peerless's compliments and wait for Rimfire Cudd to show up. By 9:30 the crowd begins to get restless but there is still neither hide nor hair of Rimfire Cudd to be seen.

Finally Sol Fishman and the Paintin' Pistoleer take a *pasear* over to the shack behind the jailhouse to see what's holding up the sheriff. They find Rimfire pacing the room, stripped to his red flannel drawers and his star boots.

"Folks are hoorawing you for a coward, Sheriff!" Sol Fishman complains. "Haul on yore duds and rattle yore

118

hocks over there so as to answer all the lies Fearless will shovel out agin you."

Rimfire Cudd looks like he's fixing to lose his breakfast. "I cain't," he groans. "Last night some mangey coyote snuck into my bedroom and stole my pants and my gun and my star. I dassn't show up at the rally in these here drawers."

Well, Sol Fishman hikes over to his O. K. Mercantile and fetches back a pair of overhalls and a hickory shirt for the sheriff, but it is ten o'clock, a full hour late, when Rimfire finally makes it to the rodeo grounds.

Fearless Peerless has been spielin' for going on half an hour, and gets a big hand from the audience. When they spot Rimfire Cudd sneakin' in, they give the old galoot a loud round of booing and hoss laughs.

"Lo these many years," Fearless Pearless orates, "you have been shelling out a salary to a sheriff who is no better than Missus Coddlewort's scarecrow over in her garden patch yonder," Peerless says. "As a matter of fact, ladies and gents, I beg to direct your attention to said scarecrow. You can all see for yourselves that it looks healthier and soberer than my unworthy opponent. In fact, it bears a striking resemblance to Sheriff Cudd."

Well, the crowd cranes its neck around to look toward Missus Coddlewort's garden patch. What they see breaks up the meetin', because this scarecrow is wearing Rimfire's Stetson and shirt and patched levis. His gun belt is buckled around the scarecrow's middle with Rimfire's old single-action .44 in the holster, and the sheriff's star is pinned to the scarecrow's shirt, flashin' like a tin pie-plate in the sunlight.

"As a means of demonstrating that the incumbent sheriff is utterly incapable of guarding a jail," Peerless says, "I entered his office last night, got the jail keys, and unlocked the cell block door and entered his sleeping quarters. With Cudd snoring there like a buzz saw hitting a knotty log, I choused his gun and badge and pants. Friends, I ask you — what if I had been a desperado bent on letting an owlhooter out of jail? Is this the kind of stupid nincompoop you want to wear the sacred emblem of the law in Stirrup County?"

Well, Rimfire Cudd turns red as a bull's tongue and shuffles over to the garden patch and recovers his gun harness and duds offn the scarecrow. He comes back to the speaker's platform and Missus Hernia Groot tries to quiet the crowd, but even when she does Rimfire just stands there tongue-tied, with his Adam's apple bobbing up and down his throat like a knot tied in a rope.

The assembled voters let Rimfire Cudd know which way the electoral wind is blowing, all right. They begin pelting the poor old cuss with ripe eggs which one of Fearless Peerless's wagoneers had smuggled into the bleachers.

Cudd, looking like an omelette, high-tails it back to the jail with his tail tucked betwixt his laigs, and holes up out of sight for the rest of the day.

That night he sneaks over to the Paintin' Pistoleer's studio, where Smith is working late to finish a canvas.

120

Cudd admits he ain't worth hell-room so far as Apache is concerned.

"After all I've sacrificed to make my stretch o' border safe for them women to raise their kids in," Rimfire wails, "they're fixin' to nail my pelt on the fence, Justin. The best y'ars of my life I've dedicated to bein' a public servant, and now that I'm string-halted and spavined up, they figger I ain't desarvin' of being put out to pasture in my sunset y'ars. Justin, I cain't endure the humidity being heaped upon me. I aim to pull my picket pin and drag my wagons come payday, which same is the day before the election."

Justin Other Smith tries hard to think up something consoling to say, but the words just won't come. It looks like Rimfire has his choice of vamoosing and making it a no-contest win for Fearless Peerless, or else waiting around for the ballots to be counted, which same is a dead cinch to bury him under a landslide.

Either way, it looks as if Rimfire Cudd is sucking on a dry bottle. The only prospect left open to him is herding sheep on his brother's range down in the Sacatone foothills, which would be quite a come-down for a man as proud as Rimfire.

Next morning is a Sunday. The Paintin' Pistoleer gets up at the crackle of dawn, wrapping his oil painting ready to ship out on the early stage. All of a sudden he hears a loud cracking noise, followed by a squall of pain like a tomcat with its tail caught between a flat rock and a wagon wheel.

Justin O. goes to the window for a look-see. It being Sunday, the main street is deserted, all except for

Samanthie Coddlewort's oldest youngun, Percy, and Fearless Peerless.

Young Percy is lyin' curled up in the dust in front of the Bloated Goat Saloon, covering his face with his hands. Peerless is setting on the seat of a tandem-hitched string of wagons, coiling his long blacksnake whip. Smith can see the red stripes where Peerless has walloped the blacksnake around Percy's bare shins.

"Don't larrup me agin, Mister Peerless!" begs Percy. "I won't ever do it agin, I promise! I was only joshin' —"

Well, Fearless Peerless stands up in his wagon box and lets out a string of cuss words that could have melted the fillings in his teeth, and hauls back his arm to belt Percy with his whip a second time. Before he can let go, though, a gun blasts out and Peerless finds hisself looking at a stub of whip handle. A bullet has snipped the thongs offn his whip and dropped them down on the whiffle trees.

Percy Coddlewort gives a timid peek through his fingers and sees the Paintin' Pistoleer leaning from his window upstairs over the Longhorn Saddle Shop. His .32 six-gun on a .45 frame is smokin' in his fist, and he looks about as mad as Fearless does.

"What's goin' on down there?" Smith hollers, cocking his gun and drawing a bead on Peerless's left ear. "A two-hundred pound bully hoss-whippin' a slick-ear button thataway! I ought to punch your ticket, you yellow-bellied sidewinder!"

Well, Fearless Peerless looks for a minute like he wants to reach for the Winchester propped agin his

122

footboard, but he has already seen a prime example of how Justin O. can handle a gun, so he pulls in his horns pronto.

"I lost my temper," he grumbles. "Young Coddlewort's been going up and down the street drawing black whiskers on my campaign pictures, Smith. I figgered the scamp needed a tanning."

Well, by the time Justin Other Smith got downstairs, he seen Fearless Peerless was applegizing to young Percy, and was handing him a 20-dollar greenback to square accounts.

"Percy has promised to go around and erase all the signs he defaced," the muleskinner says. "We're still friends, Percy?"

Young Coddlewort blinks back his tears and shakes hands with Peerless. He's saving his dinero to go to college and be a lawyer some day, and this double sawbuck is the most money he had seen in one chunk in his life.

"You bet, Sheriff Peerless!" he blubbers. "I jest wisht I was ten years older, so's I could vote for you next week."

Well, Peerless grabs his jerkline and wallops his mules out of town, heading for the Sacatone diggins with a load of supplies for the jackleg muckers over there.

The Paintin' Pistoleer is wearing a puzzled frown like he is thinking hard. He walks over to the Bloated Goat Saloon where young Percy is fixing to rub out the black mustache and whiskers he had drawed on Peerless's picture.

"Hold on a minute, son," Smith says, slow and serious. "The poster is ruined anyhow. I'd like to keep it."

Smith rips the poster offn the saloon door and folds it careful and puts it in his pocket. Then he sashays over to the county jail and rousts Sheriff Rimfire Cudd out of bed.

"Sheriff," he grins, "you are still a candidate for re-election, savvy? What is more, I aim to be your campaign manager. I figger we'll either make a spoon or spoil a horn by doing a little electioneering on your behalf."

Well, that perks up Rimfire considerable, but before he can ask Smith how he aims to jerk a miracle out of thin air, the Paintin' Pistoleer is gone. He shows up at the Wells-Fargo depot and hands the stage driver a package containing his oil painting, and also an envelope which contains Fearless Peerless's picture that Percy Coddlewort had defaced with a chunk of crayon. This envelope is addressed to Phoenix, and Smith hands the jehu a gold piece to make sure it gets delivered pronto and personal.

Well, Fearless Peerless is back in town a couple of days later with a string of loaded freight wagons which has a sign, *Put In Peerless at the Polls*, painted on their boxes. As usual he makes a beeline to the Bloated Goat and sets up the house to free drinks, including buttermilk for Justin Other Smith.

"I understand you are managing my shiftless opponent's campaign for re-election," Peerless smirks. "I can't imagine a more useless waste of time and

124

energy on your part, my friend. I got the voters tied up tighter than a badger in a bushel bag."

Justin O. shrugs and goes on sipping his buttermilk. "You talk big and fancy," he admits, "but it takes more than a glib tongue to ramrod a town this close to the Mexican Border. My candidate hereby challenges you to a target-shootin' contest this afternoon, which same will be open to the public if you got the guts to accept."

Fearless Peerless grins like his throat is cut and gives his gun belt a hitch. "I was fixing to take a string of wagons over to Nogales to pick up a shipment of Mexican wool," he says happily, "but I reckon I can postpone business for pleasure. Where is this so-called contest to be held?"

Smith allows that the corral back of the county stables is as good a place as any, using the compost pile as a backstop.

Well, this news spread like wildfire. Most people figgered it was a kiss-poor start for Justin Other Smith's campaign-managing, what with Fearless Peerless being a crack shot and Rimfire Cudd about as handy with a smokepole as a blind baboon.

That afternoon the corral fences was jammed with cowboys and town folks and a batch of miners from the Sacatone diggings, who had come down for the next day's election in full force. There was even a big delegation of Chinese muckers, who didn't have a legal vote but had come along to see the fun and root for Peerless to win, on account of Peerless selling them rice at wholesale.

The targets was beer bottles furnished by Curly Bill Grane, set up a foot apart on a plank between two whisky barrels. Sheriff Rimfire Cudd and Fearless Peerless stood alongside the back wall of the livery barn, 60-odd feet from the target, and flipped for first shots. Peerless won, and he knocked over four bottles out of six, and got a rousing big hand from the sidelines.

Justin Other Smith, who had arranged this shooting-match, was nowhere to be seen. But that didn't appear to ruffle Cudd's tail feathers none. The old gaffer braced his back against the barn wall, squinted at the row of bottles just like he could see what he was shooting at, and raised his rusty old Walker .44.

Whereas Peerless had taken his time squeezing off his shots, Rimfire Cudd fans his gunhammer with the heel of his left hand, shooting his gun empty as fast as he could trip the prong.

The eyes of Apache's citizens bugged out like pigeon eggs when the smoke cleared and they seen Rimfire's score. Six shots in Rimfire's Colt, and six bottles blasted to smithereens. Two better than Peerless had done!

"There!" Rimfire hollers, poking his gun into his holster. "I reckon that there disproves them insults you been circulatin' about my shootin' ability goin' to pot twenty years ago, Peerless!"

Fearless Peerless scratched his head, unable to figger it out. During the four-five years he had been running his freight line out of Apache, he had never seen

Rimfire Cudd hit a target yet, even if it was glued to the end of his gun muzzle.

Folks was beginning to crowd around Rimfire, slappin' his back and telling him they'd misjudged him, when young Percy Coddlewort pokes his head out of the hayloft overhead and yells:

"It's a fake, gents! The Paintin' Pistoleer was hidin' in a manger and shootin' through a knothole at them bottles! The sheriff's slugs went into that manure pile or else he was shootin' blank shells!"

Well, that fried Rimfire's goose for sure. Peerless made a little speech about a hoax being foisted off on a gullible public, and lectured them about morals in politics, and wound up by inviting one and all to the Bloated Goat saloon for free drinks on the future sheriff of Stirrup County, namely, Fearless Peerless.

Rimfire Cudd wanted a drink the worst way, seeing as how the bottom had dropped out of his chances of re-election, but nacherly he wouldn't guzzle any of his rival candidate's likker, even for free. He waits till the crowd has broke up, and then he slips inside the barn.

Justin Other Smith crawls out of a manager, looking sicker than Rimfire was, if that was possible. "How'd I know that tattle-tale Coddlewort brat was hiding up in the haymow?" he groaned. "Well, we still got an ace in the hole, Sheriff. At least, I hope we have."

Fearless Peerless didn't join the boys at the saloon; that would have cost him the Ladies' Knitting & Peach Preserves Society vote. He pulls out for the Border with his wagons, carrying a load of dead-head passengers for the trip, these Chinee muckers who couldn't vote in tomorrow's election nohow.

Rimfire Cudd retires to the jail and starts packing his war sack, figgering that come tomorrow, the electorate of Stirrup County would evict him from his happy home for keeps. Justin Other Smith, meanwhile, goes over to the Overland Telegraph office and settles down to wait, keeping Lew Pirtle on duty long after closing time.

Around ten o'clock that night, when the saloons and honkies in Apache was doing a land-office business catering to the voters who had flocked into town, a telegram come over the wire addressed to the Paintin' Pistoleer. It was the one he had been hoping and praying would show up. Smith swears Lew Pirtle to secrecy, and then he saddles up his palomino hoss, Skeeter, and rides over to the jail. Perty soon him and Rimfire Cudd lit out for parts unknown, and the town figgered they'd seen the last of that pair.

Election day dawns and the polls open in Sol Fishman's store. By noon ninety percent of the votes has been cast, but the ballot box can't be opened legal until six o'clock. Fearless Peerless ain't in town, being away to Nogales on a hauling job, and neither is Sheriff Rimfire Cudd or his campaign manager, Justin O. Smith.

When the three o'clock stage pulls in from Tombstone, out steps a six-piece Mexican band from Tombstone which Peerless has hired to play at a Victory Ball that night in the lodge hall, which Peerless had leased for the celebration of his election.

128

The voters spend the afternoon bucking the tiger and getting likkered up, waiting to learn how bad Rimfire Cudd had been whipped.

Just before six o'clock, who should come gallivanting into town but the Paintin' Pistoleer and Sheriff Rimfire Cudd. With them was Fearless Peerless, straddle of one of his wagon mules.

Peerless didn't look in very good shape to preside over the Victory Ball. His right arm is in a blood-stained sling and he's hog-tied with Rimfire Cudd's rusty old handcuffs.

Well, a big crowd surrounds them and there was talk of a lynching when they seen what Sheriff Cudd had gone and done, arresting his rival candidate on election day, but when they call on Fearless Peerless to explain, he just looks hang-dog and says nothing.

The Paintin' Pistoleer slips away somewhere, leaving Rimfire Cudd to spring his bombshell.

"It's like this," Rimfire says, making his first and only campaign oratory from the saddle of his crowbait pony. "Last night, I waylaid my unworthy opponent driving a string of Conestogas up from the Mexican Border. I demanded to inspect his freight, which same was supposed to be bales of wool, but this so-called Fearless hombre drags a shotgun out and we had to plug his gun arm."

"We," everybody knowed in this case, must have been the Paintin' Pistoleer.

All eyes was glued on Peerless, but he still didn't play his taw. With which Sheriff Rimfire Cudd reaches in his saddlebags and takes out a bunch of tiny bottles, filled with white powder.

"Before Fearless Peerless come to Apache to open his freight line," the sheriff goes on to say, "he was a border-hopper known to the Arizona Rangers as Blackbeard Bailey, who cleaned up a fortune smuggling opium acrost the Border before the Rangers caught him. Bailey busted out of Yuma penintentiary six years back, shaved his whiskers off, and went on the dodge under the name of Fearless Peerless."

Rimfire Cudd went on to explain how he had found these bottles of contraband drugs cached in the wool Peerless had cleared at customs, which opium he intended to peddle to the Chinees over at the Sacatone mines. Peerless's freight business was just a blind to conceal his smuggling activities, which was why he had talked the Apache womenfolks into nominating him for Sheriff. As a lawman, he could have opened up a stretch of Border without any trouble.

Well, the election board seen candidate Peerless locked up in the county jail. The Arizona Rangers would pick him up when they got the telegram which Rimfire Cudd got Lew Pirtle to send to Ranger headquarters over in Phoenix.

Then the board members went back to the O. K. Mercantile to unlock the ballot box, only to discover that some mangey thief had stolen the box during all the excitement.

"All the voters are here in town anyhow," suggests Jim Groot the banker, who was chairman of the election board. "We'll hold a duplicate election here

130

and now. Them as want to exercise their franchises, line up now."

Well, it was news to everybody in Apache that they even had franchises, let alone knowing how to exercise same, but they lined up and scratched their ballots all over again.

When the ballots was counted, the good ladies of the Anti-Alcohol Committee and the Wide-Awake Citizens' League was fitten to be tied. It was a landslide for Rimfire Cadwallader Cudd, the incumbent, who was a hero as a result of dabbing his loop on Blackbeard Bailey, the most notorious escaped convict in Arizona Territory's history.

There was 16 votes cast for Fearless Peerless, at that, which same represented the 16 members of the temperance-minded Knitting & Peach Preserves Society. Those biddies would have rather elected a bone-dry dope smuggler sheriff than a harmless old tippler like Rimfire Cudd.

The Victory Ball come off as scheduled that night, seeing as how Peerless had rented the hall and imported an orchestra, but it was Rimfire Cudd who called the dances and Fearless Peerless listened to the merrymaking in a cell of the county *juzgado*.

Justin Other Smith let Rimfire brag to his heart's content, but he passed up his usual dram of buttermilk to drink a shot of Blue Bagpipe whisky which Curly Bill Grane fetched over in a jug from the Bloated Goat to celebrate the occasion.

"How come you got the idea of arresting Fearless Peerless on his way back from Mexico last night,

Sheriff?" Sol Fishman was curious to find out, along with everybody else.

Well, old Rimfire Cudd was just drunk enough that he didn't try to hog all the credit for hisself. He jerks a thumb toward the Paintin' Pistoleer. "You tell 'em, Jushtin ol' pard," he hiccups.

Smith looks plumb embarrassed. "Well," he begins, in that soft Alabama drawl of hisn, "last Sunday I caught Fearless Peerless hoss-whipping Percy Coddlewort for drawing whiskers on the campaign posters the ladies had tacked up around town.

"That was a trick any younker would pull off," Smith goes on, "and it struck me as strange that Peerless should get so mad over such a picayune matter. It was as if Peerless was mortally scared of anybody seeing his picture with a full beard. Besides which, I was wondering why a busy man as prosperous as Peerless should be honin' to take on the sheriff's job in the first place.

"So," Smith says, "I mails a poster to Arizona Ranger headquarters in Phoenix, showing my portrait of the clean-shaven Peerless as he looked with a black mustache and full set of whiskers.

"The Rangers wired me back that the picture was a dead ringer for an escaped smuggler named Blackbeard Bailey that they had posted a thousand-dollar reward to recapture. Which reward, by the way, will go to young Percy for his college fund. Well, the sheriff and I took a jaunt down to the Border to check up on what Peerless might be hauling over from Nogales — and you know the rest."

Curly Bill's whisky jug goes the rounds again and it was one drop too much for Rimfire Cudd. He passes out cold as a fish and the Paintin' Pistoleer lugs him over to the jailhouse and tucks him in bed.

What Apache never found out was that Justin Other Smith had stolen their ballot box. He burned the original ballots that night up in his studio over the Longhorn Saddle Shop. He never let on to Rimfire Cudd what the first mandate of the people had been, but it tallied out 97 votes for Fearless Peerless and 2 votes for Rimfire Cudd — which same was the absentee ballots Rimfire and Justin O. Smith had left with Sol Fishman before they lit out for the Border.

The Horseless Head Man

When this here Doc & Pony show went broke and the railroad pushed it onto the side track here in Apache, Lawyer Plato X. Scrounge was right on the spot to locate a buyer for said show when the ringmaster, Colonel Krutch, said it was for sale. Lawyer Scrounge had lived in Apache long enough to know that Sol Fishman of the O. K. Mercantile was a sucker for any kind of white elephant if it could be corralled at a bargain price.

Like the time Sol bought a gross lot of snowshoes, because his liver-medicine almanac predicted a spring blizzard for Apache. It ain't snowed in this corner of Arizona Territory since the Great Ice Age, but the almanac was never wrong and Sol figgered there'd be a big demand for these snowshoes, so he stocked up heavy.

Well, it didn't even rain that year, but Sol unloaded them snowshoes on the squaws over at the Cheery-cow Injun reservation, who used 'em to make papoose cradles, and even Lawyer Scrounge had to admit that Sol was a purty smart trader.

But when this Dog & Pony Show got side-tracked in 'Pache because Colonel Krutch hadn't paid his freight and feed bills back along the line, Lawyer Scrounge got Sol to lay out $500 cash on the barrelhead to buy the circus. The deal was that Colonel Krutch would be ringmaster, putting the menagerie through its paces when it was on the road, while Sol Fishman would foot the bills and carry the title of "Head Man of the Circus."

As soon as Sol had paid over the cash to Lawyer Scrounge, he wanted to brag to somebody, so he lit a shuck over to the vacant lot behind the Longhorn Saddle Shop where his friend the artist, Justin Other Smith, was busy painting.

This morning, though, the Paintin' Pistoleer was doing a special job for a young Mexican sport name of Don Gusto. Seems this Don Gusto aimed to get married up to a percentage girl over at the Busted Flush dance hall, and take her back acrost the Border to his hacienda. He had commissioned Justin O. to paint him straddlin' a spanking palomino gelding, all decked out in his fancy Mexican trappings, for a cash fee of $500.

The painting was to be his wedding present to the señorita, and the palomino he was using for a model was Skeeter, which same belonged to Justin O. Smith. Because the hoss balked at climbing the stairs to Smith's studio over the saddle shop, the Paintin' Pistoleer had set up his easel outdoors in back of the building and was daubing away at his canvas there, with Don Gusto and Skeeter posing in the shade behind Dyspepsia Dan's restaurant.

Well, Sol Fishman didn't get a chance to brag about being the Head Man of a circus just yet, because he found Sheriff Rimfire Cudd busy pounding Justin O. Smith's ear.

"The Phantom Rustler's gang made off with another jag of Buck Speeglebaum's Diamond S mossyhorns last night," the sheriff was blubbering. "That's in my county, and them cattle vanished in the Sacatones, headin' for Mexico. Lawyer Scrounge has got Speeglebaum into the notion of suin' me for malfizzance in orifice, whatever that means."

The Paintin' Pistoleer looks up from his daubing. "Malfeasance in office," he explains, "means that Lawyer Scrounge is out to force you to resign your star, Sheriff. This here Phantom Rustler has been robbin' the ranches blind and you ain't done a thing to dab your loop on them raiders. You can't hardly blame the Cattlemen's Association for wantin' a new sheriff."

Rimfire Cudd's face gets so long that Smith accidentally used him for a model instead of his horse, before he noticed his mistake of putting a tobacco-stained mustache on the palomino's muzzle in this pitcher he was painting.

"No sheriff could track the Phantom Rustler when his trail peters out in Cactus Crick, which same leads to a hundred foot waterfall at the end of a box canyon," Rimfire Cudd moans. "I'm a danged fool for even tryin' to buck anythin' Lawyer Scrounge sticks his horn into. It's bad luck when that shyster steps in."

Sol Fishman don't like the sound of this last remark. It's a fact, bad luck and Plato X. Scrounge wear the same collar; you always find 'em together, like cuspidors and a splattered carpet. Mostly because Lawyer Scrounge is always ready to twist somebody's misfortune to his own profit. He's about as popular in Apache as a red-hot rock in a settin' hen's nest, and Sol Fishman begins to regret how he give Scrounge a box of his best three-for-a-nickel stogies as a bonus for making him Head Man of the Dog & Pony Show.

But anyway, after the sheriff left, Sol tells the Paintin' Pistoleer about his bargain. Justin O. allows that it's about time to pack up his paint box for the day, what with Don Gusto being tired of posing, and he promises Sol that he'll take a *pasear* over to the railroad station and look over his circus.

Don Gusto climbs down offn the palomino and says to Justin O., "I geeve you a t'ousand seelver pesos for thees *caballo*, Señor."

But the Paintin' Pistoleer just grins and shakes his head. All week, Don Gusto has had his eye on that palomino. "I wouldn't part with Skeeter for all the silver in the Sacatone diggings," he tells Don Gusto. "You be back here tomorrow mornin', *amigo* and we'll get this picture finished for your bride-to-be."

Well, after he stables Skeeter over in Curly Bill Grane's barn behind the Bloated Goat Saloon, the Paintin' Pistoleer lets Sol Fishman take him over to the railroad depot to look over the Dog & Pony Show which he has brought.

It turns out that this Colonel Krutch is an old-time animal trainer, and he claims that his 28 dogs and 15 Shetland ponies will make a fortune for Sol Fishman, tourin' the frontier tank towns. Quite a passel of folks is around watching the colonel exercise his animals, the ponies walking on balls and barrels and waltzing to the music of a hurdy-gurdy and such-like.

Colonel Krutch says it won't pay to put up the circus tent here in 'Pache, though, because the Sacatone miners won't have any spendin' money until payday, and the cowboys from the outlying ranches are all busy patrolling their range day and night to make sure this Phantom Rustler gang don't steal any more cattle.

There won't be another train through Apache for a week, though, which means that Sol Fishman will have to rustle up feed for this property he has acquired. Justin O. allows that will force Sol to butcher a steer for the dogs, and buy baled alfalfy hay for the ponies.

Sol Fishman agrees with the Paintin' Pistoleer that maybe he's bought hisself a pig in a poke, especially when he looks over the contract Lawyer Scrounge got him to sign and discovers he has agreed to foot Colonel Krutch's unpaid railroad bills.

Sol perks up a little bit that night, over at the Bloated Goat Saloon where he's roundsiding with the boys, when word gets out that Jim Groot, the banker, has captured hisself the world's biggest rat in a patented trap which Sol Fishman has the exclusive agency for.

This rat trap which Sol has been trying to peddle around town is a wire-cage affair called the Rodents' Nemesis, and sells for ten bucks without bait. So far, the sample traps Sol has loaned out to folks around 'Pache has only succeeded in ketching Missus Hernia Groot's pet setting hen, Lew Pirtle's youngest boy

Cootie, and a blind tomcat belonging to Sol himself. Which record hasn't done much to boom the rat-trap business.

"Jim Groot's on his way over here now with his Rodent's Nemesissy," announces Curly Bill Grane. "Claims he trapped the fattest rat ever seed in the Territory, just before he closed up the Stockman's Bank this evenin'."

This pleases Sol plenty, because there are lots of rats around town, and with a prominent citizen like Jim Groot buying one of his Nemesises for ten bucks, lots of other folks will want one too.

Sure enough, Jim Groot comes into the Bloated Goat carrying his big wire cage. Inside it is unquestionably the biggest rat what ever gnawed a nibble hereabouts, and Apache is a rat-ridden burg of which there ain't no whicher west of the Pecos.

This rat of Groot's must weigh five pounds, is about a foot long not counting the tail, and has eyes as big as marbles. It started scratching one ear with a hind laig when Groot sets the cage up on Curly Bill's bar for the boys to see.

"Sol, I'm proud to be the first citizen in this community to invest in a Rodents' Nemesis," Jim Groot says. "I'll let you display this rat in the window of your O. K. Mercantile to draw trade. This rat has lived in my bank for years."

Jim Groot hands Sol a crisp new sawbuck, and several other boys has their pocketbooks out, when Justin Other Smith speaks up. "First time I ever seed a rat wag its tail," he says. "Or one that wears a collar."

Just then Colonel Krutch comes into the saloon to wet his whistle. He takes one look at this giant rat in Groot's trap, and liked to blew his cork.

"Where'd you get my pedigreed Mexican hairless puppy?" the colonel bellers, yanking open the lid of the cage and hauling out Groot's champeen rat. "This here is Foochie, my waltzing Chihuahua dog. He chawed his leash in two this evenin' an' I been combin' the town lookin' for him."

Well, that made Jim Groot so mad he slammed the Rodents' Nemesis over Sol Fishman's head and stomped out of the saloon in company with Krutch and little Foochie.

The boys in the Bloated Goat got out their wire cutters and managed to pry the rat trap offn Sol's noggin, skinning his ears up considerable in the process, and Sol appreciated that so much he set up the house to a round of Blue Bagpipe Scotch. Everybody pitched in to help Sol drown his troubles except the Paintin' Pistoleer, who stuck to his usual dram of buttermilk.

Sol was beginning to perk up some when the batwings slammed open and Lawyer Plato X. Scrounge 'poked his turkey neck into the barroom and crooks his trigger finger at Curly Bill Grane, who was minding his own business back of the bar.

"Mr. Grane, a delegation from the Apache Ladies' Knittin' & Peach Presarves Society is waiting outside the portal of this infamous house, to slap a writ of habeus corpses on you!" Lawyer Scrounge announces in that pompous courtroom cackle of his. "You better

140

come out here peaceable an' see if we can settle this here litigation outside o' court. I am the legal counsel representing the plaintiffs in this action."

Curly Bill looks plenty scared, knowing the Knitting & Peach Preserves Society is out to close up his saloon. He's never heard of this here writ of halibut's corpuscles, so he picks up his sawed-off shotgun from the backbar just in case, and goes outside. The boys follow him, wondering what orneriness Lawyer Scrounge has cooked up now.

Waiting out by the hitch-rack are three women who look as mad as banty hens who've had a bucket of slop throwed on 'em. There is Samanthie Coddlewort, and Lew Pirtle's Missus, and Hernia Groot, the three ramrods of the Society. Each one of them is holding a glass of some kind of drink or other, and glowering at Curly Bill mad enough to chew nails and spit tacks.

Curly Bill, he looks at Rimfire Cudd for moral support, but the sheriff slinks off, not wanting any part of this ruction. What with a recall election in the offing to oust him from office, backed by all the cattlemen in the county who have been the victims of the Phantom Rustler's raids, Rimfire Cudd had an excuse for not tangling with these she-blisters.

"All right, ladies," Curly Bill bluffs, hiding his double-barreled greener under his bar apron. "What can I do for you fine people this balmy evenin'?"

The women all start squawking and gabbling at once, brandishin' their drinkin'-glasses at Curly Bill. Lawyer Scrounge finally manages to back them into the traces and quiet them down some.

"Mr. Grane," Scrounge says to the defendant, "these fine, upright, unsuspecting ladies purchased five gallons of punch from you this afternoon, to serve as refreshments at their Society sociable tonight. They are hereby indicting you for spiking said lemonade with alcoholic spirits, which same is a breach of federal statoots, or maybe a pair of breaches, depending on what judicial precedent I can dig out of Blackstone."

Curly Bill turns as sickly a green as he did the time he caught a live skunk in the garbage can under his free-lunch table.

"I'm innercent!" Grane protests weakly. "There was nothin' in that punch but lemon powders an' sugar an' well water. I even washed my hands before I stirred up the batch, knowin' the ladies was persnickety."

Hernia Groot bats Lawyer Scrounge out of the way and waddles over to Curly Bill, who hauls out his shotgun and backs away as wobbly-laiged as if his kneecaps was missing.

"Is that so!" Missus Groot hollers, and pours her glass of lemon punch over Curly Bill's head. "Well, every one of the temperant, law-abiding ladies at our sociable who quaffed your witches' brew are now seeing hallucinations. I defy you to take a drink of this so-called harmless concoction and then come down to our sociable and see what you can see!"

Well, Curly Bill takes a glass of punch from Samanthie Coddlewort and downs it at a gulp, gagging a time or two. The Paintin' Pistoleer volunteers to swaller the drink Lew Pirtle's wife has brung along for evidence.

142

"Now, by grab!" Curly Bill says, wiping his mustaches. "Let's sashay over to the sociable and take a gander at these here Lucky Nations you have reference to."

So Lawyer Scrounge and his clients march off down the street to the lodge hall, where the Knitting & Peach Preserves Society is throwing its party. The lodge hall is crowded with womenfolks who are caterwauling like they've et loco weed. Next door to the hall is Lew Pirtle's Overland Telegraph office, and it is here that the Bloated Goat delegation finds the Society ladies gathered.

"Look up yonder," Lawyer Scrounge says, pointing toward the sky. "Justin Other Smith and Curly Bill Grane will see something the rest of you gentlemen can't see, not having drunk any of this doctored-up brew which the defendant foisted off on the plaintiffs."

Well, Curly Bill and the Paintin' Pistoleer, they take a look up to where Scrounge is pointing, and they seen there was no doubt about it. Hallucinations was crawling all over the sky, plain as day in the moonlight. To be exact, two fuzzy white animals were walking back and forth in mid-air teetering along the Overland Telegraph wires.

Curly Bill would have took to his heels just then, if it hadn't been for what Sol Fishman has to say.

"Them animals ain't Lucy Nations!" Sol yells, "I ain't had nothin' to drink except a pint and a half of whisky neat, but I can see them critters walkin' them telegraph wires!"

143

Just then Colonel Krutch steps out of the crowd and whips off his silk stovepipe hat. He gives a whistle, and the two hallucinations bark with joy. They reverse direction on the telegraph wires, walk over to the roof of Lew Pirtle's office, and hop down. Then they clumb down the rungs of a ladder which Lew has leaning against the eaves, and come running over to where Colonel Krutch has started passing the hat to take up a collection from the boys.

"You ladies an' gents have just witnessed a spectacle sponsored by Fishman's Dog & Pony Show," Krutch says proudly. "Allow me to present Spiffy an' Toby, the only Tight-Wire-Walkin' Canines in Captivity. They sneaked out of their kennel tonight and took theirselves an evenin' stroll along the bobwire fence which leads over from the railroad yard. Any small contribution you good people wish to make for this aerial extravaganza —"

Well, you'd have thought that ought to have throwed Lawyer Scrounge's writ of habeus corpses out of court, but Samanthie Coddlewort, she was riled up fit to kill, claiming the ladies had been publically humiliated by a bunch of barflies. She got Lawyer Scrounge's promise to start a court action agin Sol Fishman, the Head Man of the Circus which owned the dogs, and agin Curly Bill Grane, who had been impolite enough to bust a gallus guffawing. The crowd busted up and the male half of it went back to the Bloated Goat to celebrate, but they found that serious trouble had come to roost in Apache. Buck Speeglebaum and a big delegation of up-county stockmen rode into town for a powwow with Lawyer Scrounge, who would have been hard pressed to have fried catfish for all the clients he had hollerin' for his legal services that night.

Seems the Phantom Rustler had shot and killed Buck's cavvy wrangler out on the sage flats. The trail had vanished, as usual, over Cactus Crick way. The stockmen were out to throw Sheriff Rimfire Cudd into the discard as a no-good nincompooper.

Nobody in Apache got a wink of shut-eye that night, what with all the local hound-dogs and gutter mongrels congregating around the Dog & Pony Show car to get a glimpse of the city slickers and show girls camped in their midst. The noise they made visitin' back and forth was one for the books. Sol Fishman was being cussed by every man in town, including himself, before daylight come.

The Paintin' Pistoleer got up next morning to find out that bad luck had kicked him in the face, too. First off, it turns out that Don Gusto and his dance-hall jessie-belle had got the padre to marry 'em last night and had eloped, leaving Smith with a half-finished painting that wasn't paid for. Worse yet, when Justin O. goes over to the barn to feed his palomino, he found Skeeter had been stole, along with a $150 kack.

Colonel Krutch had skipped town during the night with Sol Fishman's $500, leaving the Dog & Pony Show with a Head Man but no ringmaster. Everyone tooken for granite that krutch had rode off on Justin O.'s palomino, but a windstorm during the night had wiped out his tracks, so there was no way Smith had of knowing what direction Krutch went to.

The Paintin' Pistoleer was up in his studio, tearing his hair out from worry over his stolen horse, when Sheriff Cudd come banging up the steps with a telegram he had been handed by Lew Pirtle, addressed to the sheriff of Stirrup County.

It seems this telegram come from back East, from the owners of the Dog & Pony Show. The railroad had notified them how they had cut the circus adrift here in Apache, Arizona, and the owners wanted the local sheriff to take the show and its boss into custody because this Colonel Krutch had run off with the menagerie back in Texas some place and had been pocketing all the gate receipts. The telegram went on to say that the owners were rushing a couple of Pinkerton detectives out to take Krutch back to jail.

"This puts Sol Fishman's tail in a helluva tight crack," Rimfire Cudd says. "With Colonel Krutch stealin' your hoss and skedaddling for parts unbeknownst, this means Sol will have to buck these here Pink-Tongue detectives when they show up. And the only lawyer in town to defend him is Plato X. Scrounge, which same is like askin' a hangman to fix your necktie for you."

But the Paintin' Pistoleer is too far sunk in his own misery to worry much about what happened to Sol Fishman. He knows the Cattlemen's Association has given Rimfire twenty-four hours to haul in the Phantom Rustler for murder, or submit to a recall election.

All of a sudden, the Paintin' Pistoleer jumps like a rattler has crawled up his pantleg. He's looking out the

146

studio winder at the time, and over in the livery-stable corral he sees a pinto mare which he recognizes as the nag which Don Gusto always rid into town when he come to court his dance-hall sweetheart.

"Saddle up, sheriff, an' meet me out front in ten minutes!" Justin O. says. "We're goin' to make ourselves a spoon or spoil a horn. Colonel Krutch didn't steal my palomino after all!"

Well, the sheriff rigs his crowbait and when he gets back to the Longhorn Saddle Shop, the Paintin' Pistoleer is waiting for him, wearing the .32 Colt on a .45 frame that he's made famous throughout the Territory, and he's riding Don Gusto's pinto mare.

"I figger Don Gusto stole my horse and left his own nag behind," Justin O. says. "I've got a hunch if I give this mare her head, she'll strike out for home, where Don Gusto is."

Well, Rimfire welcomed the chance to get out of town for the day; so he follows Justin O, across the mesquite flats as Smith gives Don Gusto's mare its head and it lines out for the Sacatones.

All morning the mare hoofs it acrost the desert, until she hits Cactus Crick, which same is the last spot where the sheriff has been able to find any trace of the county's stolen cattle. For ten miles or so, Don Gusto's pinto splashes up the creek, until she reaches the end of the box canyon, where Hosstail Falls tumbles down over the cliffs.

This is dead end, but Don Gusto's paint hoss don't let the waterfall faze her. She plows right on through, giving Justin O. and the sheriff a bag dousing in water that's brings them into a big cave which was formerly the subterranean course of Cactus Crick.

Smith whispers for the sheriff to dismount, and they foller Don Gusto's nag afoot. About a hundred yards farther on the cave takes an elbow bend and there, hid in the heart of the Sacatones, is the purtiest green graze you ever seen, a 50-acre basin lined with cliffs a thousand foot high, which is why no man ever laid eyes on this spot before.

The Paintin' Pistoleer tells Rimfire to keep back in the shadders, and watch. They see Don Gusto's pinto head over to where there is a corral and an adobe shack with smoke coming out o' the chimbley. There are several head of saddle horses in the corral, including Smith's palomino, and out in the basin a sizeable herd of cattle are grazing. Four-five Mexicans are busy over a branding iron fire, reworking the brands these mossyhorns arrived with.

"Don Gusto's mare led us to the Phantom Rustler's hide-out," Smith explains to the bug-eyed sheriff. "We're south of the Mexican line here. The Phantom chouses a jag of steers through the waterfall without leavin' any sign, they blot the brands in this holding-ground and market their wetbacks down in Sonora."

Well, seeing that they can sneak up on the rustler's shack and keep out of sight of the Mexicans at work a mile away, Justin O. Smith orders Rimfire to cover him from the cave while he has a look in the 'dobe.

Peeking through a window, Smith sees Don Gusto and his bride eating tortillas and drinking *pulque*

148

inside. They both look petered out from their 40-mile ride over from Apache, and this is their wedding breakfast.

Smith takes out his Colt and kicks open the door, putting the bride and groom under a cold drop before they know what's up. Don Gusto makes like he's going to draw, but he thinks better of it, having heard too much about the Paintin' Pistoleer's gun rep to risk swapping lead with this grinning hombre from Apache.

"I've come for my hoss, Don Gusto," Smith says in that easy-going Alabama drawl of his. "I'm going to gag you and your wife and leave you tied up here. Then I'm going back to Apache and send the sheriff and a posse out here to nab you and your brand-blottin' crew. You see, I know you're the Phantom Rustler."

Well, Don Gusto winks at his bride and they submit meek as milk to the Paintin' Pistoleer tying them back-to-back and stuffing gags in their mouths. They know the Mexican waddies will show up around nightfall, and that it will be day after tomorrow morning before Sheriff Cudd can possibly get a posse back here. Even so, a single man with a rifle could keep an army from coming through the cave behind the waterfall.

"You ain't so smart, Phantom Rustler," Smith says, when he has them hog-tied and gagged. "If you'd waited around town one more day, you could have stole the Dog & Pony Show animals. Sol Fishman has tooken them over to the sheep camp owned by Rimfire Cudd's brother Chewie, where they can get graze and mutton. If you'd have rustled that circus, you could have got $5,000 apiece for them trained ponies."

Don Gusto's eyes kind of glitter; it's plain he's hatching up an idea of some kind. The Paintin' Pistoleer leaves. He don't tell Rimfire Cudd about finding Don Gusto and his wife. He just insists on Rimfire leaving the rustler's roost with him and asking no questions. Only this trip, the Paintin' Pistoleer is forking his own Skeeter palomino.

They get back to Apache after dark, and right off Smith goes into a powwow with Sol Fishman. The upshot of that was that Sol loads his dog kennels on a buckboard and hitches the cavvy of Shetland ponies to it, and gets Rimfire Cudd to drive out of town with the Dog & Pony Show menagerie, heading for his brother Chewie's sheep ranch ten miles away.

After the sheriff left, the Paintin' Pistoleer really goes to work, busy as a rooster in a hen yard. He swears Lew Pirtle to secrecy, and gets Lew to doctor up that telegram about the Pinkerton detectives coming after the Dog & Pony Show.

Lew shows this telegram casual-like to Lawyer Scrounge, who is eating supper over at the Feedbag Café. It states that the Dog & Pony Show has been stolen and that the owners are putting up a $10,000 cash reward for information leading to its return.

Within ten minutes, Lawyer Scrounge shows up at the O. K. Mercantile, where Sol Fishman is busy working on his books.

"Sol," the shyster braces Fishman in mournful tones, "in view of the fact that my client, Colonel Krutch,

150

turned out to be a crook, I am morally bound to make amends to you. Not only have I persuaded the Ladies' Knittin' & Peach Presarves Society to drop their lawsuit agin you an' Curly Bill, but I am willing and ready to pay you back the five hundred dollars you give my absconded client. All I ask in return is a bill of sale naming me as sole owner and Head Man of said circus, just to make everything legal and above-board. It's the only fair thing a man of conscience could do."

Well, Fishman allows that was right white of Lawyer Scrounge, and he signs a bill of sale and gets his money back. Scrounge is so tickled over this sandy he had put over on Sol that he goes right-off to the Overland Telegraph office and pays Lew Pirtle a $50 bonus in return for Lew's promise not to mention the telegram to Rimfire Cudd or nobody else around 'Pache.

Soon as Lew tipped 'em off how things stood, Sol Fishman an' the Paintin' Pistoleer lit out acrost the desert to Chewie Cudd's sheep camp. They found the Shetland ponies and the caged-up dogs penned up in Chewie's brush corral.

Well, the night drags along and nothing happens. But along about sunrise, the Paintin' Pistoleer spots half-a-dozen riders topping the ridge from the direction of Cactus Crick. The sheriff and his brother are hid out in the chaparral near the corral and they recognize Don Gusto and his Mexican rustlers. They are palavering in Spanish, but Justin Other Smith has picked up the lingo since he come West for his health three years back.

151

"This will be our last raid on the gringos, amigos," Don Gusto is saying. "The Apache sheriff will lead a posse to our hide-out by sundown, so our rustling days are over in this part of the Border. But we will all be rich when we sell these circus ponies. Señor Smith told me they are worth $5,000 apiece. Why should we worry about risking our necks to steal cattle at $20 a head?"

Well, Don Gusto and his outlaws climb out of stirrups and surround the sheepherder's shack, but find it empty. They figger Chewie has gone to town to buck the tiger, leaving the coast clear for this raid. The Mexicans are all laughing and chattering betwixt theirselves when they walk over to the corral.

A gun cracks in the brush just then and Don Gusto's sombrero goes kiting off his head. Before the rustlers can run for their horses, a Winchester starts working from behind a woodpile where the sheepherder is bellied down, and that stampedes the rustlers' broncs from hell to breakfast.

Don Gusto and his men see they've run into a trap, and that start for the adobe shack to fort up. But three of them get their hats shot off before they cover a dozen steps and they recognize that brand of shooting. They're bucking the Paintin' Pistoleer and maybe a big posse, and they give up pronto.

Rimfire Cudd steps out from behind a sheep-shearin' shed just then and Don Gusto gets boogery and lets fly a shot, but the slug hits the turnip watch which Cudd has in his vest pocket and he's picking hairsprings an' bits of glass crystal and cogwheels out of his hide for a month after that. The Paintin' Pistoleer shoots the gun

152

out of the Phantom Rustler's hand, though, so Don Gusto joins his compadres in surrender.

When they get back to town they find Buck Speeglebaum and his Cattle Association ranchers all fixed to start their recall election agin Rimfire Cudd, but they call off that arrangement pronto when they see the sheriff herd the Phantom Rustler and his wild bunch into the Apache calaboose.

Rimfire is braggin' and struttin' like a pouter pigeon, neglecting to give Justin Other Smith any credit for trapping the Phantom, but the Paintin' Pistoleer don't mind that. He knows the Cattlemen's Association has posted a $1,000 dead-or-alive reward on the Phantom Rustler's topknot, and he aims to make Rimfire Cudd split that bounty with his sheepherder brother and Sol Fishman and Lew Pirtle, who had a hand in the plot. All Smith wanted was his palomino back, which was reward enough for him.

Well, it was open house at the Bloated Goat that night, with the county ranchers setting up the house to Blue Bagpipe Scotch and making a big hero out of Sheriff Rimfire Cudd. Every man in town was there to celebrate the end of the rustlers' reign of terror.

Everybody, that is, except Lawyer Plato X. Scrounge. It seemed that Apache's legal light was very unhappy. A couple of Pinkerton range dicks had dropped off the Wells-Fargo stagecoach at sundown, hunting the Head Man of the Dog & Pony Show which Colonel Krutch had stole back in Texas. Lawyer Scrounge was Johnny-on-the-spot with his bill of sale to prove he was sole owner of the Dog & Pony Show, and for once Sol

Fishman was glad he was what Smith termed a "horseless Head Man."

After these detectives had handcuffed Lawyer Scrounge and set off acrost the desert to dab their loop on the Dog & Pony Show, Sheriff Rimfire Cudd come back to the Bloated Goat to make his report to the boys.

"Lawyer Scrounge is goin' to need every bit of skull-duggery in his bag of tricks to get his neck out of this trap them Pink-Tongue detectives set for him," chuckles the sheriff, who is more or less in his cups by now. "And he ain't bucking anything as simple as one of Sol Fishman's Rodents' Nemesissies, neither."

Go West, Young Woman!

It was plumb redic'lous, of course, trying to convert Apache from a two-bit Arizona cow town into a refined, fashionable center of culture. But when those pedigreed society bluebloods sashayed out from Boston, Mass., to size up the town, civic pride made Apache folks come rompin' out of the chutes with ettyquette an' eddication oozin' from their ears.

Venting Apache's brand just warn't in the cards, of course; but they run a perty good bluff, at that, considerin' they was betting deuces back-to-back agin a Bostonian royal flush.

It all started four years back when Lew Pirtle, who runs the Overland Telegraph office, decided to send his son Lucius Jr. off to a highfalutin school in New York State, to file off his rough edges and cram his knothead full of sofistication and book-larnin' and how to hold a teacup without dislocatin' his little finger, and other essentials of gracious livin' which was a mite hard to come by in an uncurried frontier settlement like 'Pache.

Well, it kept Pirtle's nose to the grindstone, answering Lucius's distress signals for extry dinero to buy hisself overhalls he called "tuxedos," and perfoomy hair-lotion instead of the biled goose grease which the young bloods around here use, and books enough to pave hell a mile, and such fol-de-rol.

But anyhow, young Lucius finally dabs his loop on what he calls a "diploma," after spending four years and a mint of his dad's hard-earned cash. Lucius comes back to Arizona Territory all duded up fitten to kill, in spats and tight pants and a vest and a hard derby hat, and takes on a job as clerk in the Stockman's Bank, of which Jim Groot is the ramrod.

Lucius was a plumb likeable cuss before he corralled this new Oxford accent, though, so the town calculates he'll settle down in the harness eventual and get hisself re-civilized.

But it seems that Lucius Pirtle, Jr., had made quite a splash back at this here school where he got a "bachelor's degree" slapped on his hide. During his last summer vacation, Lucius had posed for a picture which our local artist feller, Justin Other Smith, was painting for a magazine cover. Smith had painted Lucius as an Injun fighter wrasslin' with Geronimo on the brink of a cliff.

It seems this here magazine showed up at Croton-Oil-on-Hudson, the college Lucius was attending, and them Easterners got the idea that Lucius was a two-gun rough-rider from the wild and woolly West, who could shoot Buffler Bill into the shade, ride anything with hair on, and sleep of nights on a soogan stuffed with the skulps of Injuns he'd sent to the happy huntin' grounds as soon as he outgrowed his cradle.

Instead of admittin' to his college pards that he had just posed for Justin O.'s painting, Lucius modestly admits that he's got a big repitation out West as a redskin hunter.

This makes Lucius the hero of the campus, and a filly name of Spetunia, from a Boston society fambly, she cuts Lucius out of the herd while he was soaking up refinement at Croton-Oil-on-Hudson, and got herself engaged to marry up with Lucius as soon as he got settled in his bank job out in Arizona. Which is proof right there that his "bachelor" degree wasn't worth the sheepskin it was printed on.

Well, Lucius stalls off sending word to his Boston sweetheart to rattle her hocks out West for the weddin'. After a few months, Spetunia's old man, who is a Boston financial magnet name of Marmaduke Archibald Spoot III, he sends a telegram to Lucius saying him and his wife are heading West by train, bringing Spetunia with 'em, to prove that Lucius is a tinhorn fourflusher instead of a hero.

Of course Lucius's dad, being the Overland Telegraph operator, he lets this news leak out pronto. Most folks in 'Pache figger that Lucius can sizzle in his own juice, ifn he had tried to pass hisself off as the bull of the herd back home.

Seeing as how the Paintin' Pistoleer's magazine cover had been the cause of Lucius getting in his jam back East, young Pirtle decides it's up to Smith to help unravel things. Justin O. has a studio upstairs over the Longhorn Saddle Shop, and that's where Lucius braces him.

157

"I got as much trouble as a stump-tail bull in fly time," Lucius begins doleful-like, without a trace of his Oxford accent showing through. "Here this beautiful young social butterfly, Spetunia Spoot, is wingin' her way out West, and she expects to find me the leadin' citizen of Apache, instead of being the tinhorn sport an' cheap incomepooper her folks say I am. Her pa and ma like to swallered their cuds when Spetunia busted the news to 'em that we aimed to get hitched in double-harness after graduation."

Justin O. knows his usin' Lucius as a model for his painting is the thing that the kid blames his difficulties on, so he feels he's sort of been dealt a hand in this game.

"Just what," Smith asks in that soft Alabama drawl of hisn, "did you tell Miss Spoot about yourself and your home town?"

Well, it takes considerable scratchin' to dig the truth out of young Pirtle, but he finally owns up that he'd made out to Spetunia's folks that he had single-handed cleaned the Injuns out of this corner of the Territory, and that he was the bravest hombre this side of the Rocky Mountings, bar none.

"Mister Spoot tells her I'm a yeller-livered braggart, ascairt of my own shadder," Lucius mourns. "The reason for that opinion bein' that when I first visited 'em in Boston, last Christmas, they tried to git me on one of them new-fangled electric tram cars which run along Beacon Street. Nacheral, seein' a vehicle movin' without hosses or an en-gine hitched in front, I shied in the traces an' skun up a tree in Boston Common."

158

Justin O. tugs his lower lip, frowning plumb serious. "I can well savvy your trepidation," he allows. "Any other reason why Spoot figgers you ain't man enough for his daughter?"

Lucius scratches his noggin with a hossshoe nail, pondering. "We-ell," he admits sheepish, "when I got to their house in Boston — which hogan is twict as big as the Wells-Fargo livery barn — Spetunia showed me into what I figgered was my bedroom. It was kind of smallish, but nacheral I was too refined to say anything — that would be what they call in Latin a *fox's puss*.

"But when I got into this room, Spetunia pushes a button an' the hull thing riz clean to the roof! It tooken a bottle o' smellin'-salts to rally me around. Later I found out this corntraption was what they called a 'elevator,' but I told 'em that out West we used ladders to git into attics with, an' that's what I would use in Boston, thank you just the same."

The Paintin' Pistoleer has a coughing spell at that.

"An' here's a telegram," Lucius groans, producing same, "which I got today. It says the Marmaduke Archibald Spoots III are on their way out to size up my home range. They're expectin' me to be the town hero, an' they're likewise expectin' to find Apache is a mee-tropolis as straight-laced as Boston an' twict as refined. Ain't I got my nose knee-deep in trouble?"

Well, Smith makes certain of two things: that Lucius has told Spetunia the real truth about himself not bein' an Injun fighter, and also that he loves this gal something fierce, which Smith allows is what counts in the long run.

159

"You leave this to me, Lucius," Justin O. says. "When the Spoots arrive, I guarantee they'll believe that Apache, Arizona, is the cultural capital of the West, and what's more, that you're the boss wrangler on this spread."

It's a mighty big order, mighty big, even for a clever hombre like the Paintin' Pistoleer. Apache is just a wide spot on the stagecoach road, and its hairy-eared inhabitants ain't exactly got their brands registered in no Society Blue Book as yet.

Well, Smith starts out by rounding up his cronies in what passes for the civic forum, namely Curly Bill Grane's barroom at the Bloated Goat Saloon. There's Sol Fishman, who owns the O. K. Mercantile, and Jim Groot the banker, and Sheriff Rimfire Cudd, and Dyspepsia Dan of the Feedbag Café, and a few other rannihans.

"What we got to do is spruce up a little," Justin Other Smith explains. "You galoots got to get haircuts and maybe take a bath, and launder yore overhalls for the first time in years, and otherwise impress these visitin' Bostonians that you're elite upper-crust gentlemen of breeding. Most of all, boys, we got to convince this Marmaduke Archibald Spoot III that his prospective son-in-law is the bravest hombre who ever burned a pistol cap."

Well, Sol Fishman grumbles that Lucius Pirtle, Jr., ain't worth it. But him and the others changed their minds when Smith p'ints out that Apache's muni-sipple prestige is at stake.

160

"We don't want them Boston puritans to give our community a hosslaugh," Smith augers. "What's more, we need fewer bachelors in this burg nohow, if Apache is goin' to grow up with the country. From what Lucius says, this girl Spetunia is cut the right way of the leather. All she needs is a chance to shake the dust of Boston offn her bustle, to be right civilized."

Well, anyway, the Bloated Goat bunch gits to work. Sheriff Rimfire Cudd takes a *pasear* over to the Cheery-cow Injun reservation, and has a powwow with the kingpin, Chief Ache-in-the-Back.

After he has bribed the chief with chawin'-tobacco and a quart of Curly Bill Grane's redeye whisky (which last is strickly illegal, and could have cost the sheriff his star), the old Injun agrees that when the app'inted time comes, him and forty-fifty Cheery-cow bucks, in warpaint an' feather bonnets, will raid Apache and pertend like they want to count coup on the Boston Palefaces.

These Injuns will be driv off single-handed, of course, by none other than the town hero, Lucius Pirtle, Jr., who will stand ace-high with Marmaduke Archibald Spoot III when he rescues Spetunia from them tomahawk scalp-hunters.

Meanwhile, Lucius being the dutiful son he is, he takes his mother into his confidence. Missus Pirtle is the new president of the Apache Ladies' Knitting & Peach Preserves Society, and she is proud as a mare with a two-headed colt over her boy fixing to marry up with a Beacon Street debutanty.

161

Missus Pirtle palavers with Samanthie Coddlewort and Hernia Groot, and they decide it's their civic duty to make the town look more aristocratic. They begin their campaign by having Justin Other Smith paint up a batch of signs.

Cowtail Alley, which leads from the railroad station to the stock pens, becomes *Park Avenue Boulevard*. The sign on the town's one and only hotel, which for 40-odd year has read *Cowboy's Rest Rooming-House, Guaranteed Bugless*, is changed to *The Waldorf-Plaza Arms*.

Hernia Groot rousts Sol Fishman out of the two front rooms, where he has batched for 20 year, and the womenfolks spend two days cleaning out that boar's nest. They label the door as *The Royal Bridle Sweet*, which same the Spoot IIIs will occupy when they show up in 'Pache.

The Bloated Goat Saloon has a canvas tarp slung acrost its false front to hide its vulgar sign, and on this tarp is lettered *Apache Literary & Book-Lovers' League*, although this makes Curly Bill Grane so starch raving mad he gets drunk and threatens to perforate the Spoots with his double-barrel greener, on sight.

Sol Fishman voluntarily rechristens his O. K. Mercantile into the *Exclusive Paris Emporium & Fashion Salon*. He even goes so far as to rig up a window display of the latest red-flannel drawers and high-buttoned women's shoes he's got in stock, although it's plumb doubtful if the Bostonians will do much window-shopping while they're out West, the glass being so fly-speckled and cobwebby.

162

The main detail, of course, is convincing these Spoot IIIs that their would-be son-in-law is the real McCoy as a bold Lochinvar out of the West, afraid of nothing that breathes. Sheriff Cudd's arrangement with Chief Ache-in-the-Back's warriors may turn the trick, but when Lucius hears about that scheme, he's dubious.

"You see, I've already bragged to Spetunia's folks that I've made Apache too hot for a redskin to git within a hundred mile of the place," he explains. "I told them the Arizona red men call me 'Thunderbolt Bad Medicine,' and that their squaws warn their papooses as soon as they're borned to steer shy of my stampin'-grounds, at the risk of losin' their topknots."

Well, it's too late to call off the Cheery-cow raid for fear of offending old Ache-in-the-Back, him being a touchy old buzzard. But Justin Other Smith promises that after the powder smoke settles, he'll assure these pilgrims from the Hub o' the Universe that the Injun raiders were Comanches from Texas, who have come acrost country to see if they was skookum enough to nail Lucius's hide to a fence — to the tribe's everlastin' sorrow.

The whole scheme has leaked out by now, what with the womenfolks being let in on it. As a result of this, the best idea of all is hatched up by an hombre who is a newcomer to Apache, the night hostler at the Wells-Fargo barn, name of Swede O'Flannagan.

Swede O'Flannagan is an ornery-looking galoot with notches on his gun butts, who has had Sheriff Rimfire Cudd scairt sleepless ever since he come to town a month ago. Rimfire thinks mebbe this O'Flannagan is a wanted owlhooter, hidin' out from the law. Swede drinks like a blotter, but just the same, he comes up with this prime idea for backing Spetunia's folks into Lucius's stall.

"Young Pirtle works at the bank, as I savvy this layout," O'Flannagan tells the boys who are roundsiding at the Bloated Goat. "Why not arrange for Pirtle to kill a masked bandick durin' a holdup while the Spoots are lookin' on? The robber, of course, will be Justin O. Smith, your champeen gun slinger."

Well, the boys put that idea on the back of the stove to simmer awhile, and Lucius, who is swigging buttermilk along with the Paintin' Pistoleer, he allows the scheme has merits, at that.

"Sheriff Rimfire Cudd will be in the bank at the time of this phoney holdup," Swede O'Flannagan warms to his subjeck. "Every spalpeen in the bank — includin' Lucius an' Cudd an' the Paintin' Pistoleer — will have blank shells in their shootin'-irons, savvy?

"Spetunia will see a rootin', tootin' Western gun fight, with Smith pertendin' to salivate the sheriff. When Rimfire falls dead, the gal will realize the town ain't got a lawman to defend it, and she'll realize likewise that the outlaw's li'ble to make off with *her*. An' that's where young Lucius Pirtle steps into the picture. He kills the masked bandick, usin' a shotgun with blank loads in it. Faith an' begorra, men, I can hear the weddin' bells a-janglin' in the Baptist church right this minute!"

Well, everybody gits enthusiastic over the idea, including the Paintin' Pistoleer. Next morning they pull

164

off a rehearsal in the bank, with Justin O. climbin' in through a winder and shooting Rimfire Cudd, finally getting his needin's from the dashing hero, Lucius Pirtle, Jr.

Swede O'Flannagan, dressed in gunnysack skirts to play the part of the bride-to-be, he embarrasses young Pirtle considerable when he kisses him an' begs him to corral a preacher pronto, but the rehearsal is pronounced a big success. Needles to say, Lucius figgers the wedding is a cinch, forty ways from the jack.

The night before the Spoot IIIs are to arrive in 'Pache, a little hitch develops. Chief Ache-in-the-Back sends a runner over from the Cheery-cow reservation to say that his braves don't want to pull off no humiliatin' retreat unlessen they get paid for it, five bucks a head. So the town took up a collection, with Justin O. making up a $45 deficit out of his own pocket, and sends the dinero over to the Injun camp — enough to hire 40 warriors, including the chief, who has upped his ante to $15 and a bottle of forty-rod.

Well, that's how things stack up when the Rainbow Flyer stops on flag the next morning, the first time that's happened since the Skunk Gulch trestle caught fire. The whole town is out to greet the Marmaduke Archibald Spoot IIIs, the men wearing new galluses, and the ladies of the Knitting & Peach Preserves Society drawed up like a 20-mule team alongside the baggage-room platform.

Lucius Pirtle, Jr., wearing this git-up he calls a tuxedo — which looks like the coroner's buryin'-clothes — he's waiting at the coach steps when his sweetheart leaps into his arms. Spetunia's as perty as a little red wagon, about 18, with eyes as shiny as Rimfire Cudd's nose. She's sweet enough to eat raw, for a fact.

Next to show up is Spetunia's mother, and the contrast is something fierce. The III in Missus Spoot's name must be the tally count on her three chins. Her nose is stuck up so high she'd have drowned pronto ifn Arizona had had a halfway rainy climate. She's peering over the crowd through a pair of eyeglasses she's got rigged up on a kind of a stick, which is maybe why she trips coming down the steps and sprawls headlong, bowling over the conductor and busting a plank in the station platform.

She bounces to her feet as dignified as ever, though. She's wearin' a bustle the size of a mail sack at seed-catalogue time, and totes a little postage-stamp parasol. Mebbe she's blue-blooded, but there's a passel of squaws over to the Injun reservation who could have spotted Missus Spoot III a hundred pounds of tallow and still beat her comin' an' goin' in a free-for-all beauty contest.

Last off the train is Marmaduke Archibald in person. He's a mousy little hombre, bald as a turkey egg. Mebbe he's a big business magnet out in Boston, but in Arizona he's a ganted little maverick who'd be cut out of any herd as a cull for the glue works.

Marmaduke's wearing a Boston Watch & Ward button, and under his arm he's got a copy of *Alice in Wonderland*, which he aims to censor as being indecent. When he steps off the train he appears at first glance to be sawed off at the knees; but this turns out to be an optional illusion, him having stepped into the hole in the platform which his wife had caved in a minute before. He's stuck there tighter'n a cork in the bottom of a glue bottle.

Well, while the sheriff and Justin O. Smith are busy prying Mr. Spoot out of this hole, Lawyer Plato X. Scrounge reels off an official address of welcome, pertending he's the city mayor. Scrounge can spiel off more big words than arybody else in 'Pache, and he outdoes himself today, impressing these dudes considerable.

The Spoots are looking down their noses at the crowd — the old folks, that is — but they pert up some when they are loaded into a yellow buckboard which has been donated by the livery stable, and they ride in state for the 50 feet from the railroad depot to the shack which is now called the Waldorf-Plaza Arms.

Missus Spoot III has a little trouble negotiating the rickety stairs up to the Royal Bridle Sweet, but the manager, Crowfoot Hoskins, he explains that the reg'lar elevator had caught the eye of His Royal Highness the Prince o' Wales, who spent his two-weeks' summer vacation in 'Pache this year, and the Prince bought the elevator to take back to Buckin'ham Palace, and they ain't got delivery on a new one yet.

The main event on the program that evening is a formal banquet at Dyspepsia Dan's Feedbag Café, now wearing the name of *Ye Olde Gourmet's Inn, Henri Delmonico, Matre d' Chef.* This shindig ain't open to the public, only the famblies of the bride and groom. But the Apache folks who push their noses to the winders and drool in their whiskers, they see that Dyspepsia Dan has fixed things up brown.

Dan is all bibbed and tuckered out like a French sport in a black suit he borried from the undertaker, and along with the grub he dishes up a lot of elegant talk about horse's doves, cover charges, table of oats, and such-like, which is over the heads of everybody present except the Spoot IIIs, who savvy it easy.

While the Spoots and Pirtles are having their snack of bait, Sheriff Rimfire Cudd is out in the mesquites riding herd on Chief Ache-in-the-Back and his Injun warriors, who are due to pull off their big raid as soon as the visitors polish off their chow.

Things git perty suspenseful when the banquet finally busts up, with Lucius Pirtle leading Spetunia out into the street. Missus Spoot is picking her false teeth with a fancy gold quill, with Marmaduke Archibald trotting along behind like a dog on a leash, and they size up Apache's Great White Way.

Missus Spoot sees that Apache's womenfolks are dressed in the latest style, too. All the Knitting & Peach Preserves Society members are out promenading, and they've all got their spectacles rigged up on sticks, just like Missus Spoot. "Lung-nets," Hernia Groot says is the name for them.

Well, out in the chaparral back of the Busted Flush Dance Hall, Sheriff Rimfire Cudd gives the high-sign to the Injuns. Out of the brush they come, a-hossback. There's only six-seven of them, though, instead of the 40 which the town has rented. Seems the Injuns figgered that as long as they'd been paid off already, there was no use riskin' pneumony by shedding their blankets, so most of the bucks were squattin' along the street to watch the fun.

Anyhow, Chief Ache-in-the-Back and six warriors come riding down the main street hell-for-leather, shivering without their blankets, and doing more coughing than war-whooping. The Apache ladies scream, "Run for your lives! We'll all be scalped alive!" and skedaddle like a flock of hens when a buzzard hawk shows up.

Everybody runs, that is, except the Spoot family and Lucius Pirtle, Jr., who find themselves surrounded in front of the Longhorn Saddle Shop by these here red-skins.

Them bucks are a decrepit-looking lot. They got a few chicken feathers stuck in their hair, and are smeared up with axle grease and corn starch as an imitation of warpaint.

The chief's horse shies and bucks Ache-in-the-Back tail over tincup onto the ground at Missus Spoot's feet, knocking the wind out of him, but he picks hisself up finally and waves an ax with a broke handle which he's passing off for a tommyhawk.

"Injuns want-um p-p-paleface scalps!" the chief stammers the speech he's memorized, acting as nervous as a kid recitin' poetry at a church sociable. "Big chief ketch-up squaw for his wigwam." Then he ad-libs quick-like, "I mean this young squaw, not the fat one. Ugh! Heap good! Wah-hooo!"

Well, the other bucks slide offn their crowbait nags, shivering in the cold, their scrawny ribs all over

169

duck-bumps. Chief Ache-in-the-Back, having delivered his blood-curdling announcement, gets an acute case o' stage fright and just stands there scratching the flea bites on his pot-belly.

Young Lucius is frantic, trying to signal the chief to attack him. Ache-in-the-Back finally gits wise, and makes off to draw his scalping-knife, which same he carries under the waistband of the cut-off levis he's wearing. The blade slashes his belt in two, and from there on the chief is got his hands full holding his pants up.

One of the Injuns squatting over on the saddle-shop porch puts in his two cents' worth, "Build-um heap big fire, burn palefaces at stake! Wah-hoooo!" Right this minute, them teeth-chatterin' Cheery-cow bucks look like they needed a warm fire, at that.

Well, Lucius draws in a big breath, shoves Spetunia safely behind him, and gets set to make his hero play. Before he can move, though, Missus Marmaduke Archibald Spoot III waddles past him and bops Chief Ache-in-the-Back acrost the noggin with her parasol, bowling him offn his feet. That redskin really bit the dust, as Shakespeare said onct.

"Begone, you filthy hinterland barbarians!" Missus Spoot III screeches. "What do you mean, appearing in public with nothing on but your underwear? Scat, the whole vulgar lot of you!"

Well, Ache-in-the-Back picks himself up, almost losing his pants before he makes his saddle. The other braves scramble to fork their nags, with Missus Spoot a

170

jabbing their rumps with her parasol, never once lowering her lung-net eyeglasses.

Thirty seconds later there ain't nothin' left of that bloodthirsty band of Injuns but a few chicken feathers floatin' in the dusty air. Them Cheery-cows lit out for their reservation and didn't come out of hidin' till the fall beef issue at the agency.

Lucius shows up at the Bloated Goat a while after that, looking plumb miserable. He says that the Injun attack was what he calls a "fiasco," and that Marmaduke Archibald is over at the hotel going after Spetunia hammer and tongues for wanting to marry a no-good coward who would let his mother-in-law drive off a gang of mother-nekkid hoodlums. Seems them Boston aristocracks ain't even caught on that Chief Ache-in-the-Back's outfit was supposed to be redskins, mebbe because they was blue with cold. The Spoot IIIs figger they was fugitives from a bathhouse, judgin' from the towels wropped around their middles, or something.

"Furthermore," Lucius moans, "they're callin' Apache a plebeian, decadent, jerkwater, bucolic, low-caste, hog-waller of which there ain't no whicher on the map of the U.S.A., and be damned if they'll stand for their daughter comin' to live in such a run-down camp."

Swede O'Flannagan, he treats Lucius to his first shot of forty-rod, and tells the kid to pert up, that the big "bank robbery" tomorrow will fix things up proper. The town goes to sleep on that, plumb humiliated but hopin' for the best.

Turns out, next morning, that Lucius don't have to lure the Spoots over to the Stockman's Bank on no pretext or other. All three of the Spoots are perched on the bank steps when Jim Groot shows up at nine o'clock to open the place. Marmaduke says he wants to git a traveler's check cashed, so's he can buy a return ticket for Boston, Mass. Seems there ain't another train due through 'Pache until next Thursday week, so the Spoots aim to take a stage over to Tucson and ketch a train there, takin' Spetunia with 'em.

Well, Jim Groot stalls them off while Lucius hustles over to the jailhouse and wakes up the sheriff, telling him that the fake bank robbery has got to be staged earlier than they'd planned. Things moved mighty rapid behind the scenes then, with the Paintin' Pistoleer fixin' up his robber's mask and makin' sure his gun was loaded with blanks, and getting over to the woodshed alongside the bank where he will wait for Lucius to signal to start the robbery.

The sheriff, he lights a shuck over to the bank, his guns loaded with blank ca'tridges, and strolls in casual-like. He finds Spetunia sobbin' her eyes out, with Marmaduke and the old woman fumin' because Jim Groot is taking so long to cash their check.

Well, Lucius opens the alley window, to signal Justin Other Smith. Lucius feels a heap relieved when he sees his masked bandick step out of the woodshed, brandishin' his six-guns an' winkin' at Lucius. It's now or never, Lucius knows, so far as winning his bride is concerned. He figgers mebbe even Spetunia is beginning to peg him for a iggorant deceiver.

172

Well, Jim Groot and young Pirtle are back in the vault getting out their dinero, when all of a sudden a two-gun man wearin' a sombrero an' batwing chaps and with his face covered with a dirty red bandanna comes straddlin' in through the alley window.

"Reach for the roof!" he hollers. "This is a stickup!"

The Spoots really get their corks to bobbin' when they look into the bores of them two Colt .45s. Missus Spoot drops her lung-net glasses an' busts 'em, she's in such a hurry to raise her arms. Just then Rimfire Cudd slides off the corner stove where he's been warming his britches, and heads toward the bad man with his six-guns barkin' an' smokin'.

The bandick swings his Colts toward Rimfire Cudd and yanks triggers. Rimfire chokes out, "Yuh got me, podnuh!" claws his chest, an' pitches to the floor like a coat slidin' off a hook. This is too much for Marmaduke, who keels over in a dead faint.

The sheriff's feelin' hotter than a four-bit pistol about now, because he distinctly heard a couple of *bullets* drill the stove behind him! Something has slipped up — maybe because Justin O. was called away from his studio so sudden — because it's plumb obvious that the Paintin' Pistoleer's guns ain't loaded with blanks.

Over in the vault, Jim Groot and Lucius see the bullet holes in the stove, and Lucius ain't acting very heroic when the masked bandick backs them into the vault and tosses them a gunnysack, tellin' 'em to fill it up pronto with legally tender dinero.

173

"*Pssst!*" whispers Jim Groot, shaking like a cat spitting peach seeds. "You got real loads in them hoglegs, Smith!"

"Close-hobble yore trap!" snarls the bandick, and belts Jim Groot acrost the noggin, layin' him out cold.

Well, Lucius goes green aroundst the gills and likes to claws his fingernails off filling the bandick's sack with greenbacks and specie. Spetunia is watchin' him through the window of the teller's cage, scairt pea-green, figgering her lover is going to get his chips cashed in any second now.

The bandick shoulders his sack of loot and backs out of the vault, fires a couple shots to ventilate the ceilin', and bellers, "I've just kilt the sheriff of this burg, an' I'll do the same to ary galoot who tries to foller me, savvy?"

With which he crawls out of the window and vamooses out acrost the desert on a hoss he had stashed in the 'squites, taking along mighty nigh onto $10,000 of the bank's liquid assets.

After a good safe wait, Sheriff Rimfire Cudd screws open one eye. Then he hauls hisself to his feet and sprints out the front door. This makes Missus Spoot III bat her eyelashes, plumb puzzled. Rimfire's a mighty lively corpse, even for a healthy climate like she's heard Arizona Territory has got.

Anyway, out in the bank's woodshed, Rimfire Cudd finds the Paintin' Pistoleer. He's laid out with a lump on his noggin, having been knocked out colder'n a pawnbroker's heart.

174

Cudd pours some whisky down Smith's gullet, which rallies him pronto. By this time Curly Bill and Sol Fishman and the other boys in on the hoax have gathered around, wondering what went wrong.

"Swede O'Flannagan come into the woodshed just as I was getting my mask on," says the Paintin' Pistoleer, who's really on the peck. "This whole idear of a fake holdup was O'Flannagan's scheme to double-cross us into puttin' blanks in our guns, so's he could pull off a real robbery. We're a bunch of jugheaded fools, and I'm the biggest fool in the herd."

Well, Lucius's matrimonial chances are blowed higher than the tail feathers of a soarin' eagle now, but that ain't no-ways important. While Sheriff Cudd is trying to round up a posse to chase this O'Flannagan, the Paintin' Pistoleer bolts a kack on Skeeter, his palomino, and streaks out of town on his own private man hunt.

With him rides Lucius Pirtle, straddlin' the fastest bronc he could rent at the livery stable. Lucius says he cain't bare to look Spetunia in the eye ever agin, and that he don't aim to ever go back to Apache. Claims he's going to rip his college diploma out of its frame an' — well, he's figgered up a practical way to utilize that document, he says.

As soon as the Paintin' Pistoleer cuts Swede O'Flannagan's tracks — which are headed toward the Mex'can Border — he gives his palomino the spurs and leaves Lucius in a cloud of dust, Skeeter being the fastest hoss in Stirrup County.

Lucius keeps joggin' along, feeling flatter than a week-old flapjack. He figgers Mexico is as good a place as any for him.

Along about noon, he sees a big dust boiling up out of the Sacatone foothills, an' perty soon he sees the Paintin' Pistoleer ridin' back toward town. Smith's trailin' a man on foot, with a lass' rope around his neck. His prisoner turns out to be Swede O'Flannagan, who's totin' his bag of bank loot. O'Flannagan ain't tryin' to auger about this arrangement, neither, for he's had a chance to find out that Smith's famous .32 on a .45 frame ain't loaded with no blanks. Not this trip.

"Swede got set afoot when his bronc busted a laig in a gopher hole," Justin O. tells Lucius. "No difference, I'd have trailed the walloper clean to Chihuahua ifn I'd had to."

The Paintin' Pistoleer grabs O'Flannagan's gunnysack and tosses it to Lucius Pirtle.

"You burn the trail back to 'Pache, son," he says. "You got time to make it before Spetunia pulls out on that four-o'clock stage for Tucson, I reckon. And turn this dinero back to Jim Groot's bank, so's it can start accumulatin' interest agin."

Well, Lucius lines out for 'Pache like a turpentined terrier. It's a tedjus ride for Smith, slowed down like he is by Swede O'Flannagan's having to hoof it, so it's after dark when he shows up in Apache. He turns the bank robber over to Sheriff Rimfire Cudd, who claps O'Flannagan in jail pronto. O'Flannagan is glad to get there, actually, his hoofs being wore down plumb to the frawgs.

176

Feelin' the need for some nourishment, like say a glass of buttermilk, the Paintin' Pistoleer sashays over to the Bloated Goat Saloon. He notices that the *Apache Literary & Book-Lovers' League* sign has been tore down, along with all the other phony pedigree trappings around town. That tells him for shore that them snobby Spoots have high-tailed it back to Boston, Mass.

Shoulderin' through the batwings, Smith finds the barroom jammed to the rafters. Marmaduke Archibald Spoot III, the Boston financial magnet, is treating the house to Blue Bagpipe Scotch. He's got one arm around Lew Pirtle's neck, just like they was social equals, and he's plastered to the eyeballs.

It's quiet enough to hear a bumblebee belch for a minute, and then Spoot III greets young Smith:

"Come join our bachanal, young man! We're celebrating the marriage of my daughter, who is now en route to Tucson on her honeymoon with the hero who went out into the desert alone and slew that bank robber, bringing back the miscreant's ill-gotten boodle as proof of his deed. Spetunia's a lucky young woman."

Smith bats his eyes a time or two, not thinking Marmaduke Archibald could have possibly got himself that tipsy. But Mr. Spoot lost his holt on Lew Pirtle's neck just then, and fell flat on his face on the barroom floor. Cocking one eye up at the Paintin' Pistoleer, he spits out a mouthful of sawdust and hiccups:

"What I personally am celebrating, stranger, is that my good spouse has retreated to the purlieus of Beacon

Street, leaving me free to draw the first happy breath of my hen-pecked career!"

With which Spoot passes out cold.

Rain, Rain, Come to Stay!

Yessir, the cow town of Apache, Arizona Territory, ain't likely to forgit that first week in January, the winter of the Big Drought. The skinning that burg took was plumb complete, the tail going with the hide.

Them seven days seen the post office robbed, an economic crisis the which there warn't no whicher in the history of Stirrup County, a miracle of Nature, and a shootin' scrape throwed in for boot. And the whole ruction started because two of 'Pache's prominent citizens, Sol Fishman and Justin Other Smith, happened to both be working late on New Year's Eve. Else the county would be bankrupt flatter'n a bride's biskit today.

Sol Fishman is Apache's postmaster, the post office being a cubbyhole in his O. K. Mercantile, betweenst the feed room and the harness counter. It seems this New Year's Eve the weekly mail stage come in ten hours late on account of the jehu having to keep his team at a walk acrost the desert, because the Big Drought had dried up the Wells-Fargo water hole at Neverfailing Springs.

Most of the town was at the Bloated Goat Saloon or the Busted Flush dance hall, seeing the Old Year out and trying to forgit the drought which was ruining the county. But when Sol Fishman has a mail-sorting job to attend to, you couldn't pry him from behind them pigeonholes ifn you promised to dunk him in bourbon to the ears. Sol takes his dooties plumb serious, besides which his eyesight is getting poorly and it taken him longer to read the postcards than it did ten-twelve years ago.

This same night, Justin Other Smith was working late in his artist's studio, upstairs over the Longhorn Saddle Shop. Seems he had a picture to paint for a calendar-publishin' outfit back East, and was bucking what he calls a deadline, and had to make shore this painting got off on the Lordsburg stage, which same pulls out before daylight, holidays or whatever.

Anyhow, after wropping up his canvas and slapping the publisher's address on it, Justin O. sees a light is burning in Sol Fishman's store even though it was midnight, to judge from the guns goin' off down at the dance. He decides he'll take care of mailing the package tonight so's he can sleep in *mañana*.

When Justin O. reaches the O. K. Mecantile he raps on a winder and hollers for Sol to open up. Not getting an answer, he is all set to rattle his hocks over to the Bloated Goat for his buttermilk toast to auld lang syne, when he notices Sol's front door is open a crack. Scratching a match on the seat of his pants, Smith sees further that the lock has been jimmied open, and right off he figgers mebbe the place has been burgled while Sol is out celebrating.

180

Smith debates a second whether he orter fetch Sheriff Rimfire Cudd to the scene, but just then he sees the top of Sol Fishman's bald head showing through the post-office window, and figgers the old codger has dozed off while wading through his batch of postcards.

Anyhow, the Paintin' Pistoleer lets himself in, and goes over to the post-office corner. Then he sees that Sol ain't sleepin' voluntary. He's got a bloody welt on his noggin, a bandanna gag around his face, and he's laced to his chair with lass' rope, tighter'n a corset on a three-hunderd-pound spinster.

The next thing Justin O. Smith knows, *wham!* he don't know a thing. Something conks him from behind and his nose is rammed to the hilt in a knothole in the floor. When he comes to he's laid out behind the cracker bar'l, gagged and trussed up like a fryin'-hen.

He hears Sol Fishman squirmin' in his ropes, and since Smith ain't bolted down to anything solid, he manages to h'ist hisself to his feet. He gits rid of his gag by snaggin' it ag'in a pitchfork tine, an' then he pokes his head in at the post-office window and sees Sol a-makin' frantic signals with both eyeballs, motionin' Smith toward the door leading into where he is at.

"You sit tight," Smith says after he's hippity-hopped into the cubbyhole, "while I chaw a knot loose on your rope."

Sol sits tight, all right, fuming and sputtering behind his gag, while Smith gnaws on the rawhide until Sol is able to work one hand loose. It's short work then with the post-office scissors to cut both of 'em loose from this hog-tyin' deal.

181

"Anything wrong?" the Paintin' Pistoleer wants to know, rubbin' a knot on his noggin the size of a pullet aig. "Or do you always see the New Year in liken unto this?"

"I'll be chawed up an' spit out ifn I know," Sol confesses. "I dozed off tryin' to decipher a postcard — it was from yore Aunt Feebie in Alabama, Justin. Her erisypilas is actin' up agin an' Cousin Pootie's colic is worse. Nohow, when I woke up I was like you seen me. Damn if I know what happened."

The Paintin' Pistoleer pulls at his lower lip and allows sober-like, "This is right serious, if it involves the U.S. Mail. Reckon anything's missing?"

Well, something's missing, all right: a whole bag of third-class mail which Sol hadn't got around to sorting out. Fishman gets a good laugh out of that.

"The robber didn't make much of a haul," he says. "That sack he stole was this year's shipment of new Almanacs from the Doctor Dingle Hoss-Liniment concern, yak yak!"

The Paintin' Pistoleer, who's got hisself considerable of a rep hereabouts as an amachoor detective, he scouts around the store, finds Fishman's loose change is still in the till, the safe ain't molested, and furthermore there ain't a solitary clue to be found. It's plumb obvious the robber — or robbers — vamoosed with the sack of Doctor Dingle almanacs, thinking it was valuable parcel post. The way things stood, Apache didn't lose anything except the main item in the community's reading-habits for months to come.

"Nacheral, this has got to be reported to the law," Smith says, looking at his watch and seeing it's close onto daylight. "Maybe we've missed some clues by lantern light."

"No — I dassn't haul the sheriff in on this," Sol Fishman groans, scared bug-eyed as a thought hits him. "You know how Plato X. Scrounge has been wreckin' his brains trying to figger a way to be postmaster. Them U.S. postal inspectors find out I let this disgrace happen to me, they'll hand my job to that lawyer sure."

Well, they augered some, but finally Justin O. Smith agrees to let this robbery be his and Sol's secret, neither of them wasting much love on this shyster Plato X. Scrounge, who has been bit by the political bug and figgers the postmastership of Stirrup County is as good a toehold as any if he's going to be prosecutin' attorney.

"I'm plumb sorry about Doctor Dingle's new Almanac bein' choused, though," Smith tells Fishman before he leaves. "On account of I painted a beaut of a cover for Doc Dingle this year. It shows Lew Pirtle, our telegraph agent, posin' as one of the Defenders of the Alamo. I been keepin' that Almanac cover as a surprise for Pirtle's friends."

Well, durin' the next few days there was too much excitement around town for Sheriff Rimfire Cudd to get wind of the fact that robbers had busted into the local post office, which was probably all to the good so far as Rimfire's peace of mind was concerned.

Of course, Samanthie Coddlewort and Hernia Groot and some of the other womenfolks around town noticed that Smith and Sol were sportin' identical

183

lumps on their skulls, which made them raise their eyebrows plumb to the back of their necks and whisper around town that these two citizens had got drunk and fell on the brass rail over at the Bloated Goat on New Year's Eve.

This excitement which turned 'Pache upside down had nothin' to do with Doctor Dingle's Almanac failing to show up, but was due to the Big Drought. Water was running out over at the Sacatone diggings, where they mine with hydraulic hoses, and 'way last fall the big syndicates let it be known that if rains didn't come by January first, the reduction mills would close down for lack of ore and the muckers would be paid off, said pay-roll dinero having already been shipped down to the Stockman's Bank in Apache by a heavily guarded Wells-Fargo stage.

Well, it hadn't rained and none was in prospect, so the town began to fill up with out-of-work miners, waiting for payday. The north-county cattle spreads was hard hit, too, and a wholesale stock auction was scheduled for the following day, the ranchers being forced to dispose of their beef because the drought had burned out their winter graze. So, what with cowboys and miners arrivin' in Apache thicker than flies at a hawg-scaldin', nobody had time to remember that Doctor Dingle's Almanac had missed showin' up on New Year's Day, like it had done for generations.

Three days after the post office was robbed, something a mite out of the ordinary happened — that was the day before the miners was to be paid off at the Stockman's Bank. A shiny red and gold wagon drawed

184

by two spankin' blacks rolled into town from Tucson way, driv by a red-whiskered hombre in a silk hat an' Prince Albert coat. Writ on the sides and tailgate of this wagon was a big sign in gold letters: *Prof. J. Pluvius McCloud, Guaranteed Rain-Maker — My Scientific Method Always Brings Results!*

Nacheral, nobody was gullible enough to pay him no notice, ticketing him for a faker who probably sold snake-bite medicine on the side. But the Perfessor minded his own business, stabling his blacks at the livery barn and paying in advance for their groomin' and grainin', and rented hisself the best sweet of rooms in the Cowboy's Rest Hotel, Guaranteed Bugless, at a dollar-six-bits a day.

McCloud's red wagon was parked in the alley behind the Overland Telegraph office, but everybody in town got a gander at the picture painted on its sides. This job of art wasn't in the class with what Justin O. Smith daubs up, but it showed a fair-to-middlin' likeness of Prof. J. Pluvius McCloud riding in the basket of a balloon, prodding a cloud with a pitchfork and making it give off rain onto a desert full of cactus and sand dunes.

If the Perfessor was a medicine man, he didn't act like it. He et a snack of bait at Dyspepsia Dan's Feedbag Café and left the waitress, a cartwheel for a tip. That evenin', when he showed up at the Bloated Goat and treated the house to a couple rounds of Blue Bagpipe whisky, the Perfessor suddenly found himself the most popular rannihan in town.

185

Of course the Big Drought was the main topic of conversation, and it wasn't long before the talk drifted around to the subject of rain-making, and after a little prodding by Jim Groot the banker, who was plumb worried about what the drought was doing to the mines and ranches he had loaned dinero to, the Perfessor loosened up and give out a little info about hisself.

"I am en route to the Rio Hondo country in New Mexico," the Perfessor says, biting the end off a two-bit cigar. "The cattle outfits over in Lincoln County are butcherin' their beef on account of their water holes have dried up for want of rain. I will be paid the sum of five thousand dollars in legally tender dinero for causing the skies to cloud over and precipitate a few inches of *aqua pura*."

Well, the only man in the place who didn't think it could be done was old Chief Ache-in-the-Back, who was in town from the Cheery-cow Injun reservation trying to wheedle some firewater offn Curly Bill Grane. The old redskin shakes his head and says, "Me rain-maker too. Make-um rain dance. No good. It ain't gonna rain no more this year. Range dry as Ache-in-the Back's tongue is now."

The Perfessor joins in the laughter and when things quiet down he says, "My secret of inducing moisture from the cirro-cumulus, sub-stratospheric regions happens to be in the realm of science, not black magic," he tells the old chief. "I use explosives to compress the air and produce clouds, by means of free balloons."

Well, that made everybody's ears pert up. This corner of Arizona Territory ain't had a sprinkle to speak of in goin' on two year, and there was considerable concern in 'Pache that mebbe the wells would start drawin' dust, to say nothing of the Sacatone mines closing down and the cow spreads in a bad way.

"How," inquires Plato X. Scrounge, the lawyer, "do you bring this scientific miracle about, Perfessor?"

McCloud grins behind his red whiskers and looks wise. "As I told our red brother here, sir, that is my secret. I send dynamite charges up ten thousand feet by means of balloons. The composition of this explosive, and the means by which I detonate it at the proper time and elevation in order to induce the atmosphere to give up its humidity content in the form of rain, is, as I say, my professional secret. It never fails."

Well, Sheriff Rimfire Cudd is slightly under the influence and he hauls out a wad of greenbacks and hiccoughs, "I'm ready to bet my last blue stack that you cain't make a smatterin' of rain settle the dust anywhar in Stirrup County."

The Perfessor raises his hands for quiet. "Keep your mazuma, my friend," he says, friendly-like. "You would be bucking a sure thing. I have made a cloudburst occur in Death Valley, Californy, where rain never fell before. I have made clouds form in Chile, South America, where rain never occurs. If I had the time and inclination, Sheriff, I could deluge your fair town in a torrential downpour. I could bog down your stock in hock-deep mire overnight. Yea, verily, I could make your desert bloom like a rose garden, with swamp grass and skonk cabbage replacing the cactus and sagebrush, an' coyotes would grow web feet."

With which Perfessor J. Pluvius McCloud spills some gold money on Curly Bill's bar, yawns, and says he must retire for the night, seeing how far him and his team have traveled since daylight, without so much as a drop of water to cut the alkali dust out of his craw.

The Paintin' Pistoleer has been taking all this in while he sips his buttermilk, and as the Perfessor is headin' for the batwings, he sings out in that soft Alabama drawl of hisn, "How long does it take you to produce rainfall, startin' from scratch?"

McCloud shrugs and flicks a grain of dust offn his coat. "Within thirty minutes after I get my balloons up, the heavens darken with gathering moisture that shrouds the sun and is dispelled only when the firmament disgorges its liquid bounty on the parched earth, my friend. And now, I must bid you all good night, gentlemen. It is with regret that I will leave Apache come high noon tomorrow, but I must be on my way to New Mexico to save its drought-blighted denizens from dehydration."

Well, the Perfessor left the saloon crowd buzzin' like a squashed hornet's nest. The upshot of it was that next mornin' a big crowd of Sacatone miners, beef shippers, and Apache folks was gathered around the Cowboy's Rest Hotel when Perfessor J. Pluvius McCloud come downstairs for breakfast.

Plato X. Scrounge, dolled up in a clawhammer coat to match the rain-maker's, meets McCloud on the top step.

"Perfesser McCloud," Plato X. booms out in his best courtroom manner, "I am legal counsel for the following, to wit: The Sacatone Mining Syndicate, et al; the Stirrup County Cattlemen's Association, et ux; the Home Garden committee of the Apache Ladies' Knitting & Peach Preserves Society; and the miscellaneous citizens of this community who take baths, turn out washings, raise vegetables, or otherwise, somehowever, and to wit are dependent upon water."

The Perfessor takes off his silk hat and bows, plumb impressed by this string of highfalutin wordage. "Please continue, Mr. Barrister," he says. "This farewell gathering in my humble honor is overwhelming, considering the transient nature of my visit in your midst."

"Now, whereas," Plato X. Scrounge goes on, snapping his gallus and puffing up like a peacock, "Perfessor McCloud, the organizations an' individuals I have the privilege of representing are ready to pay you the sum of five thousand dollars in coin when, if, and providing, to wit that you bring rain to Stirrup County."

Over in the edge of the crowd old Ache-in-the-Back waves his tommyhawk and hollers, "Medicine man with red hair on chin no can do. Dry time, rain no come. Injun try. No rain."

The Perfessor says slow and regretful, "I am very sorry, gentlemen, but I cannot tarry long enough to accept this contract, much as I should like to. You see," he reminds the assembled multitude, "it is a long and weary journey to Lincoln County, New Mexico, and my team and equipage travel slowly."

A hum of disappointment runs through the crowd, which gives Sheriff Rimfire Cudd his cue to step into the limelight.

"Last night you claimed it tooken you only thirty minutes to whip up a man-sized cloudbust," Rimfire says. "You likewise said you aimed to pull out around noon, which same is four hours off."

Perfessor McCloud bows again, in Cudd's direction. "True, true, my esteemed minion of law and order," he says. "But inflating my balloons, preparing my explosives — this takes time, more than I have at my disposal. Sorry, gentlemen, I —"

Rimfire Cudd rattles his pair of rusty old handcuffs under McCloud's whiskers. "Then it is my bounden duty to arrest you as a fraud an' a swindler," Cudd says pompous-like. "Either you can make rain or you can't. Plato X. Scrounge, here, is the local justice of the peaces, and he can delay you for thirty days in the county jail on fragrancy charges, ifn he sees fit. This kentry is desprit for rain, Perfesser. I can't be responsible for what this mob might do to you ifn you turn us down."

Well, McCloud gulps once or twice. He sees the crowd is in a lynchin' mood, especially the Sacatone miners who are drawing their final pay this afternoon, and the cowhands who will likewise be out of a job after tomorrow's beef sale.

"Okay," McCloud says. "I will release my balloons at eleven o'clock sharp. If my scientific rain-making method doesn't produce rain by noon, the sheriff may incarcerate me in the local bastille. If my rain falls as

190

scheduled — which it will — I will make you a present of it, gladly. If I only succeed in forming clouds enough to appreciably obscure the sun, then all bets are off. Is that fair enough?"

Well, Apache agreed unanimous, having nothing to lose, and McCloud nothing to gain but his freedom. While the Perfessor is dawdlin' over his breakfast at Dyspepsia Dan's, Sol Fishman gets busy and announces a special sale on umbrellas and raincoats, for today only, and does a land-office business. Everything else in town is locked up tight.

By 10:30, everybody and his grandmother has trooped out to the old rodeo grounds and seated themselves on the bleachers, to watch Perfessor McCloud get to work. His little red wagon is rolled up in front of the grandstand, and just before eleven o'clock he comes out of the wagon with four white rubber balloons, which same he percedes to swole up with some kind of gas he carries in metal drums, until they was about six foot acrost and was tugging at their anchor ropes with enough pull to have h'isted a yearlin' leppie sky-high.

Perfessor McCloud needs help in attachin' his bundles of dynamite and the clockwork machine which sets off his charges, and summons the Paintin' Pistoleer out of the crowd to loan him a hand. While this work is going on, J. Pluvius explains to Smith that he originally started out in this balloon business as an advertising stunt for a traveling circus. He would send up balloons loaded with circus posters, which would come fluttering down over a town where the show would be playing in about a week.

"One time over in the Oklahoma Panhandle, just for the hell of it, I sent up a stick of dynamite," he tells Justin O. "It exploded about a mile up and formed a cloud in the blue sky, which cloud give off with rain. I quit the circus-advertisin' business and have been rain-makin' ever since."

Well, the crowd really pounded its gums when the Perfessor cut his guy ropes and released his four balloons, which went shootin' up into the sky like a Fourth of July rocket and kept goin'. There wasn't a cloud to be seen, a hot dry day that looked plumb impossible for a rain-maker to peddle his wares, but Perfessor J. Pluvius McCloud looked as confident as a hound dawg eatin' hawg scraps. He didn't even let Chief Ache-in-the-Back's hecklin' from the stands git under his skin.

Them four balloons, white as snowballs, started driftin' south toward the Mexican Border when they got about a mile high, which brung a-plenty of cheerin' from the Sacatone miners, who figgered McCloud's rainstorm was going to soak down the diggings and reopen the mines for shore. The direction them balloons was travelin' made the north-county stock ranchers glum, but Perfessor McCloud assured everybody the whole district would git deluged.

Well, it begun to get dark, that was for shore. By 11:15 the rooster over in Missus Coddlewort's chicken yard began herding his hens toward the roost, thinking night was coming on, but plumb puzzled about it being

192

such a short day, even for January. So far as the 'Pache folks could see, though, there wasn't a cloud or even a thin haze anywhere in the sky.

All of a suddent four little clouds appeared, high up, like the spots on a dice. A big cheer went up, until the noise of four explosions come thumping back to earth, close together, and the crowd realized it was just the Perfessor's time bombs going off.

It was gettin' darker an' darker. All of a suddent, at exactly 11:22, a miracle happened. The sun, which nobody had bothered to squint at, went dim and then went out like a candle under a squirt of tobacco juice. Just like that. One minute it was shinin', and the next minute it had vanished, except for a bright circle in the sky, like a halter ring.

"The world is comin' to an end! Let us pray!" screeches Jim Groot's wife, who was setting with the Apache Ladies' Knitting & Peach Preserves Society. The women and kids began caterwaulin' in the dark, plumb loco, while Perfessor J. Pluvius McCloud bellered through a megaphone to set tight, that there was nothin' to be afraid of because night had come and the stars was out in all their glory at midday — the Perfessor said it was just a dense haze his rain-makin' gadgets had whomped up.

Well, everybody had their umbrellers up and their oilskin saddle-slickers on, ready for the rain to come. But even the cowhands and the tough miners was getting spooky. Above all the commotion in the darkness, something like a muffled blast busted out over across town somewhere, enough to make the bleachers shake. Nobody paid any attention to that, though, because the crowd was dangerous close to stampedin' like a bunch of longhorns in a Texas norther.

Justin O. Smith hollers in McCloud's ear, "This ain't any of your doing, Perfessor! Looks to me like a total eclipse of the sun!"

Well, right when Perfessor McCloud was telling Smith that it was all part and parcel of his rain-making, a corner of the sun peeked out, and within another five minutes day had come back to Arizona, showing the far-off Sacatones on the south horizon. The crowd calms down, sheepish as hell. Missus Coddlewort's rooster give out with its second sunrise crow of the day — a mite off-key this time — and sent his hens back to their scratchin'.

Right over the town, another balloon was drifting straight up, a bright-red one this time. The Perfessor explained that he had kept this special secret balloon in reserve, inside his wagon, which same had to be released at the critical moment when it got dark. This red balloon, he explains, is the McCoy; it will shake the rain out of the sky, or he'll be damned for a wall-eyed leppy.

Well, the day kept gettin' brighter, and hotter, and dustier. The red balloon drifted off toward the Border, heading toward Gunhammer Pass. Not so much as a drop of moisture had showed up by high noon, which was the deadline the Perfessor had set for hisself.

J. Pluvius McCloud looked like he wanted to crawl into a gopher hole and pull it in after him. In full view

194

of the crowd, he slinks over to Sheriff Rimfire Cudd and holds out his hands.

"Slap yore bracelets on me, Sheriff," he groans. "I have failed utterly, for the first time in my rain-making career. I will take the consequences, as agreed. I am at your mercy."

Well, the crowd was in a merciful mood, seeing as how the world hadn't come to an end, so they bellered for Cudd to be a good sport and let the Perfessor out of his deal. After all, ifn he was skookum enough to put out the sun for five minutes, what the burned-out old heck? It went without saying the $5,000 wouldn't be paid to the rain-maker. The old Injun, Ache-in-the-Back, was so tickled he went into a war dance on the top bleacher, fell off, and broke a leg.

J. Pluvius McCloud made a little speech of thanks, explaining with tears in his eyes that ifn he pulled off another failure in New Mexico next week his rain-making career was shot forty ways from the jack. He promised to write back what happened.

The paymaster of the Sacatone mining syndicate announced that the jackleg muckers would be paid off at the Stockman's Bank as originally scheduled, and the Cattle Association ramrod follers up by saying the stock auction was coming off tomorrow.

Everybody scattered, most of the men heading for the Bloated Goat Saloon to drown their sorrow over the Perfessor's failure. Wasn't long, though, before Apache got set on its ear agin.

When Jim Groot and the Sacatone paymaster got over to the bank to fetch out the pay-roll dinero, they

195

found a window busted in and the vault blowed open with nitroglycerin, its big door hanging slanchways on one hinge. The syndicate pay roll, one bag containing $50,000 in greenbacks, was gone, along with all the handy dinero in the vault.

Well, Rimfire Cudd rousted up a posse and sent riders in all directions, pealin' their eyes for any dust that would show where the bank robbers had vamoosed to. In all the excitement, nobody but Justin Other Smith seemed to remember the muffled explosion which had shook the grandstand, just after the sun went out. That explosion, he knew now, was the TNT going off in the bank.

Smith, being suspicious of strangers right off, had himself a good thorough look inside the Perfessor's red wagon, though of course the bank loot wasn't in there. After all, the wagon and the Perfessor had been over at the rodeo grounds, in plain sight of everybody, including Smith, at the time of the bank robbery. But in emergencies like this, with so much at stake, the Paintin' Pistoleer was takin' no chances.

The only other stranger Smith couldn't account for was a one-eyed saddle tramp who had been kicked off a freight train two days before, but he claimed he had been at the rain-makin' demonstration. The one-eyed hombre was scared, though, so he bummed a ride on the Perfessor's wagon when it pulled out around two o'clock, headed for New Mexico and another stab at rain-making.

Along about sundown, Rimfire Cudd and his posse began driftin' back to town, empty-handed. They hadn't cut any suspicious tracks or spotted any getaway dust nowhere around.

Well, the Paintin' Pistoleer was up in his studio all the time the posse was out, busy mauling the whole business around in his head, when all of a sudden a hunch strikes him. He fishes around in his desk and brings out a little book he'd got in the mail, which he scans for a couple minutes.

Then he jabs the book in his pocket, straps on his famous .32 Colt on a .45 frame, bolts a saddle on his palomino hoss, and rides over to the jail to roust Rimfire Cudd out of a nap.

"We got a ridin' job ahead of us, Sheriff," Smith says, excited-like — which was onusual for him. "I got a hunch."

Well, Cudd knows better than to ask Smith damn-fool questions when he's astraddle of a hunch. Nobody seen them ride out of town a little later, follerin' the tracks of Perfessor McCloud's red wagon. There was plenty of starlight, which was lucky, because a few miles out they seen where the wagon had turned south toward the Sacatones, instead of keepin' east toward New Mexico.

Around midnight they found the wagon, minus its team, about sunk out of sight in a quicksand *sumadero*. The trail of the two black hosses led straight toward the Mexican Border.

"This rain-maker an' his one-eyed passenger are prob'ly camped over in Gunhammer Pass," the Paintin' Pistoleer says. "We ought to overtake that pair around daylight."

197

Sure enough, just after dawn, the sheriff an' Justin O. locate McCloud's black hosses picketed down, and a couple bedrolls. The rain-maker and his pard wasn't nowhere around, though. Their tracks, afoot, led off up the rocky wall of the Pass.

Through the field glasses he packed in his saddlebags, the Paintin' Pistoleer ketches sight of J. Pluvius and the one-eyed saddle bum, scramblin' from ledge to ledge about a mile beyond. What they were after was a big splash of bright red which stood out like a boil on Rimfire Cudd's nose, up in some talus.

"It's that red balloon," Justin Other Smith says, handing the glasses to the sheriff. "We might as well wait here for them to come back for their broncs."

Around noon, J. Pluvius McCloud and the saddle tramp come back. They'd left the balloon, which had deflated before it come to earth, back where they'd found it. But McCloud and his pard was takin' turns toting a gunnysack which this balloon had carried.

They was fixing to roll their soogans back at camp, both of 'em perty nigh tuckered out, when the Paintin' Pistoleer and the sheriff stepped out from behind a rock between them and their hosses and throwed their guns on the rain-maker and the one-eyed buckaroo.

"We'll take over that gunnysack full o' bank loot," Rimfire Cudd says important-like, "an' likewise you two rannihans."

Well, McCloud yanks a gun and so does the saddle bum. Before they could squeeze off a shot, the Paintin' Pistoleer's little .32 exploded twice, one slug nippin' the saddle bum's off ear, his other shot tearin' the big

198

hogleg out o' McCloud's fist. Neither hombre had ever seen shootin' the likes of that there, so they submitted to Rimfire Cudd's handcuffs meek as buttermilk.

"How'd you git wise, anyhow?" McCloud wants to know. "I figgered we had thunk up a perfect crime."

For answer, Justin Other Smith shows McCloud the little book he'd been toting in his hip pocket, and sight of same makes those two crooks fold up like an accordeen.

Well, it was cloudin' over and perty dark an' windy by the time they got back to Apache. Rimfire Cudd clapped the Perfessor and One-Eye in the calaboose, and then lit a shuck over to the Bloated Goat Saloon where a perty sorry-actin' crowd of Sacatone miners and out-of-work cowhands was roundsiding.

Rimfire Cudd really set their corks to bobbing when he hands Jim Groot, the banker, a gunnysack containin' the $50,000 bank loot, down to the last red cent. Nacheral, they wanted explanations, and Justin Other Smith kept quiet while Rimfire, as usual, hawgs the credit for all the detective work.

"It was like this," Sheriff Cudd brags. "This one-eyed jasper was a safecracker turned circus clown, in the show McCloud worked for. He blowed open Groot's vault while the Perfessor was holdin' the crowd over at the rodeo grounds. Instead of hidin' the loot or vamoosin' with it, One-Eye ties it to a red balloon he was packin' and lets it fly off.

"This here balloon had a pinhole in it, which kept leakin' hydrogen gas until it deflates an' come down in Gunhammer Pass, else it woulda drifted to the Gulf o'

Mexico. McCloud knowed about how long this red balloon would stay aloft, an' the gen'ril direction it was driftin', and bein' red it was easy to locate in the badlands. All they had to do was head cross-country after it."

"What I cain't savvy," Sol Fishman speaks up, "is why you trailed that rain-makin' cuss in the first place, Rimfire."

Well, the sheriff didn't have the answer to that one. It involved the post-office robbery on New Year's Eve. With Sol Fishman's permission, the Paintin' Pistoleer explains how McCloud an' One-Eye snuck into town on New Year's Eve an' stole the mail sack containin' Doctor Dingle's Almanac.

"I got to wonderin' about the whole set-up," Justin O. says. "The robbery had to take place durin' the eclipse of the sun, but how come us folks in Apache didn't know about that eclipse, whereas McCloud had read about it in the big city papers? The answer to that was simply that we would git our information about eclipses and such from Doctor Dingle's Almanac, all of which had been stolen.

"It so happens I had an advance sample copy of the Almanac, mailed to me by Doc Dingle on account of I painted the cover for it. I takes a look at it, and sure enough, right there in bold print it predicted an eclipse of the sun, visible in this corner o' Arizona, totality lastin' five minutes sixteen seconds, starting at eleven twenty-two a.m.

"Well, the Perfessor had got wind about the big Sacatone mining payoff scheduled for Apache the same day as the eclipse, and with fifty thousand bucks at stake, he teams up with this one-eyed safecracker and they thought up this rain-makin' scheme to end the Big Drought. They had to keep us Apache folks in ignorance about an eclipse comin' our way, so they waylaid Doctor Dingle's Almanac, knowing it always arrives at post offices on December 31, year in an' year out."

Which reminds the Paintin' Pistoleer to show the boys his copy of the Almanac which he'd packed in his hip pocket. He hands it to Curly Bill, who squints at the January page.

"Hey!" Curly Bill hollers, "this Almanac predicts rain for Arizona Territory for tonight. This Almanac ain't worth the paper it's printed on, as any fool kin see. It ain't gonna r —"

Grane's words is blotted out by a clap of thunder an' a stroke of lightnin', and rain began peltin' down liken to wash 'Pache offn its foundations. Out in the middle of the street the boys found old Chief Ache-in-the-Back going through his rain dance, crutches and all. That pleased Curly Bill so much he risked a jail term by giving the old redskin all the rotgut whisky he could swill down.

Well sir, that rain lasted four days and five nights, got the Sacatone mines runnin' full-blast agin, an' saved the calf crop for the north-county cattle spreads.

Perfessor J. Pluvius McCloud and his one-eyed amigo tried to hog credit for that life-savin' rainstorm when their trial come up, but the judge an' jury didn't let that nonsense dampen their ardor for seein' justice done.

Them polecats drawed 15-year stretches at Yuma for grant-larson an' robbin' the U.S. Mails, an' when last heard from was drivin' water wagons to irrigate the pen's truck garden.

Cupid Can Be Stupid

Yessir, the first time Justin Other Smith clamps eyes on this lucious lass from deep in Dixie, ol' Cupid had him corralled in a corner an' hog-tied for brandin'.

Her name was Magnolia Malarkey, accordin' to what was writ on the big hosshide trunk, all plastered with hotel stickers, which the Wells-Fargo driver unloaded from the stage boot. Apache's whittle 'n' spit club was holding a meeting on the station porch when Magnolia stepped outen the Concord, and her appearance started a rash of mustache-wipin' and bandanna-neckerchief-adjustin' the like of which you never seed.

This Magnolia filly was a peachy looker, no denyin' that. She had frizzled bangs and a pert little nose and a hour-glass figger that made Jim Groot take another look at his ever-lovin' wife, Hernia, and go on a drunk that night.

She looked as cute an' helpless as a leppie calf bogged down in a mud waller, a-standin' there so shy in her frills an' finery, an' there warn't a male hombre in that crowd who wouldn't have been stirrup-drug through the portals of perdition for a chance to of helped her git wherever she was goin'.

Magnolia swells up them gorgeous lungs of hern with a drag of Arizona ozone, and says timid-like to nobody in partiklar, "So my dream has come true at last! Here Ah am in Apache, the home town of the greatest painter in all America, Justin O. Smith. Do any of you kind gentlemen happen to know that celebrity of the art world?"

Well, matter of fact, Justin O. was right there in the foreground, his eyes buggin' out over his cheekbones as he sized up her lovely lines from an artist's p'int of view.

Lew Pirtle, the Overland Telegraph agent, he gives Justin a shove and sings out envious-like, "This is him, ma'am. Around 'Pache we calls him the Paintin' Pistoleer, though, on account of him bein' the champeen pistol shot of the hull Territory."

Well, Magnolia turns her big innocent blue eyes around to oggle Smith, who is pawin' the dust with his boot toe and grinnin' as bashful as a barefoot kid askin' a gal if he can carry her books home from school. Her teeth flash out in a smile that stiffens the Paintin' Pistoleer like a sage hen bein' charmed by a bull snake, and when she had him himpmatized good and thorough, she says in a voice that reminded everybody present of blackstrap molasses dribblin' out of a jug:

"So *you* are Mistuh Smith! Ah have admired yo' Western paintings for yeahs, suh. You look like a chivalrous man as well as a famous artist. Would you be so kind and condescending as to help poor little me carry her luggage?"

204

It taken another kick in the rump by Lew Pirtle to budge Smith out of his transom. He warn't exactly shiverless right then.

"Uh — de-lighted, ma'am, I'm shore," the Paintin' Pistoleer stammers out. He prances over and fixes to pick up her trunk, which same must have been packed with hossshoes and old anvils from the way his knees buckled before he h'isted it to his shoulder.

"Where would you be going, ma'am?" he puffs out, purple in the face. "The Cowboy's Rest is the only lodgin's in town —"

Magnolia reaches down to where Justin O. is bent over so steep his nose is draggin' dust, and slips her cute little gloved hand under his elbow. Smith tries to straighten up, and his backbone give off with a noise like a marble rollin' acrost a xylophone, the weight of her trunk was that fierce.

"My Auntie Prunella Peebles and I," she twitters in her mockingbird trill, "have come to Apache for a summer's rest. We have leased the old Snodgrass Mansion, if you know where that is."

Smith knowed where the Snodgrass Mansion was, all right, same being a run-down three-story brick eyesore with an iron-railed cupola on top, setting on the hill back of the munisipple garbage dump. It had been built by Old Man Snodgrass, the loco prospector who discovered the Sacatone silver lodes in '72, and who was worth a cool million before he drunk hisself to death a few years back. Since then his mansion has been boarded up.

205

Ifn Smith had had his brains about him, he would have fetched his palomino saddler over from the stable to tote Miss Magnolia Malarkey as well as her trunk, but the poor walloper was too messmerized to think of other means of transport. Magnolia's fluttering eyes and honeysuckle voice had him petrified solid from the eyebrows north.

It was a pitiful spectacle, the Paintin' Pistoleer staggerin' off down the street bent double under that trunk, but there wasn't a soul who wore pants that wouldn't have traded places with him. At any rate, Smith was spared the shock the others got when the filly's aunt, Miss Prunella Peebles, stepped out of the stage.

The rest of the boys seen right off that Magnolia was no pat hand, if a joker like her Aunt Prunella went with the deal.

She stood around six foot, with skin like dried boot leather and a jaw you could have plowed hardpan with. She had a fuzzy mustache, and beady eyes that glittered like nail heads in a coffin lid. Her face would have looked a sight more nacheral with a split-ear halter, hangin' over a manger chompin' oats.

Ordinary, Justin O. couldn't of made it to the Snodgrass Mansion under his own steam, packin' that freight. But love hath charms, as the feller says, and he was plainly under the influence. Ever step of the way up the hill past the garbage dump, Magnolia was cooing in his ear about how she had been in love with all the magazine covers and calendars and other pitchers he had painted, and she had chosen 'Pache for her summer vacation in the hopes she would get to meet her idol.

When he finally made it to the porch of the Snodgrass Mansion, the Paintin' Pistoleer collapses on top of the trunk. He would have straightened up, only he couldn't unkink his back. So he pertends he's givin' Auntie Prunella a deep bow when Magnolia interdooces this she-blister who had been trailing them.

Auntie Prunella gives a whinnying noise through her nose and produces a key from her muff which opens the front door.

"You are mighty sweet," Magnolia drools, giving Smith's nigh ear a playful tweek. "Now, if you'll be kind enough to locate a scrubwoman to do some house-cleaning for us, Auntie and I will be much obliged to you, kind suh."

Auntie Prunella reaches for the trunk, grabs it by one handle, and flips it over her shoulder like it contained a feather.

"If this young whippersnapper has any sense of courtesy," Prunella sniffs, "he will volunteer to help us straighten out this filthy hole himself, honey-chile."

Needles to say, the Paintin' Pistoleer spent the rest of that horrible day sweepin' an' scrubbin' and window-cleanin', and when he finally shows up on Main Street that evenin' his tongue was hangin' out a foot and his boots was draggin' furrows in the dust. He had dishpan hands, housemaid's knee, and an empty belly.

Feelin' the need of nourishment after this labor of love, the Paintin' Pistoleer lurches into the Bloated Goat Saloon and orders a dram of buttermilk. All the boys was in there roundsiding, as usual, and when they seen how bad Smith was stove up, Curly Bill Grane the bartender says anxious-like:

"Them she-males gang up on you in that ha'nted house, Justin? You look like you been wrasslin' with a carload o' brimmer bulls."

Smith just pulls in a deep breath, wipes the slobber offn his chin, and rolls his eyes toward the ceilin'.

"She's gorgeous, boys," he says, in an exstatic voice like a drunk with delirium trimmings. "A veritable Venus. A nymph from New O'leans. Ethereal. Flawless. And innocent to boot. Never seen a woman who could hold a candle to my Maggie."

"Yore Maggie!" snorts Sol Fishman, who runs the O. K. Mercantile. "By Jupiter, son, you're in bad shape. Ifn Doc Grubb was sober I'd recommend you seein' him for a complete fizzical check-up. You better let me sell you a dose of spring tonic."

Smith's hat falls to the floor when he swigs the last of his buttermilk. He bends down, flips his cigarette stub into the Stetson, and claps Curly Bill's brass cuspidor over his head, which was luckily empty at the time. The cuspidor, that is, not his head. Well, come to think of it, the description fits both objects, at that.

"Miss Malarkey is a famous New York actress," Justin O. goes on, his mind a million miles away from the saloon — or up on Snodgrass Hill, to be exact. "She portrays ingénue rôles."

"Whatever kind of an en-gine she is," remarks Sheriff Rimfire Cudd, "she's shore rollin' you forty ways from the jack."

Smith ignores the sheriff. "She's resting up for her fall and winter engagements," he says. "Which means that for three solid months, Apache will be blessed with her presence. Boys, I'm a lucky man. Magnolia has asked me to dine at the mansion tomorrow night. Just think — I'll be supping at the same board with the toast of Broadway!"

Sol Fishman, who thinks a heap of Justin O., waggles his head sorrowful-like, realizing the Paintin' Pistoleer has jumped the track and is in need of a strait jacket pronto.

"How about that ganted old mudhen who's sharin' this gal's roast?" Sol wants to know. "I wouldn't enjoy eatin' no Broadway toast or any other vittles, with my feet under the same table with that bile-complected bag of bones."

Smith looks insulky at this. "Auntie Prunella," he says huffy, "come along as Magnolia's chaperon. And don't any of you sports git any ideas of serenading Magnolia under her window some balmy evening. Auntie Prunella squashed a rat runnin' up a rafter this afternoon with a doorknob she yanked out by the roots. And that Snodgrass place has a heap of doorknobs left for ammunition." He sighs. "I know, because I polished sixty-seven of 'em."

Well, up to now the Paintin' Pistoleer had made hisself a perty decent livin' sellin' his art work. Like Magnolia said, he was on his way to bein' a nation-wide celebrity. But the next day, when a delegation consisting of Sheriff Cudd and Lawyer Plato X. Scrounge called at his studio upstairs over the

Longhorn Saddle Shop, they seen that Smith's talent was sleddin' down the greased skids toward a bankrupture.

"What in tarnation is *that* supposed to repersent?" Scrounge blurts out, sizing up the canvas Smith is workin' on. It had started out to be a buckaroo forkin' a wild bronc at a rodeo, but you'd never know it to look at it now.

"This painting is entitled *Ride 'Em Cowboy*," Smith says. "It has been contracted for by a Denver bootery for their forthcoming cowboy catalogue. The five hundred smackers it will fetch is goin' to buy a pearl necklace for my Maggie."

Well, that daub could just as well have been called *A Ripe Eggplant Spilling Out of a Skillet*. The horse was purple with green tail and mane, and the sky in the background had a big cloud floatin' acrost it that was the spittin' image of Magnolia Malarkey's face, and the cowboy had three arms already that Scrounge and the sheriff could count, with another one bein' sketched in.

"We come to remind you," the sheriff says polite-like, "that the hull community is waitin' down behind the Busted Flush Dance Hall to see you win yore shootin' match with that pesky drummer from Phoenix. Or had you forgot that you assepted a challenge to a public exhibition of target-shootin' for today?"

Well, it had slipped Smith's mind, all right. This drummer, a cocky galoot name of Fleegleheimer, was canvassin' the Territory representin' a line of ammunition for a wholesale house in Omaha. The minute he hit 'Pache, a couple days back, he began braggin' that there wasn't a rannihan west of the Pecos who could out-shoot him, and he backed his claim with legally tender dinero.

Nacheral, this Fleegleheimer hadn't heard of the Paintin' Pistoleer, or he would never have done his boastin' in 'Pache, of all places. So the Bloated Goat crowd, playin' him for a sucker, got their bets down in advance, each one covered by Fleegleheimer. Sol Fishman, his retail agent, was holding the stakes.

When Smith got down to the target range, totin' his famous .32 Colt on a .45 frame, everybody in town was hangin' on the corral fence behind the dance hall, waitin' to see Fleegleheimer get massacreed. The target was a printed bull's-eye bearin' Fleegleheimer's advertisement, and was set up agin a bale of alfalfy hay about 90 foot from the back steps of the Busted Flush, where the contestants was to stand.

Fleegleheimer, a fat dude in a derby and checkered pants, he shakes hands with Smith and they tossed a coin for first shots. The drummer won. Using a double-action Remington .44 and his own line of ammunition, this drummer chalks up four bull's-eyes out of his five shots, and he steps down off the porch feelin' perty spry.

"I scored eighty out of a possible hundred, Smith," he rubs it in. "Let's see you top that."

The audience, they rub their hands together and start grinnin' like a pack of boar apes, already figgerin' out what they'd spend the money on they'd win from Fleegleheimer. A target match like this was duck soup for the Paintin' Pistoleer, as any fool would have knowed except a stranger from outside the Territory.

Well, Smith twirls his .32 absent-minded around the trigger guard, and without hardly squintin' at the target, lets go his first shot. Smack center to the bull for 20 points! Fleegleheimer gulps, but there's still four shots to go before he loses.

Just then, the Paintin' Pistoleer catches sight of a flash of gay color over by the corral fence. There is Magnolia Malarkey, all decked out in a pink parasol and a gauzy dress that drug the dirt. Her Auntie Prunella is hoverin' in the background like a tame jenny mule taggin' her around. Magnolia blows Smith a kiss.

Wellsir, the Paintin' Pistoleer, who is usually as cool as an icicle in competition, he starts to shiver like a cat lickin' a cactus. Instead of keepin' his eye on the target, he draws a bead whilst his eyes are makin' sheep-talk to Magnolia.

What follered was a disgrace to Apache, no less. Smith's second shot punched out a window light in the back end of Samanthie Coddlewort's chicken house, a block away. Later Samanthie finds her favorite Buff Orphington brood hen setting on its nest, minus its head.

Justin O.'s third bullet was closer by fifty yards to the target, but that didn't qualify it. It knocked the ventilator offn a privy behind the Feedbag Café and brought Dyspepsia Dan's Chinee cook, Aw Gwan, bustin' out of there with the newspaper he had been readin', scared stiff, thinkin' a tong war had busted out.

212

Fleegleheimer starts to snicker after the fourth shot hit the dirt. The boys along the fence rail began edgin' for the nearest alley, to get out of the way of this wild-flyin' lead the Paintin' Pistoleer was sprayin' the landscape with. Fact was the safest place in the range of that .32 was the target tacked to that bale of alfalfy.

When his firin' pin finally clicked on a empty chamber, with the target only sportin' that first puncture, Smith shoves his hogleg in holster and zigzags like a sleepwalker over to where Magnolia Malarkey was fluttering her eyelashes at him.

"Justin, my dove," she was hearn to coo, "Ah never befo' in all mah borned days seen such shootin', Ah swear Ah ain't."

Well, neither had the boys who had laid bets on Smith to win at ten-to-one odds. Fleegleheimer carried better that $600 of Apache folks' hard-earned cash out of town that day, and it was obvious to all concerned that the Paintin' Pistoleer's celebrated gun rep was blowed higher than the brass ball on the courthouse flagpole.

And, things went from bad to worse! Durin' the next few days, Smith quit his studio to wait hand an' foot on this Magnolia filly. He reshingled a leaky patch on the Snodgrass roof, payin' for the same out of his own pocket, and he leased a gentle-broke hoss at the Cloverleaf Stables for Magnolia to joy-ride over the surroundin' desert with Smith during long summer evenings.

Magnolia wasn't popular with anyone else in 'Pache, though, because she was too stand-offish. The Ladies'

Knitting & Peach Preserves Society invited her to their sociable, and she never showed up. Her aunt, Prunella Peebles, started a charge account at the O. K. Mercantile and she bamboozled pore old Sol Fishman into deliverin' their vittles up the hill every day, on threat of takin' their trade elsewhere. Elsewhere meaning Tucson, but all the same old Sol become Prunella's faithful errand boy, and all he got out of it was an occasional lemonade which Prunella would stir up for him. For an old soak like Sol, that was addin' insult to injury, but he seemed to thrive on it.

One day a telegram come offn the wires addressed to Smith. It was from this cowboy bootery up in Denver, and what they had to say practically melted the wires, Lew Pirtle said:

> *Returning your parcel via express collect. Surely must be some ghastly error. We ordered rodeo scene titled quote Ride 'Em Cowboy end quote. You shipped us canvas used to catch drippings from your easel. If this your idea of joke your humor in remarkably poor taste. Please rush quote Ride 'Em Cowboy end quote as our catalogue is ready to go to press. Otherwise our contract with you canceled forthwith.*

Pirtle slid that telegram under the door of Smith's studio, but it's plumb doubtful if he seen it. Smith has talked Magnolia into settin' for a portrait, Sol Fishman reports, and has packed all his paintin' gear up to Snodgrass Mansion. For two weeks running Smith ain't turned out a tap of work, unlessen you count all the rug-beatin' and clothes-washin' and butter-churnin' and odd chores that kept him busy as a goat in a tin-can dump from daylight to dark.

Well, the boys had finally give up Justin Other Smith for lost, and was in at the Bloated Goat hoisting some Blue Bagpipe in his memory one evenin', when something happened.

The batwings fan open and in comes the stroppin'est big hombre ever seed in these parts. He wore a black hat, string tie, an' clawhammer coat, and was totin' a carpetbag all plastered up with hotel labels the same as that hosshide trunk Magnolia Malarkey had brung to Apache with her.

"Greetings and salutations, gentlemen!" this king-sized giant booms out to all and sundry. "I just alighted from the California Flyer. My name is Cedric Dangerfield Peebles. Often billed as Peebles the Great. No doubt you have heard of me. I am of the theatuh."

Well, the boys just look blank at each other. There ain't been a road show come to 'Pache since the Baboon Cage Opery House was converted into a haybarn ten years or so back.

"What kin we do for you, Señor?" Curly Bill speaks up.

This actor twirls his long black mustaches just like he is fixin' to larrup pore old Uncle Tom with a blacksnake.

"I have come to join my wife, who is vacationing in this bucolic resort," he says, flashing his gold teeth.

215

"Could I trouble you gents to direct me to the Snodgrass Mansion?"

Sol Fishman gags like he's found a dead bat in his beer. "You ain't married," he says, jealous as billy old hell, "to Miss Prunella Peebles, are you, Peebles?"

Cedric Dangerfield Peebles shudders with horror. "The Lord forbid!" he chuckles. "Prunella, bless her heart, is my father's sister. I am sure she is doomed to a life of single blessedness, considering her spinsterlike attributes."

It was quiet enough in the Bloated Goat then for a man to have heard a flea foragin' around in Heck Coddlewort's whiskers.

"My wife," Peebles goes on to explain, "travels professionally under the name of Magnolia Malarkey, the Belle of the Bayous. Surely her sojourn here has not gone unnoticed?"

This bombshell flabbergasts the boys, for shore. They were all thinkin' about the Paintin' Pistoleer, as game a little rooster as ever drawed breath, a-settin' up there in the moonlight on Snodgrass's veranda right this minute, sparkin' with this here giant's lawfully wedded spouse.

T'warn't likely Smith would be packin' a gun tonight; and the way he had been goin' to pot of late, it wouldn't have done him much good ifn he had of been. Smith has been sucked into one of them triangle love affairs, that was plain to see, and he wouldn't stand no more chance in a tangle with this Peebles jasper than a hen egg under a steam roller.

"I-I'll be g-glad to t-take you up to the Snodgrass Mansion," Sol Fishman jitters out. "J-Jest one second, M-Mister Peebles."

Sol hustles Rimfire Cudd out of earshot and whispers for the sheriff to light a shuck up to Snodgrass Mansion and dab his loop on Smith. Fishman says he'll lead Cedric Dangerfield Peebles up the hill by a roundabout way, to give Rimfire time to take a short cut and snatch Smith's bacon out of the fire.

Well, the scheme would have worked, too, ifn Rimfire Cudd hadn't of blundered into an open garbage pit alongside the mansion. The sheriff was bogged down in that hip-deep mess when Sol Fishman and the big actor arrived at the mansion.

Inside, the Paintin' Pistoleer was just fixin' to set down to supper with Auntie Prunella and Magnolia, when Cedric Dangerfield Peebles comes bowlin' into the kitchen and strikes a pose.

"I got your telegram, honey-chile," he booms, holding out his arms, "and I came without delay."

Well, the Paintin' Pistoleer can't believe his eyes when he sees Magnolia scamper acrost the room and put on a clinch with this chimney-high stranger, just like she was playin' a torrid love scene behind the footlights.

Sol Fishman is in the background, makin' frantic signals behind Peebles's back for the Paintin' Pistoleer to high-tail out the back door while he can. Instead, Smith is workin' up a mad.

When Magnolia turns around to leer at him, huggin' and squeezin' this giant from out of nowhere, Smith inquires in that soft Alabama drawl of hisn, "I presume this man is a brother you haven't gotten around to telling me about, Maggie darlin'?"

Peebles draws hisself up like a stage villain about to put the heroine under the buzz saw. "Darlin'? You call my wife darlin'?"

Auntie Prunella, knowin' the thunderbolt is about to strike, scuttles over to where Sol Fishman is standing and says, "How about us taking a little stroll in the moonlight, Sol, dear? We must give Magnolia and her husband some privacy after their long separation. They're such a devoted couple."

Before Sol knows what's happenin', Prunella is draggin' him toward the back door. Passing Justin Other Smith, the old biddy whispers to him real gentle, "I'm sorry for you, you pore kid. I tried to discourage you from courting my niece, but you wouldn't listen to an old maid like me, remember?"

Smith is glued to his tracks. His breakin' heart is showin' in his eyes, like a hurt puppy. When Magnolia puckers up and kisses Cedric Dangerfield, the Paintin' Pistoleer looked liken he wanted the floor to swaller him up. He growed up in that moment, Smith did, like many a jilted suitor before him.

"You — you two are *married*?" Smith squeaks in a voice like a newborn kitten.

Peebles looks down at Magnolia from up by the ceiling, and says in a voice like gravel on a tin roof, "Has this runt-sized Romeo been pestering you, sugarplum?"

Magnolia sniffs, "Not only that, Cedric beloved — but every day for the past three weeks he has been writing me passionate love letters, begging me to marry him!"

Peebles's face gits purple. Smith backs off, realizing he should be adding to the distance which separates him from that Goliath while he's still in one piece.

"Just one minute, small stuff!" sings out Magnolia, and her voice is like a hissin' snake fixing to strike. "You can't back out of your whirlwind courtship this easy. How would you like it if I let the citizens of Apache — say the old biddies in the Knitting & Peach Preserves Society — get a look at those love notes I've got locked in my trunk upstairs? Huh? Would you?"

Smith turns green around the gills. He ain't so numb he can't realize that just one of them letters, let alone the whole batch, would make him the laughin' stock of Arizona Territory. Even with his heart bustin' to bits inside his brisket, Smith sees where he's been deliberately led on by this man's wife, fattenin' him up for the slaughter.

"You were showing me your passbook from the Stockman's Bank, Justin," Magnolia reminds him. She glances up at Peebles. "He has salted away a very comfortable balance, Cedric, which he has been yearning to spend on my honeymoon trousseau. I've got that in writing, if he tries to deny it."

Cedric nods. "So you wrote me, chickadee." From the grin on Peebles's pan, it's plumb obvious that Magnolia has been in cahoots with her husband all along.

219

"Jim Groot opens the bank at nine in the morning, I believe," Magnolia goes on. "You withdraw your total deposits, Justin Other Smith, and have it up here by ten o'clock sharp, or by tomorrow noon your mushy letters will be in the hands of every gossiping old witch in this town!"

Smith never remembered how he got out of the Snodgrass Mansion and down the hill to town. Instinct told him to head for the Border and keep goin'. When he got to his studio, he found two friends waitin' for him — Rimfire Cudd, smellin' horrible from his dunking in the garbage pit, and Lawyer Plato X. Scrounge.

The Paintin' Pistoleer felt like kissing Plato, he was that glad to see a lawyer. As best he can, he tells his amigos what kind of a hell-fire jam he's in. They agree it's plumb desprit.

"I'd hate to tell you about them letters," he groans. "I didn't see anything suspicious about Maggie beggin' me to put my tender sentiments on paper. I poured out my soul in them letters. Signed 'em Smitty-Witty and Cookie Dumplin' and some other puppy-love names I blush to remember."

Scrounge starts pacin' the floor, his legal brain at work.

"Blackmail, that's what it is!" the lawyer says. "Or mebbe they've cooked up an alienation-of-affections suit, I dunno. However way we look at it, son, you've got your tail kinked in a dozen knots an' caught in a tight crack. Mebbe you better head for Mexico until this blows over."

Justin O. groans like a mule has kicked him.

"No, by grab!" roars Sheriff Cudd. "Smith ain't no crook, that he has to run. As sheriff of Stirrup County, it's up to me to git them love letters back, ifn I have to arrest them skunks."

Smith speaks up, snatchin' at straws, "Them letters are locked up in her hosshide trunk, I know that. She was to give me an answer to my proposal of marriage by tomorrow. Instead she must of telegraphed her husband that the trap was ready for springin'."

Rimfire Cudd slaps his gun holster and heads for the door. "I'll git them letters," he promises Smith. "I'm goin' up and jail them blackmailers right now, on a fragrancy charge."

Plato X. Scrounge puts the kibosh on Cudd's zeal. "You may tote a star, Sheriff, but you can't do anything without a legal complaint. They'd deny any blackmail charges. After all, Smith here was courting another man's wife. Ignorance of her marital status is no excuse under the law. Searching the house without a warrant would leave you open to burglary charges. No, I'm afraid Smith will have to buy them letters back, like Magnolia has been schemin' all along."

Thinkin' back, the Paintin' Pistoleer realizes now that he had been picked out for the slaughter before Magnolia even got to Apache. She'd heard of Smith and knowed he prob'ly had a good fat bank account laid away for all the art he'd sold in the past.

Cudd brightens up. "We could set fire to the Snodgrass Mansion," he suggests. "Destroy the evi-dunce."

"The first thing Peebles and Magnolia would save would be that batch of letters," p'ints out Plato X. Scrounge. "Arson ain't the way out of this dilemma."

Well, the boys augered this way and that until well after midnight, when finally the Paintin' Pistoleer scum up a scheme.

"We'll go up to the mansion tonight," he says, "and sneak into the house. I know where Magnolia keeps that hosshide trunk of hers — in the library on the third floor. Once I get hold of those letters, I can thumb my nose at them blackmailers."

There wasn't any lights showin' in the Snodgrass Mansion when the Paintin' Pistoleer and the sheriff and Plato X. Scrounge clumb up the hill. They snuck around to the back, and find a pantry window unlatched. The mansion is a reglar beehive of rooms and halls and stairs, but Smith has scrubbed and dusted that wickiup from cellar to attic enough times to know his way around, even with it being as dark as a gorilla's armpit.

Finally they snuck up three flights of stairs and Smith leads his pards to a door under the cupola.

"This is the library," he whispers, "where Magnolia keeps her trunk. This is goin' to be easier than I deserve."

Plato X. Scrounge is nearest to the doorknob and he opens the door, and stands blinkin' into a blaze of light. Cedric Dangerfield Peebles is settin' there on Magnolia's open trunk, rifflin' through a batch of letters — Smith's love letters.

"Egad!" the actor bellers out, looking at Scrounge glued to the doorway. Smith and the sheriff are back in the shadders where Peebles ain't spotted them yet. "Who in Tophet are you?"

Scrounge gulps, thinkin' fast. "Uh — a carpenter," he says. "Miss Prunella ast me to come up and repair a squeaky shutter —"

"At two o'clock in the morning?" thunders Peebles. He hauls a pepperbox pistol out of his coat. "Begone, you interloping scum of creation, before I make you a candidate for the coroner!"

Scrounge turns around and slams into Smith and Rimfire, who race pell-mell after him down the hall. Purty soon they are all bawled up to beat hell in the various twistings and turnings of this rat maze, completely mixed up. Finally, breathin' like stove-up cow-critters, they bump into a door at the dead end of a corridor.

"We're fools for luck," Smith wheezes. "This door opens to safety — an outdoor fire escape. Come on before that Peebles jasper shows up and salivates the three of us. Hurry!"

Smith opens the door — to find they're back at the library, with Peebles still settin' on the trunk, busy stuffin' Smith's love letters into a cardboard box.

The three burglars tumble over each other getting out of that door. This time Peebles is right after them, his pepperbox pistol blazing. Justin O. got lost somewhere in the shuffle, mebbe with a slug in him, for all Plato and the sheriff knowed; but them two kept goin' like the devil was after them, stumblin' an' shin-bangin' hell-for-leather and whoopin' like Injuns.

In the dark, with bullets whistlin' all around, they miss a turn and hit a door goin' full gallop. It caves in and Cudd and the lawyer find themselves out on a balcony overlookin' the yard.

"This way, Plato!" yells Rimfire. "Straddle this rail. We can shinny down this lightnin' rod."

Rimfire gets hold of said lightnin' rod and in two shakes he's slid down to terror firmer. He hears Plato's boots slidin' down the brick wall and he ducks, but there is a gosh-awful slam-bang and a splash off to one side and Cudd sees Scrounge jackknifed upside down in a rain barrel, drownin' before his very eyes.

By this time Peebles is leanin' over the balcony rail three stories up, shootin' up the landscape. Rimfire hauls Scrounge out of the barrel and they rattle their hocks down the hill out of range.

"Why didn't you warn me there was a bar'l at the bottom of that dod-blasted lightnin' rod?" Scrounge gargles out, coughin' water.

"You damned iggorant yahoo, you slid down the gutter pipe!" retorts the sheriff. "Ifn I hadn't risked my hide, you'd be a water-logged corpus wedged in that bar'l right this minute."

Scrounge applegizes. "By rights," he says, "we orter sashay back thar an' see what's happened to poor Justin O."

"Yeah," Rimfire agrees. "We can't leave him in that fix with a loony tick gunnin' for him."

By this time lights are blazin' all over the mansion, and they figger Smith's fish is fried for shore. After makin' several false starts and losin' their nerve, Cudd and Scrounge decide to go back to the sheriff's office and fortify themselves with a drink.

First thing they see when they reach the jailhouse is Magnolia and her husband, waitin' for 'em. Scrounge heads for the mesquites, but Cudd reins up when he hears what Peebles has to say:

"I'm here to swear out a warrant for the arrest of John Doe and Richard Roe. A carpenter and his helper who feloniously broke into the Mansion and stole some valuables from my wife's trunk!"

Plato starts grinnin', a bright light dawning in his knothead.

"What kind of valuables?" Rimfire asks. "It wouldn't be a package of love letters, now, would it?"

Just then there is a jangle of spurs coming around the corner of the calaboose. It's the Paintin' Pistoleer, jaunty as a jaybird. He's carryin' a rusty tin can he's picked up on the munisipple dump, and it's fumin' smoke and flame.

The Paintin' Pistoleer bows to Magnolia, and hands her the tin can. It's so hot she drops it. Out spills a mess of ashes.

"I'm returning the letters I snatched out of your trunk while your husband was busy chasing my fellow burglars," Smith says smug-like. "My masterpieces of prose were so passionate that spontaneous combustion consumed them."

Magnolia and Peebles stare at each other like the world has caved in on their shoulders. They realize all their connivin' and plottin' to steal Smith's bankroll has gone up in smoke tonight.

"I think," speaks up the sheriff, "that you bad actors — ifn you'll pardon the pun — won't find Apache a very healthy spot for holiday purposes. There is a stage leavin' for Lordsburg at daylight. You'll find the climate cooler over in New Mexico."

Magnolia Malarkey and that husband who was built like a brick smokehouse, they pulled out of 'Pache on that Lordsburg stage, all right. And Justin Other Smith wasn't around to see the light of his life go out. He was fast asleep up in his studio.

It was after sundown when Justin O. finally woke up. He seen all his accumulated mail, including the Denver telegram, and he remembers his paintin' gear is still up at the mansion.

He sashays downstairs and the first thing he seen, steppin' outdoors, was the big crêpe funeral wreath hangin' on the doorknob of the O. K. Mercantile.

"What happened?" Smith asks Plato X. Scrounge, who was on his way to the Bloated Goat just then. "Did Sol's heart give out on him?"

"It did. At three-fifteen this afternoon," Plato says doleful. "Come into Curly Bill's. We'll hoist a few to Sol (sob), wherever he is."

The Paintin' Pistoleer is too shocked to see straight. "I ain't got time," he blubbers. "I got a month's work to ketch up on — Poor Sol. I can't imagine him bein' dead an' gone."

Plato X. Scrounge daubs at his eye with a handkerchief. "He's worse off than dead," he says. "As justice of the peace, I couldn't refuse to tie the knot. Sol got hitched in double harness to Prunella Peebles at three-fifteen in my office. They've eloped to Californy for a honeymoon. God rest his soul."

Smith grabs Plato and practically drug him into the Bloated Goat. Curly Bill reaches for the buttermilk jug, as usual.

"Make mine whisky — neat," says the Paintin' Pistoleer, and all the boys relax, knowing he's his old self agin. "And hold the chaser. Belly up, boys, and help me celebrate my good luck. I might be in the same boat with poor old Sol Fishman tonight."

Innocents Abroad in
Los Scandalous

Inside of two shakes after Justin Other Smith had got his telegram from the lawyers telling him that his Aunt Feebie had died and left him a million-dollar legacy over in Los Angeles, Californy, every galoot in Apache knowed about it. Lew Pirtle, the Overland Telegraph operator, seen to that.

"There's a ketch to the deal," Pirtle tells the bunch in at the Bloated Goat Saloon, "which is why Justin O. is up in his art studio right now, packin' his carpetbag to ketch the Flyer for Loose Angels. O' course, I cain't tell you what the ketch is."

With which Lew clams up tight, allowing it ain't ethical to repeat what was in Justin O.'s telegram. But Sol Fishman, who is the 'Pache postmaster in addition to running the O. K. Mercantile, he threatens never to let Lew read another postcard, and that's all the coaxing needed to make Lew elabberate.

"It's like this," Lew whispers, drawing the boys in clost. "Seems this Aunt Feebie kicked the bucket, and her last will and testimonial was opened by a law outfit

228

name of —" Lew takes a gander at his copy of the telegram — "name of O'Leary, Shnoggle & Z-m-t-j-f-s-k-i. Accordin' to this firm of legal bannisters, ifn Justin O. don't claim his inheritance inside of a week, Aunt Feebie's entire es-tate will go to the Pasadena Pedigreed Poodle Asylum, which same Aunt Feebie helped organize."

Well, it's plumb obvious why Justin O. aims to ketch tonight's Californy Flyer, what with havin' a chanct to dab his loop on $1,000,000. That sum would make Justin O. the richest hombre in Stirrup County, richer even than Jim Groot, who runs the Stockman's Bank. O' course, Justin O. makes a good livin' as it is, illustratin' magazine stories and calendars and almanac covers and such-like.

"Needles to say, this jackpot won't give Justin O. a swellhead," comments Curly Bill Grane, the bartender. "But I hate to connemplate such a likeable kid as him goin' all by hisself to a big wicked me-tropolis like I've heard this here Los Scandalous burg is. He's li'ble to git stirrup-drug by some city slicker before he can fetch that million-buck leg-I-see home."

Well, that remark gives the boys something to think about. Especially Rimfire Cudd, the sheriff. The Paintin' Pistoleer has pulled Cudd's tail out of a tight crack more'n once, and he feels a moral obblegation to watch out for the young feller.

"It would insult Justin O. ifn I was to suggist taggin' along to Los Scandalous with him as a bodyguard," Rimfire says. "But it's tooken for granite that Justin is too young an' innercent to be turned loose in Californy with one million bucks in legally tender dinero. What ifn he *is* the champeen pistol shot of the Territory? That wouldn't do him no good if a gang of Los Scandalous hoodlums jumped him. Something has got to be did."

Well, the more the boys in at the Bloated Goat think about it, the certainer they are that the Paintin' Pistoleer, for his own good, has got to have an escort to git him and his dinero home safe. The problem was, how to keep from hurtin' Smith's feelin's.

Plato X. Scrounge, the lawyer, finally dug up an answer.

"The sheriff here has got to disguise hisself, so he can foller Smith to Loose Angels without bein' recognized," Scrounge says. "Dark glasses an' false whiskers should do the trick."

The Bloated Goat Saloon bunch chaw that over thorough, and decide Scrounge is right. Rimfire Cudd lights a shuck for the jail house pronto, to see about whompin' hisself up a disguise.

After he's gone, the boys get to palaverin' amongst theirselves, and decide that Rimfire Cudd's eyesight and trigger finger ain't no-ways dependable; Rimfire needs a pardner to go along and help ride herd on the Paintin' Pistoleer. The up-shoot of this discussion is that the boys draw straws to see who'll be Rimfire's pardner in disguise. Curly Bill Grane is the winner.

"I'll fix up like an Injun, same as I done at the Hallowe'en dance last fall," Curly Bill says. "My Cheery-cow git-up won fust prize at that shin-dig, you reckoleck."

230

Well, Rimfire and Curly Bill was busy as roosters in a pullet pen the rest of the evenin'. Curly Bill goes over to the Longhorn Saddle Shop and dyes his face and neck and ears and hands with a brown stain they use for coloring harness leather. Then he wrops up in a blanket from Sol Fishman's store, and puts on a pair of Jim Groot's house slippers for moccasins, and he's on his way to being a dead wringer for a Cheery-cow Injun buck.

Doc Sigmoid Grubb, the town medico and barber, he shaves Curly Bill's head except for a scalplock in the middle. Of course an Injun wears an eagle quill, but Dyspepsia Dan, who runs the Feedbag Café, he sez he can fix that up.

Dyspepsia Dan takes a *pasear* over to Samanthie Coddlewort's henhouse when it gits dark. There is a lot of cacklin' an' gobblin' goes on from Samanthie's flock, but Dan comes back with a turkey feather he's yanked from the tail of Samanthie's biggest Tom, and sticks it in Curly Bill's scalplock.

He makes a purty passable redskin, so much so that when he goes back to the Bloated Goat Saloon where Justin O. Smith is settin' up the gang to Blue Bagpipe Scotch by way of celebratin', the boys think Curly Bill is old Chief Ache-in-the-Back from the Cheery-cow reservation, tryin' to bum some firewater, and they throw him out on his blanket-wropped rump.

That tickles Curly Bill plenty. He sneaks over to the county jail to see how Rimfire Cudd is makin' out with his disguise.

The sheriff has cut off his crowbait saddle hoss's tail and has sewed a lot of hair on one of Sol Fishman's skull caps, to make a wig, and likewise a set of sorrel chin whiskers to match his own handlebar mustaches. He has smoked a pair of spectacles over a lamp chimbley and set them astraddle his nose. This nose sticks out of that brush of hair and whiskers like a tush-hawg's snout, but there is nothing he can do to disguise that proboscis short of takin' a pole ax to it.

Lawyer Scrounge has loant him a Prince Albert coat, and one of the gamblers down at the Busted Flush Casino a pair of striped pants and knee boots, and when Rimfire puts on Lucius Pirtle, Jr.'s derby hat, you wouldn't think he was the sheriff of Stirrup County. Cudd looks more like the scarecrow in Hernia Groot's garden patch than anything downright human.

Well, the whole town, including a batch of cowboys from outlyin' ranches and a passel of miners from the Sacatone diggin's, they turn out at midnight when the station agent flags down the westbound Californy Flyer, the fust time that had happened in nigh onto 20 year. The Paintin' Pistoleer clumb up the coach steps, lookin' mighty pert in his white Stetson and shop-made cow-boots and new overhalls.

Justin O. gets a rousin' big hand from the crowd, him bein' a mighty popular hombre even before he come into this money, and during all the commotion, Curly Bill Grane and Sheriff Cudd sneak down to the baggage car and crawl under, makin' theirselves comfortable on the rods like a couple of hoboes.

232

Perty soon the Flyer is highballin' acrost the desert, takin' Justin Other Smith to Los Angeles and the fortune his Aunt Feebie had left him. He finds himself sharin' a seat in the parlor car with a husky feller wearin' a blue uniform with gold buttons.

"First trip to Californy, eh?" this stranger says, when he seen the conductor punch Smith's ticket. "Allow me to interdooce myself, friend. I'm Monterey Q. Sizzle, a police patrolman in the city of Eternal Sunshine, Los Angeles. Just gettin' back from takin' an outlaw back to Texas. Not wanting to brag, but how old would you take me to be, young feller?"

Smith, wanting to be polite, he sizes up Officer Sizzle and makes a stab. "Forty-eight?" he guesses, underbidding his hand.

Officer Sizzle lights up a big stogie and grins. "Come July tenth," he says, "I'll be a hundred and fifteen years old. Yessir, for a fact. Born and raised in Californy, before the gold rush. When I hit my hundredth birthday, I went back to Iowa to visit my birthplace. Caught the cholera and died, yessir."

The Paintin' Pistoleer has heard that Californy is full of loco characters, so he's too polite to act doubtful. "You're a mighty well-preserved corpse, Officer," he says.

Officer Sizzle hands Justin O. a cigar. "This may sound exaggerated, young man," he goes on, "but I had left instructions for my remains to be shipped back to Sunny California an' buried there. You can believe this or call me a liar, but they had hardly planted me before the fertility of the California soil brung my corpus

233

bustin' out of the grave, to enter a public career. That was fifteen year ago. There's somethin' about the California climate that makes a monkey out o' the Grim Reaper."

Officer Sizzle was still boastin' about bein' a native son of the Sunshine State the next morning, when the train left Arizona at Yuma and headed into Californy. It was rainin' cats and dogs, though, so Justin O. couldn't see much of the scenery this policeman has been braggin' about.

Well, along about sundown the Flyer pulled into Los Angeles and the Paintin' Pistoleer clumb down out of the coach and give the town a look-see. There was a bad drizzle rollin' in from the ocean, what Sizzle called a high fog, so that Justin O. couldn't rightly judge the City of Eternal Sunshine; but he seen by the depot signboard that the population was over 10,000, which same put Los Angeles out of the class of cow towns like Apache, Arizona, anyhow.

"Here's the address of the hotel where I bunk, Smith," Officer Sizzle says. "Ifn you need ary help, look me up. Precinct Six."

Smith thanks Officer Sizzle and starts gropin' his way along the depot platform past the baggage car, when his attention was drawed under the car by a pitiful sound of moanin' and groanin'. A minute later the Paintin' Pistoleer is helping two hoboes climb offn the rods, both of 'em black with cinders and about froze stiff.

One of these hoboes is an Injun, wropped in a Cheery-cow blanket. The other was a freak in dark

234

glasses with a long sorrel beard and scraggly hair which fell over his ears and eyes like stuffing out of a straw mattress.

"Me heap big chief Swayback Buffalo," grunts the redskin, grinning to expose a set of gold teeth which was a dead wringer for the choppers wore by Curly Bill Grane back at the Bloated Goat Saloon in Apache.

Smith didn't appear to notice this coincidence, though. He was too busy starin' at the long red nose which stuck out of the hairy hobo's face like a nozzle on a fire hose.

"Paleface's brand is Handsome Harry," explains the Injun. "Him heap sad case. Handsome Harry is deaf and dumb, likewise blind as a post."

Smith tugs at his lip and says, "In view of his afflictions, I feel safe in commenting that a certain friend of mine would be jealous as billy old hell ifn he knew anybody else west of the Pecos had a proboscis to match his," Smith says. "The name of this feller being Sheriff Rimfire Cudd, the homeliest critter God ever created."

Handsome Harry bristles, almost like he had heard what Smith said, which was of course impossible for a deaf-mute. Chief Swayback Buffalo pushes in betwixt Smith and his pardner, and the Paintin' Pistoleer says, "Handsome Harry will soon be the picture of health if he soaks up enough of this California sunshine."

With which Smith turns up his collar agin the cold "fog," picks up his bag, and heads off past the depot.

The main street leading into town is hock-deep in red mud. As Smith slogs along, he sees that he is bein' follered by a couple of shadows who duck into alleyways whenever he looks around. Smith is packin' his famous .32 on a .45 frame, though, and he's had plenty of warnin' about the tough hoodlums who make Los Angeles their stompin'-ground, so he ain't particular worried.

Passing a saloon winder, Smith looks around quick and sees that these toughs who are trailin' him are none other than the two hoboes he helped offn the California Flyer back at the depot.

Shaking these two polecats is easy enough. Smith ducks into a honky-tonk until he seen the Injun and his pardner shuffle on by, actin' mysterious as hell and sniffin' for sign like a couple broken-down bloodhounds.

Bein' a stranger on this range, Smith looks up the hotel where Officer Sizzle lives, rents hisself a room, and turns in for some shut-eye.

Next morning the sun is trying to break through the fog which is making a river out of the streets, but it has to give up. Smith eats breakfast and then he lights a shuck over to Olvera Street, to visit the offices of the law firm which is handling his Aunt Feebie's estate.

He finally locates a sign painted on a door in the back of an adobe fandango parlor in the Mexican quarter: O'LEARY, SHNOGGLE & ZMTJFSKI, *Attorneys-at-Law. Exclusive Agents for Bonanza Gold Mines, Ltd.*

Just as Smith is knockin' on the door, he sees something in the back end of the alley that makes him groan. Chief Swayback Buffalo and Handsome Harry are scroochin' down there in the shadders. From their bedraggled looks, Smith knows them hoboes must of spent the night in this alley.

A voice says to come in, which Smith does. He finds hisself in a two-by-four cellar facin' a couple doors marked *Private*. There is a girl setting at a desk there, lookin' at a map of the Mother Lode country where the gold rush was in '49.

Smith forgits all about the two suspicious characters who are tailing him when he gits a second look at this filly. She's part Mexican, judging from her black hair and eyes and her fancy red and gold dress, which fits her like the hide on a hoss. She's got more curves than a side winder fixin' to strike, an' Smith lays odds she's prob'ly as deadly.

"Welcome to sunny California, Señor!" she greets him in a voice that would have hardened the arteries of a wooden Injun. She glances at a writing-tablet on her desk and comes up with, "You'll be Brown, the young yachtsman from Utah, no?"

"No," the Paintin' Pistoleer agrees, taking off his Stetson. "I'm Smith, the aging artist from Arizona."

The girl's face lights up like a brass spittoon and she comes slinking over, as willowy and slick as an eel in a lard bucket.

"I am Señorita Conchita Pepita Zmtjfski," she gurgles.

Smith shakes hands. "Howdy, Miss Zmtjfski," he says, gargling the monicker like his mouth is full of hot hoe-cakes. "I wondered how you pronounced that typographical error you use for a name. It's easy when you know how. And right purty, too."

Just then the door squeaks open syruptitious-like and Chief Swayback Buffalo and Handsome Harry sneak into the office on tiptoe, trying to hide behind a coat rack before Smith discovers them.

At sight of Conchita Pepita, the blind man pulls off his smoked glasses and blinks, while the Injun smacks his chops and rolls his eyes up and down like he's et some loco weed recently.

"One moment, Señores," Señorita Zmtjfski coos, and taps a bell on her desk. Two doors pop open and out step a pair of shifty-eyed city dudes with long sideburns and striped pants.

"Take care of these clients, please?" Señorita Zmtjfski says, and Smith sees Handsome Harry and his Injun sidekick dragged into the private offices like they been lassoed from a movin' train.

Señorita Zmtjfski turns to Justin O. and says, "Thos' gentlemens were my partners, O'Leary and Shnoggle. I presume, of course, you weesh to learn about your dearly beloved Aunt Feebie's million-dollar legacy, no?"

Smith was startled to hear the deaf-mute, Handsome Harry, augerin' like a brimmer bull in a brandin'-pen, inside Mr. O'Leary's office. Seems like this California climate has fixed up his afflictions pronto. Similar ructions is taking place inside the office where Mr. Shnoggle has collared the Injun chief.

"That's what I came to California to ascertain," Smith agrees. "That and to get myself a sun tan."

Señorita Zmtjfski daubs some powder on her cheeks and picks up a briefcase from behind her desk.

238

"It ees so noisy here, no?" Conchita Pepita pouts, linking her arm through the Paintin' Pistoleer's. "I know of a romantic leetle bistro at the end of Olvera Street where we can be alone, Señor Smith, and discuss our business affairs privately."

Her and Smith sashay out onto the street. Purty soon they are seated in the corner of a Mexican honky-tonk, at a table with a perfumed candle burnin' in the end of a beer bottle, which same makes Conchita Pepita's eyes glimmer like lanterns on the tail end of a cow-train caboose.

"I had no idea my Aunt Feebie was so well fixed," Justin O. says, after a waiter had soaked him a five-spot for some *tequila* and fish cakes. "I knew she left Alabama for her health, but I thought she was livin' on a Civil War widow's pension out here in sunny California."

Señorita Zmtjfski swigs down a shot of wine and titters. "O'Leary, Shnoggle & Zmtjfski know better," she says. "Your sainted aunt, shortly before her death, invested her meager savings in the Bonanza Gold Mining syndicate. Our firm represents Bonanza. I am very hap-pee to inform you that your Aunt Feebie's stock is now worth one million dollars, and it is all yours, as her sole living heir. With the stipulation that if we could not locate you, her fortune was to go to the Pasadena Pedigreed Poodle Foundation."

Smith tries to take his eyes offn a half-nekkid Mexican soprano who ekes for a living in this hot spot. He sees Conchita Pepita open her briefcase and haul out a batch of stock certificates, each one worth

$1,000, accordin' to the figgers printed on 'em. And there was enough of these guilt-edged securities to choke a hoss.

"This is very sweet of Aunt Feebie," Justin O. says, "especially as I am not her sole living kin. You see," he explains, "I am the youngest of thirteen kids, all living back in Alabama. That's how I got my name. When the Doc delivered me, he called me 'just another Smith.' My Ma was running short of monickers by that time, so she named me Justin Other."

"Regardless of that, the terms of your late aunt's will cannot be contested in court by your brothers and sisters, Señor Smith," she reassures him, stroking his hand with her long-nailed claws. "O'Leary, Shnoggle & Zmtjfski will protect you in case of litigation by jealous heirs, you can bank on that."

Justin O. looks plumb relieved. He shuffles through the bale of mining stock and finally says, "I should have brought my carpetbag from the hotel to carry this fortune away in."

Conchita Pepita scoops all the paper back into her briefcase. "It ees not quite so easy, Señor," she tells him, filling his wine glass again. "You see, your Aunt Feebie left certain debts such as funeral expenses, which O'Leary, Shnoggle & Zmtjfski must take care of. There are also our legal fees, you understand."

Smith shrugs that off easy-like. "As a millionaire, expenses don't bother me," he says airily. "Just you help yourself to enough of that Bonanza stock to settle Aunt Feebie's fees and your debts, or vice versa. I'll even add

240

a thousand-dollar bonus for you, Señorita Zmt-etc., to buy yourself a new dress with."

Conchita Pepita slithers around the table and snuggles down on the Paintin' Pistoleer's lap, real cozy-like.

"These stocks are not redeemable at their face value until ninety days have elapsed," she whispers, running a finger around the inside of his collar. "All debts and legal fees must be paid in cash, according to California law. How — er — how much money did you bring from Apache, Señor?"

Smith hauls out his poke and counts out 49 bucks and some-odd change. "O' course," he says, feeling Señorita Zmtjfski showing signs of cooling off pronto, "I've done purty well with my art career since I come West. I got, say, five thousand on deposit at the Stockman's Bank in 'Pache, that I could draw by telegraph, I reckon."

That runs up Señorita Zmtjfski's temperature until she's got a skinful of steam, all right. "By a strange coincidence, five thousand dollars will almost exactly cover the sum needed," she coos, and gives a quick gander at the frogskins Smith has on the table. "The exact figure, I believe, was five thousand forty-nine dollars and fifty cents."

Well, Smith hated to leave the cozy saloon and Conchita Pepita's charms, but business was business. As Señorita Zmtjfski pointed out, they had a deadline to meet, or else Aunt Feebie's fortune would have to be turned over to the alternate beneficiary, namely this pooch emporium over in Pasadena.

So, Conchita Pepita steers Smith out through the rain, acrost the Plaza, and winds up at a branch office of Wells-Fargo Express. There, Señorita Zmtjfski helps Smith compose a telegram to Jim Groot the banker in Apache.

"This time tomorrow, I'll have the dinero here," Smith says. "Which gives us quite a bit of time to see the sights, gorgeous."

Señorita Zmtjfski says she would adore to be his guide on a tour of Los Angeles, but unfortunately in private life she is Missus Aloysius Shnoggle, and her husband is a very jealous man, prone to challenging competitors to duels and the like of that there.

"I can tell by looking at you, darling," she says to the champeen pistol shot of Arizona Territory, "that you are a peace-loving gentleman who doesn't know one end of a peestol from another. It would not do for my hosband to catch us together, off duty."

So Smith escorts Conchita Pepita back to her office, and it being so blamed cold and foggy, he goes back to the hotel.

Next morning when he woke up and dressed, he steps out into the hall to discover that some varmint has tied a string to his doorknob. This string leads around the corner and Smith follers it to where it snakes under the sill of a fire-escape window.

Smith runs up the sash and looks out. The string's other end is tied to the big toe of an hombre who is sprawled out on the fire-escape balcony, fast asleep. It is Swayback Buffalo, the Injun chief, and the funny thing

242

is, his face and hands are red-skinned, but his bare foot is white as a goose's wing!

Swayback Buffalo is using Handsome Harry's backside for a pillow. The blind deaf-mute's sorrel chin whiskers have come askew, and his muddy Prince Albert coat has come open to expose a patched and faded blue denim shirt. These two hoboes are using the Injun's blanket for a mattress, and they're snorin' like a trombone duet. The jerk of the openin' door on the string tied to the Injun's big toe wasn't worth shucks as an alarm clock.

The Paintin' Pistoleer stifles an impulse to drive his cowboot where it'll do the most good, and decides to let the two tramps sleep.

When Smith gives his key to the hotel clerk, that rannihan has the nerve to applegize about the weather, which he says is "very onusual for California in June." But by now, Justin O. has heard that windy so blamed often he ain't in the mood to palaver about it.

He buys hisself a buffalo-robe overcoat at a hock shop, and kills most of the morning at breakfast. Finally at noon he presents hisself at the Los Angeles office of Wells-Fargo.

Going through the revolving door, he almost slams into two jaspers coming out the other side. They are Chief Swayback Buffalo and Handsome Harry, the latter wearin' his smoked glasses on his forehead now. They are both busy countin' a fistful of greenbacks which they must have got from the Wells-Fargo cashier.

Like he expected, Smith has got a draft for $5,000 waitin' for him, sent by telegraph from 'Pache by Jim

Groot the banker. There is also a telegram signed by Sol Fishman, Plato X. Scrounge, Dyspepsia Dan, and Lew Pirtle, and the Apache Ladies' Knitting & Peach Preserves Society, wishin' him luck and warnin' him to be careful not to let any swindlers hornswoggle him in Los Scandalous.

"Funny Rimfire Cudd and Curly Bill Grane didn't add their good wishes for my welfare," Smith grumbles, as he leaves Wells-Fargo.

On his way over to Olvera Street to see Señorita Conchita Pepita Zmtjfski, the Paintin' Pistoleer drops in at Precinct Six of the L.A. Police Department and chews the fat for a few minutes with his friend from the train, Patrolman Monterey Q. Sizzle, telling him how much he's enjoyed the City of Eternal Sunshine, among other things.

When he gets to the offices of O'Leary, Shnoggle & Zmtjfski, he don't see hide nor hair of Handsome Harry or the Injun, but when he goes inside he hears that pair jabberin' like magpies in the private offices.

"You brung the five thousand and forty-nine dollars?" Señorita Zmtjfski greets him, planting a big kiss on Justin O.'s cheek. "I have the papers all ready for you to sign, Señor. You will walk out of that door a millionaire, Señor. I congratulate you."

Smith pats his inside coat pocket and pinches the Señorita's left cheek playful-like. "I got the cash, Señorita Zmt-etc.," he says. "It's a shame, you bein' Missus Shnoggle in private life. I can think of several ways you and I could celebrate my good fortune."

Conchita Pepita is rubbing her hands together and is so nervous she can hardly set still.

"I've got a friend outside who can serve as a witness to our signatures, Señorita," he says, and opens the door to let in none other than his 115-year-old friend, Officer Sizzle.

"Yo're under arrest, ma'am," Sizzle sings out, drawing a six-shooter, "for defrauding the public with phony minin' stock."

Conchita Pepita lets out a scream which brings Shnoggle & O'Leary bouncin' out of their doors. Shnoggle spots the tin star on Officer Sizzle's blue coat and he gets a .41 derringer out of his sleeve in nothing flat, aiming to use the law badge for a target.

Conchita Pepita is wrasslin' with Officer Sizzle, tryin' to claw his eyes out, but Justin O. Smith, who ain't supposed to know one end of a peestol from t'other, he whips out his .32 Colt on a .45 frame and next thing Aloysius Shnoggle knows, his derringer has been shot out of his hand.

Meanwhile O'Leary ducks back into his office and dives out the winder, smack into the arms of two six-foot Los Angeles cops waitin' there in the alley. Two more officers foller Sizzle into the place and they flush an Injun warrior out from under a table in O'Leary's office, and likewise dab their loop on Handsome Harry, who has crawled into a woodbox behint Shnoggle's stove.

The policemen haze their prisoners out front to where a hoosegow wagon is backed up to the door, and in less time than it takes to tell it everybody is behind bars at police headquarters except the Paintin' Pistoleer, who is escorted up to the chief's office by his friend Sizzle, the leader of the raid.

"We been tryin' to get the deadwood on those swindlers ever since they set up shop here in L.A.," the chief says. "They work towns up an' down the coast, gettin' the names of relatives from newspaper obituaries and sellin' 'em this fake mine stock which don't 'mature' for ninety days, by which time them swindlers have moved on to another town an' changed their names. The only evidence we didn't get on this raid was the fake mining stock, but your testimony, Mr. Smith, will be enough to convict them fakers."

"My Aunt Feebie died, all right — six months ago," the Paintin' Pistoleer explains. "I sent enough money to the Los Angeles coroner to keep her out of a grave in pauper's field, and had her remains shipped back home to Alabama.

"When I got this telegram signed by O'Leary, Shnoggle & Zmtjfski, telling me Aunt Feebie was worth one million simoleons, I knew something was rotten in the state of Denmark, as the scriptures say. That's why I picked up Officer Sizzle on my way past Precinct House Six this mornin'."

The chief beams at Sizzle and tells him he'll be promoted to a desk sergeancy for this, which ain't bad for a 115-year-old flatfoot who had already died once.

A guard steps into the office and says, "I know you're holdin' them gold-mine fakers for the penitentiary, chief, but how about their customers — the Injun and that blind man? They claim they're personal friends of Mr. Smith, here."

The chief looks startled. "Send those two hoboes in," he roars. "Just for that lie, we'll put 'em to work on the county rock pile for thirty days, on a vagrancy charge. Just imagine, those two tinhorns claiming they know the famous Paintin' Pistoleer! It's redickilous."

Perty soon Chief Swayback Buffalo and his deaf-mute pard, Handsome Harry, are ushered into the chief's office, handcuffed together and looking plumb tuckered out and scairt silly.

"I never saw these impostors before in my life," Smith says. "Well, I'll take part of that back. I did see them coming out from under a railroad car over at the depot day before yesterday, at that. Ordinary tramps, I reckon."

The chief of police snorted. "Lock 'em up, Sergeant Sizzle!" he bellers, gruff-like. "Those knights of the road will draw sixty days apiece in the county pokey, turnin' big rocks into little ones."

At this, Chief Swayback Buffalo speaks up, and he's lost all of his Injun accent. "Justin O.," he says, triumphant as hell, "prepare to witness the most amazin' transformation of your life!"

With which Chief Swayback Buffalo reaches over to where there is a mop bucket full of soapy water, and he scrubs his face good, removing the saddle stain to reveal he's really a paleface.

"Curly Bill Grane!" gasps the Paintin' Pistoleer, like he's surprised out of a year's growth. "What in hell are you doin' impersonatin' an Indian? I'd never have known you in that git-up."

Handsome Harry is busy meantime. He peals off his black derby and the horse-tail wig under it, exposing his bald dome. Then he yanks off his chin whiskers and black specs and pulls back his clawhammer coat to show his sheriff's badge.

"Sort of surprised you, eh, Justin?" he chuckles.

"*Rimfire Cudd!*" shrieks the Paintin' Pistoleer, and turns to the Los Angeles chief of police, who is getting red enough to explode by all these shenanigans. "Sir, this is a colleague of yours, a minion of law enforcement well known in Arizona. Mr. Cudd is our sheriff in Apache. This erstwhile Vanishing American is Mr. Grane, who owns the town's biggest saloon. I assure you both of them are respectable, law-abiding pillars of society."

The chief has Sergeant Sizzle unlock their handcuffs. "I still got half a mind to jail you hombres for impersonation and making a laughingstock out of the farce — I mean force," he bellers. "Can you explain this outrage?"

"Why, we disguised ourselves so as to be on hand in case our friend Smith got into difficulties in the big city, sir," whimpers Rimfire Cudd. "He's a young, inexperienced boy, not up to buckin' the slickers who infest these wicked me-tropolises. He needed the pertection of older and wiser heads, like ourn."

Curly Bill Grane puts in his two cents' worth: "And danged lucky we come along, eh, Justin?" he says. "We'll have you out of this jail in a couple o' ticks."

It wasn't until later that day, when the three pards from Apache were fifty miles from the outskirts of Los Angeles aboard a train headin' back to Arizona, that Curly Bill and Rimfire Cudd let the Paintin' Pistoleer in on a little secret.

Curly Bill unrolls his Injun blanket, and out comes a big bundle of fancy-printed Bonanza Gold Mine stock. Rimfire Cudd has a big hunk of certificates stashed inside each of his bootlegs, as well.

"Half a million bucks worth o' gilt-edged gold-mine stock, Justin O.!" chuckles the sheriff. "Redeemable in ninety days in cash, it sez here. And we'll divvy up with you, too. We snuck this fortune out from under the noses of them Los Scandalous po-lice. We'll be pardners in the richest gold mine in Californy!"

The Paintin' Pistoleer slaps his forehead with his palm and looks like he's fixin' to be seasick.

"You confounded loco stones-of-peaches!" he yelps. "These mining-stock certificates are the missin' evidence needed to convict O'Leary, Shnoggle & Zmsffft of fraud and collusion to swindle the gullible public. Those L.A. cops are fine-tooth-combin' the Olvera Street premises right this minute, searchin' for this evidence you two stole!"

Curly Bill and the sheriff bust out guffawing, proud enough to split.

"Don't worry, Justin O. — this stock belongs to us," Rimfire Cudd says. "We got receipts to prove it, signed by Mr. Shnoggle and Mr. O'Leary. Curly Bill an' me, we wired to 'Pache and got all our life savin's telegraphed to us to buy this gold mine with. And just in the nick of time, as it turned out."

Smith is too disgusted to talk back.

"Yeah," goes on Curly Bill. "I slapped a five hunderd-buck mortgage on the Bloated Goat for my share, and the sheriff's friends anted up two hunderd. Look at the profit we made — half a million bucks for an investment o' seven hunderd! And we res-cued you from them city slickers and that si-reen female to boot. Wait till 'Pache finds out what a couple o' sets of Arizona brains can do in disguise, out here in Californy!"

As it turned out, though, all the boys had to show for their jaunt to the Sunshine State was three bad chest colds. It taken considerable Blue Bagpipe cold medicine to cure 'em, too.